WHEN THE DUST SETTLED

ROBERTA KAGAN

CHAPTER ONE

Manhattan, New York June 1930

Jazz music filled the smoky room. Izzy Reznick sat at the bar in the speakeasy where he worked, and lit a cigarette. It was a hot night. He felt sweat running down his back and pooling under his arms. But despite the sweltering heat, the bar was packed. He turned and looked around at the crowd of people guzzling the illegal alcohol that the speakeasy provided. There were so many different types. There were the regulars, drunks who came every night and stayed until Joey the bartender had to go over and tell them it was time to go home. Then there were the folks out celebrating an occasion, a birthday, an anniversary, an engagement. It was easy to tell them apart. They were flushed and usually a little frightened that there might be a police raid. And then there were the men who were all dressed up and flashing money trying to impress their dates. Scattered around the bar were the other men who, like Izzy, worked for the mob. Laevsky, the head of the Jewish crime syndicate was in his office in the back. He rarely came out.

"Izzy, you want another whiskey?" Joey asked.

"Yeah," Izzy said. He lit a cigarette and then added, "Who's the new broad with Lenny?"

"Oh, her," Joey said. "Her name is Rose. She's a pain in the ass. The girl thinks she's going to be a famous dancer, and she's told everyone here at least ten times. But just look at her, she's too short. No legs. You gotta have legs to be a dancer. Anyway, stay away from her. She'll talk your ear off if you let her. I don't know what Lenny sees in her."

Izzy nodded. "Leave it to Lenny. He's always got a new one. I don't think he sees anything in any of them. He just likes variety."

Rose noticed Izzy looking her way and she smiled. He returned her smile. Lenny was busy, so Rose walked over and sat at the bar beside Izzy. "Hi, do you work the for the big boss too?"

"You mean Laevsky?"

"Yep."

"I do," Izzy said. "I hear your name is Rose."

She let out a laugh. "So you two were talking about me!"

"We were. I said you were a hot tomato," Izzy said.

"Thanks." Rose beamed. "I'll take that as a compliment. By the way, what's your name?"

"My name is Izzy. And . . . I think you look like a Ziegfeld girl." Izzy was having fun watching this girl completely melt from his flattery.

"You do? But don't you think I'm too short? I wish my legs were longer. If my legs were longer . . ."

"If not a Ziegfeld girl, at the very least I think you could be in a Broadway show."

"A Broadway show? As a dancer or as an actress?" she asked.

"Both. Either. You could be whatever you want to be. You sure are pretty enough."

She beamed. Then she said, "Say, I didn't see you at the engagement party here at the speakeasy the other night."

"There was a party here?"

"Yeah. Last Saturday night. It was a real nice party. Lots of good food and liquor. And everything was paid for."

Izzy felt as if he'd been punched in the stomach. All of sudden everything made sense. And he felt the red-hot sting of betrayal on his cheeks. He knew his face was crimson. *Lenny told me the speakeasy was going to be closed last Saturday night because the boss had to meet with a special client from Canada. He lied to me. Why? Why would he lie to me? Why would he have a party and invite everyone behind my back?* Rose was still talking but Izzy didn't hear her. He was too stunned by what he'd just learned. *It hurts like hell for me to believe it, but I'll bet Sam and Chana are tying the knot. And I'm sure Laevsky didn't want me to come because of the fistfight Sam and I had over Chana. He's choosing Sam over me again. Ever since the day Sam Schatzman first walked into this place, my life has turned to shit. If only he was out of the picture.*

"Whose party was it? Who's getting married?"

"Do you know Shatzy and Chana? Lenny says Shatzy works with you fellas. And Chana is a redhead. I would have to say that she is the prettiest girl I've ever met . . ."

"Yeah, I know Chana. I know Shatzy too." His heart sank. *I wish I would have been wrong. I wish it would have been somebody else's party. Anybody else. But I was right. And, boy oh boy, do I know Shatzy. I wish I didn't know him. I wish he'd never come into the speakeasy. Before he came, everything was different. I had a chance with Chana. Laevsky and I got along pretty good. But then Sam Schatzman strolled into my life, and he stole Chana from me. She should have been my girl. This should have been my engagement party, but ol' Shatzy with his good looks and charm put an end to any chance I might have had with Chana. Then after he robbed me of my girl, he stepped in and took my position with the boss. Basically, the bastard has stolen my life.*

"I think Lenny said his real name is Sam."

"Yeah. That's right," Izzy said. He was annoyed. Her incessant rambling was grating on his nerves. *What the hell does Chana see in Sam? Why him and not me? I know he could not possibly love her as much as I do.*

"Did I offend you or say something wrong?" Rose asked. She looked genuinely sorry. "You look upset."

"No, no, not at all. In fact, I was just thinking," Izzy said. A plan was hatching in his mind.

"About what?"

"Well, about you," Izzy lied.

She giggled.

Then Izzy went on to say, "You see . . . I just happen to know a Broadway director. He's an old friend of mine. How about you give me a number where I can get in touch with you. Then I'll give that friend of mine a ring and set up a meeting for you with him."

"Would you really do that for me? I mean I would be indebted to you. I would do anything to be in a real Broadway show. I mean anything . . ." she said seductively.

Izzy managed a smile. "Listen, just don't say anything to Lenny or anybody else about this. You understand me? Can you keep it a secret? Just between us?"

"Sure thing. Lenny and I aren't serious. I mean we aren't talking about getting married or anything like that. In fact, he's always telling me that he doesn't want to be serious with anyone ever. He says he is never going to settle down. So it's none of his business what I do."

"You want another drink?" Izzy asked, tapping on his empty glass with his finger.

"Sure."

"Hey, Joey," Izzy called the bartender over, "give us another round, will ya?"

"Right away, Izzy."

Rose was chattering like a bird chirping, but Izzy wasn't listening. He had an idea, and he was putting the puzzle pieces together in his mind in order to make that idea a reality.

Gee, Joey was right, this girl sure can talk and say nothing. She rambles like an idiot. But I don't mind because I think if I play my cards right, I can use her to get rid of Sam for good. And it won't be hard to convince her to do what I tell her. All I have to do is throw her a bone. I'll set up a meeting for her with my old friend, Ben Siedelman, the Broadway director. He has one hell of a good reputation. So when she hears that it's Ben that I'm going to introduce her to, she'll do whatever I want in order to meet him. I'll go and talk to Ben tomorrow. I'm sure I can convince him to give this broad a small bit part in one of his shows. He owes me. But just in case he gives me any problem, I'll show him a little muscle if I have to.

Rose took a pen out of her handbag and wrote down a phone number. "It's not my private line. It's a phone in the building where I live. So just call and tell who ever answers that you want to talk to

Rose, the girl in 413. Here's my address too, just in case you can't reach me by phone. And here is the number to the office where I work. If you call there, just tell them you're my brother Jim and that there's a family emergency."

"All right. Now these things can take some time. But I'll be in touch."

CHAPTER TWO

Manhattan October 1, 1930

Izzy stewed over his plan for three months, all the while hoping that Sam and Chana would break up on their own. He knew how headstrong Chana was. And he also knew that Sam wasn't the brightest man in the outfit, and he could easily say the wrong thing to Chana. It would have been far better and less risky if the relationship had gone sour without Izzy's interference. If the boss found out that he'd broken Sam and Chana up, Laevsky would not be happy. And Izzy had seen how badly other men had suffered who had angered Laevsky. So Izzy waited. But as the months passed and the wedding day grew closer, Izzy knew he had no choice but to act. If he didn't, Chana and Sam would be wed, and he would be forced to step aside. At least for now.

I must try to break them up. I can't let her go this easy I won't. I have loved her for too long, and I want her far too much.

Izzy went to see Ben the following day. He walked around to the stage door at the back of the theater and knocked. A tall girl with dark, wavy hair opened the door. "How can I help you?" she asked in a throaty voice.

"I'm here to see Ben Siedelman. He's an old friend of mine. You can tell him that Izzy Reznick is here to see him."

"Sure. Wait here, I'll be right back," she said, closing the door. A few minutes later she returned. "Come in and follow me."

Izzy followed the girl to the front of the auditorium where Ben was sitting in a seat in the audience three rows from the stage. "Izzy Reznick. I haven't seen you in years. What brings you to the theater?" Ben stood up and extended his hand. Izzy shook Ben's hand.

"I came to cash in on a favor," Izzy said, sitting down in the front row across from Ben. "I'm sure I don't have to remind you of when you first started in showbiz, and I helped you out of that tight situation with the brother of that broad you knocked up."

"How could I forget. If it weren't for you, Reznick, I'd be six feet under. That guy was huge, and he wanted to kill me." Ben shook his head. "You sure did come through for me. By the way, you look good, Izzy. I heard that you're connected now."

Izzy smiled. "Yeah, well. I'm doin' all right."

"You work for Laevsky?"

"Actually, I do." Izzy smiled then he added, "So about that favor. I need you to cast this girl in a part. She's an unknown."

"Oh yeah?" Ben said, winking. "She must be a special one if you're coming here to ask me to help."

He thinks I am doing this to get laid, Izzy thought. "She sure is." *It's better if he thinks that. Then he has nothing on me.* Izzy lit a cigarette. "It doesn't have to be a big part. A quick walk-on is plenty."

"For you, Izzy, I could arrange that!" Ben said.

"And I just want you to know that I never forget a favor," Izzy said. "So if you ever find yourself in a jam again, just call."

"Good to know."

CHAPTER THREE

A week after Izzy's meeting with Ben, Izzy was making his collection rounds. He was in charge of collecting money from the local businesses, especially the other speakeasies. They paid Laevsky for protection from the police and from other gangs. When he finished making his rounds, Izzy dropped in to see Gladys, a prostitute who he'd visited many times over the past few years. He knocked on the door to her flat. "Who is it?"

"Hi Doll, It's me."

"Hello, Izzy," she whispered, opening the door. "I'm not free right now. But I sure would like to see you. Can you come back tonight?"

"How about tomorrow?" Izzy asked.

"Sure. You tell me what time, and I'll arrange my schedule so I can be available for you."

"Two in the afternoon?"

"I'll be waiting." She was about to close the door, but then she added, "By the way, you sure do look handsome." And she smiled.

Izzy returned to Gladys's apartment the following afternoon. She'd cleaned the place. He could tell because it smelled of bleach. Her hair was still wet from being freshly washed, and she wore a clean black nightgown. "Come on in!" she said. "It's been a while since you came to see me. I was thinking you had grown tired of me."

"I could never get tired of you, doll. I was just busy with work. But let's not worry about all that. I'm here now." He smiled. *I was getting tired of her; the sex had become so routine*, he thought.

"You sure are here now and I am so glad you came. Mmm . . . you look good enough to eat." She smacked her lips.

He laughed. "I'm not here for sex today, Gladys," he said. "I'm here to talk to you."

"Why? Did I do something wrong?"

"Nope. You didn't do anything wrong. I came to see you today because I have a job for you. And . . . I think you would be perfect for it."

Izzy had been a regular customer of Gladys's for years. He liked the fact that she never expected anything from him. He didn't have to spend hours sweet talking her. He put the money on the table, and that was all she asked of him. *We've been as intimate as a couple can be, but I don't think we've said fifty words in total to each other over the last five years. Maybe that's why I was getting so bored.* He felt awkward trying to carry on a conversation. It was almost as if he didn't know Gladys at all.

"Before we go any further, I need to be sure that I can trust you," he said

"Come on, Izzy. You know you can trust me. You didn't want anyone to know that you come to see me, and I've never even told anyone. It's been five years we've been having sex, and I've never leaked a word. What is it you want today? Something a little nontraditional? You don't have to be ashamed with me."

He let out a short laugh. "No, honey, it's nothing like that. It has nothing to do with sex."

"Just tell me what you want. I can't give it to you if I don't know."

"All right. I'll tell you. It's kinda like an acting job. Are you good at acting?"

"How could you ask me that, Izzy? Do you know how many men I've had to act like I was having a good time with when we had sex?"

"Yep, I'll bet. I hope I wasn't one of them." He winked

"Of course not. You were always special to me."

He nodded. "Anyway," he said, "here's the plan. Sometime later this month, I am going to make arrangements for you to go to a speakeasy with a fella that I know. You're gonna act like he's your boyfriend. Then while you're in the speakeasy you are going to pretend to get into a fight with him. I want the fight to be loud. I want everybody in the club to stop what they're doing and turn around. Then this fella's going to hit you. I'm sorry, but he's gotta hit you pretty hard. I'm thinking in the mouth because the lips bleed a lot."

"Why would you want some fella to beat me up in a speakeasy?"

"Because when this fella who's acting as your boyfriend starts beating the crap out of you, I want you to run over to this other fella and beg him for help."

"What other fella?"

"I'll show you pictures of the other fella. It'll be easy to recognize him when you see him. Scope him out and be sure you know where he is even before the fight starts."

"All right."

"This fella I'm talking about, he works at the speakeasy. His name is Sam." Izzy put his cigarette out in the ashtray. "I know Sam, and he'll always defend a lady. So he'll turn around and punch the other guy. They'll get into a fistfight. Then once it's over and the fella who is playing your boyfriend walks out of the speakeasy, I want you to go over to Sam and make nice."

"Make nice?"

"I want you to thank him. Hug him, kiss him, play with his hair. Crawl all over him. Rub his arm. Even if he tries to push you away, don't stop. Keep it up for as long as you can. Offer to buy him a drink. Do whatever you can to keep him there with you. Does this make sense?"

"Yeah, sure."

"If you're sure you can do it, I'll give you a hundred dollars for this job. Only thing is you gotta keep your mouth shut. You can never tell anybody that I hired you to do this. The fact that this was planned must never come out. Do you understand?" Izzy pulled a picture of Sam out of his pocket. "Here, look at this fella."

"He's a handsome devil."

"Keep your opinions to yourself. All I want to know is if you're sure you can do this."

"Yeah, sure Izzy. I can do it. I promise you. I won't let you down. And I sure could use a hundred dollars. I mean that's a lot of money!" she said, smiling. Then she winked at him and put her hand on his thigh. "And . . . since you're here, how about you let off a little steam?"

"Why not?" He dug into his pocket and pulled out a ten-dollar bill. Eight dollars more than he usually paid her. He laid the money down on her coffee table.

CHAPTER FOUR

October 1930

It took Izzy a couple of weeks to put his plan together. He had to make sure that he had everything in place as soon as possible because the wedding date was November the first. But it wasn't that easy; he had to find the right fella for the job. The man had to be an unknown. It could not be someone who was a regular at the speakeasy. If the others knew the guy, there would be a chance that people would find out Izzy was behind the whole thing. The problem with finding someone unknown was that everyone in the Jewish neighborhood knew everyone else. Izzy was perplexed. But he finally decided on a man he'd met, who was a day laborer.

His name was Eddie Flynn. He lived in the Bronx with his wife and infant son. From the first time they met, Izzy had felt a kindred spirit with Eddie. Eddie was always hard up for money. It seemed like life had a way of shortchanging him. But he never knuckled under to the struggle. He was a fighter. He worked day labor; sometimes he got into fistfights with other men in the neighborhood. The men took bets and he received a percentage of the pot. Other times he hustled and helped

Izzy collect money from a reluctant tavern owner. Yes, he was not a quitter, and for this, Izzy admired him.

Early one evening Izzy went to Eddie's neighborhood. He found Eddie sitting outside his cold-water flat with a bunch of other men playing cards and gambling. Izzy walked over and asked Eddie if he could speak to him alone. Eddie got up and followed Izzy to his car. They got in, and Izzy presented his plan to Eddie. At first Eddie had refused to be a part of it. Even when Izzy offered him a hundred dollars. It took Izzy another two hundred dollars to convince Eddie to accept.

"Now, you're sure that I'm not gonna get killed for messing with some mobster's girl or nothin' like that, right? 'Cause I got a wife and kid that depend on me, Izzy."

"I know. You won't get into any trouble. Once the fight gets heated, you back down and walk out. Don't beat the hell out of the other fella. Understand?"

"Yeah."

"Here, look at this picture." Izzy showed Eddie a picture of Sam. "Memorize his looks. This is the fella."

Eddie nodded. "I got it," he said.

Now that Izzy had all his players in place, he was ready to call Rose.

When he got home, it was almost nine in the evening. He knew it was late to call, but he decided to try anyway. He picked up the receiver and called the phone in the main room in Rose's apartment building.

"Who do you want to talk to?" It was an old woman who answered. She was yelling. *Damn, she sounds half deaf,* Izzy thought.

"Rose."

"Who's Rose?"

Izzy felt his heart sink. *Did I wait too long? Did Rose move?* Frustrated, he said, "Rose, a short girl with dark hair. She dresses like a flapper. She's very outgoing. Talks a lot. She stays in room 413."

"Rosey," the old woman said. "Well, why didn't you say so?"

"Yeah, Rosey."

"Hold on. I'll go up to her room and see if she's home."

At least she's still living there.

"Hello." It was Rose.

"Well, hello there, gorgeous! It's Izzy Reznick. Remember me?"

"It took you long enough to call. I wrote you off. I thought you were just another bullshitter."

"Nope, I'm honest as can be, honey. I'm sorry, it just took me a little longer than I originally expected to arrange that meeting I promised you."

"You did it?" she asked excitedly. "You arranged a meeting for me with Ben?"

"I did. Why don't you and me have dinner tomorrow night, and after dinner I'll take you over to the theater to meet Ben."

CHAPTER FIVE

Izzy picked Rose up and then drove to a restaurant across the bridge in Brooklyn where he was sure they would not be recognized by anyone they knew. Izzy had been to this restaurant before, and he knew it was very private. It was dark inside the eatery. And Izzy asked the host to seat them in a very private booth in the back.

"What can I get for you tonight?" the waiter asked.

"Coffee," Izzy said.

"Just coffee, Izzy? I'm hungry. Can I have dinner?" Rose asked.

"Sure, kid. But I want to make this quick."

"What's the special tonight?"

"Roast beef with potatoes and carrots."

"I'll have that."

After the waitress walked away, Izzy said, "I made the arrangements for you to meet Ben. He wasn't available tonight. I can take you to see him tomorrow. You'll have to call in sick to work."

"That's no problem. I haven't ever called in at this job. So I think it should be all right."

"Well, that's good. But there's one condition. I want something from you."

"Yeah, I figured. How about I pay up after I meet Ben? So many fellas make promises. Then I let 'em get in bed with me and they never deliver."

"I don't want sex from you. I need you to do something for me. An important job."

"What?"

He reconsidered. *This girl has such a big mouth. I can't trust her. But the wedding day is almost here. And I need someone to do this who knows Chana.* "All right, first off, I want you to know that if I find out that you ever told anyone about what I am asking you to do, I'll cut that pretty face of yours, and you'll never have a chance to be on the stage again. Do you understand me?"

"Yes," she said, turning pale. "What is it you want? I mean, I want to help you. But I won't kill nobody. I can't do nothin' illegal. 'Cause I can't go to jail."

"Shut up and listen closely. There is going to be a fight at the bar next week. As soon as you see Sam get involved, I want you to run to the public phone and call Chana. I want you to tell her that Sam is in a fight, and you want her to come to the speakeasy. Don't tell her anything else. Just say, Sam is involved in a fight at the bar. I'm afraid he is going to get hurt. Maybe you should get over here right away," Izzy said staring into her blank face. "Repeat it after me," he said, frustrated.

"Sam got into a fight at the bar. I am afraid he is going to get hurt. You need to get here right away," Rose repeated.

"Good. Now that's all I want you to say. Not another word. Just shut your mouth and hang up the phone. Is that clear?"

"That's all you want?"

"Yeah, that's all I want. But I want it done right. Can you do it? Because if you mess this up, you can forget your Broadway debut. I'll introduce you to Ben. But if you fail me, he'll throw you out of the theater faster than you can blink those pretty eyes."

"I can do it," Rose said.

CHAPTER SIX

Manhattan October 20, 1930

It had been raining on and off all day. Sam had a slight sinus headache. He would have liked to go home, take an aspirin, and lie down, but he couldn't because he had set up a craps game upstairs at the speakeasy that night. So he was at the speakeasy waiting for the players to arrive. It was early, so he sat down at the bar and ordered a whiskey.

Joey, the bartender, brought him his drink. "You look tired tonight, Shatz," he said.

"It's the weather. Besides, Chana and I have been so busy with the wedding plans. If it had been up to me, we would have gotten married at the courthouse. But you know how women are. She wanted a wedding. It's been a lot of work, but if it makes her happy . . ."

"Yeah, you got to keep the wife happy," Joey said. "Mine drives me nuts spending money. She always seems to need something. But I don't fight with her. In the past I used to fight with her. So what would happen? She would throw me out of the bedroom. The result was I got a lousy night's sleep on the sofa. Then the next day we would make up. Everything would be berries. A week would go by, and then boom, she's off spending money again. Nothing changes. So why fight?"

Sam laughed.

A young couple walked into the speakeasy. Gladys wore a red flapper dress, her dark hair in waves. She hung on Eddie's arm. He wore his shirt sleeves cuffed to show off his muscles. They sat down at a table in the front of the speakeasy where everyone could see them. Sam glanced up from his drink, but he didn't pay much attention to the couple. He checked his watch. The craps game was scheduled for ten o'clock, but Laevsky always insisted that he be at the speakeasy by six.

"You want something to eat, Shatzy?" Joey asked.

"Yeah, I guess so. How about a steak?"

"Medium rare, right?"

"Yep," Sam said.

"Baked potato?"

"Yeah, sounds good. Thanks."

"I'll put in the order," Joey said.

Then Sam heard a woman curse. "You dirty good-for-nothing bastard." It was the girl in the red flapper dress. She was standing up and looking down at her dress. "You spilled that drink on me, you son of a bitch," she yelled.

"I told you to shut your mouth," Eddie yelled back at her. "You curse like a sailor. You'd like to be a lady, but you don't have it in you. Why don't you sit down and act like you were raised with some class instead of like a common whore."

"Go to hell. I don't have to listen to you; you're not my father."

"I'm your man. And you had better listen to me, or I'll beat you until you can't answer back."

Gladys started to walk away from the table, but Eddie grabbed her arm and pulled her. As he pulled her toward him, she knocked over the chair. Then still holding on to her arm tightly, he pushed her against the wall, knocking over the table. She slapped him in the face. And he slapped her back. She yelped as she cupped her cheek. "You make me sick, you two-bit hustler," she said. "You're going nowhere. Nowhere, I tell ya."

Eddie slapped Gladys again. This time he hit her hard enough to make her lip bleed. Blood dripped down her chin. Eddie grabbed Gladys and threw her down on the floor. She was cowering, but she managed to crawl over to Sam. Grabbing his hand, she said, "Help me. Please, help me. He's going to kill me."

Sam got up from his chair and walked over to Eddie. He grabbed Eddie from behind. Eddie whirled around. Sam hit him hard. Eddie returned the punch, but with only half of his strength, as he'd promised Izzy he would do. Sam stumbled backward. But he regained his footing before he fell. And again, Sam punched Eddie in the face. Blood spurted out of Eddie's nose and mouth. Eddie almost hit Sam hard enough to knock him out, but he forced himself to remember that this was all an act. If he had lost control, it would have been purely a reaction to seeing his own blood on the floor. And since he was here already, why make a mistake. Why not make sure to collect the three hundred dollars? His family could live on that for six months if they were careful.

"Get out of here," Sam said.

Eddie turned around and glared at Sam. "What are you gonna do, call the cops?" Eddie laughed because, of course, Sam wouldn't dare call the cops. The speakeasy was serving illegal alcohol.

"I said get out," Sam repeated, "and I meant it."

"To hell with you," Eddie answered, tossing his hand in the air. "I will get out. I'd rather not be in the same building as this disgusting whore." He gave Gladys a push. Then he turned and left.

Gladys threw her arms around Sam's neck. "I don't know how to thank you," she began, "You saved my life."

"Are you all right?" Sam asked.

"I think so." Gladys moaned. Then she touched his face. "You are so strong, and well . . . you sure are handsome."

"Thank you. I am truly flattered, but I am not interested. I'm getting married next week."

"Isn't that a shame." She leaned into him even further until he could feel her breasts against his chest. "I owe you so much for being my hero. I mean, heck, I owe you my life. And . . . I'm not opposed to paying. If you know what I mean. Take it as a last hurrah before you sign your life away in matrimony."

He smiled and shook his head. "Sorry, honey. I am glad I could help. But like I said, there's only one doll for me."

Meanwhile, no one noticed as Rose slipped out the door and ran down the street to the pay phone where she dialed Chana's number.

"Chana," she said, "It's Rose. Lenny's girlfriend." She sounded panicked

"Is everything all right?"

"No, no…it's not. There's been a fight at the speakeasy. Sam was involved. I think you'd better get here quick." She said. Then the phone line went dead.

When Rose arrived back at the speakeasy, no one had noticed she'd left. She glanced over at Sam. The girl was still hovering over him. Rose saw him push her away gently. But she came back and touched his face.

CHAPTER SEVEN

Chana hung up the phone and ran outside to the busy intersection to catch a taxi. Within minutes she was in a cab and on her way to the speakeasy.

Her heart was pounding so hard that her chest hurt. *Rose said Sam is hurt. Please God, let him be all right.*

When Chana arrived, she threw two dollars at the cab driver and jumped out of the cab. Then she disappeared into an alleyway and knocked on the invisible door. Lenny let her in. The musicians had not yet started to play. And all of the tables were empty. In the middle of the room, one of the tables had been turned on its side and a chair was upside down. There was a pool of blood on the floor. Chana looked up and saw Sam with a girl in his arms, who had her hands on his face and was smoothing his hair.

Sam saw Chana and their eyes locked. She shook her head in disbelief. Then she ran out of the speakeasy.

CHAPTER EIGHT

Manhattan, October 20, 1930

Blinded by tears, Chana ran into the street. She heard the screech of tires followed by a high-pitched scream from a bystander. Traffic was all around her. Then Sam's strong arms grabbed her and pulled her to safety only feet from a moving automobile. Her legs were like Jello and she could hardly stand up. But he held her steady in his arms. "What the hell is the matter with you? Geez, Chana, you almost got hit by a car," he said, squeezing her tightly to him.

"Damn you, Sam!" she said through her tears. "How long has this been going on?"

"What? How long has what been going on?"

"You and that woman. How long have you been seeing her? I wish I had found out sooner, not today, not when we are supposed to be getting married in a week." She pushed away from him. "How am I going to call off a wedding of this size?"

"You're not. We are getting married. I love you."

"Then what the hell was that all about?" Rose called me and told me that you were in a fight. She said you were hurt. I took a taxi to the speakeasy. I was so worried. And what do I find when I get there? You, with some girl in your arms."

"Oh, Chana. Listen to me. Please. I'll tell you what happened," Sam said as a car whirled around to avoid hitting them.

"Yes, Sam, why don't you try to explain."

"I will. But I think we'd better get out of the street before we both get run over." He pulled her off the street and onto the sidewalk. It began to rain.

"Chana, I know you think that I've been having something to do with that girl. But believe me, you're wrong. She came in with some fella. They started fighting. He slapped her and she slid across the floor. He slapped her again a couple of times. Nobody stepped in to stop him. She came over and asked me for help. What was I supposed to do? I had to help her. I can't stand to see a man beating up a girl. So I hit him a few times. When he left, she put her arms around me and thanked me. I tried to peel her off, but she kept on coming back. Right before you arrived, I told her to leave me alone. But then you saw what you saw, and you misinterpreted the whole damn thing. Come with me."

"Where are we going?"

"Back to the speakeasy," Sam said. "Why don't you ask Joey, the bartender. He saw what happened."

"I think he'd lie for you."

"Then ask Rose or Laevsky. Laevsky would tell you if I was cheating on you. He'd tell you after he killed me. Laevsky loves you almost as much as I do. You can trust him."

"You're right. I do trust him."

They walked back to the speakeasy. The blood on the floor had already been mopped up, and the table and chairs had been put right. The customers had returned to their tables and the bar was full again. Izzy was huddled in a back booth alone. Rose was sitting with her back to the door. Chana walked up to her. "Rose, I have a question for you."

"Sure," Rose said, but she sounded nervous.

"Have you ever seen that girl before. The one that was here earlier?"

"What girl?"

"The one with the red dress that was hanging all over Sam?"

"No, but she's the reason that there was a fight."

"Yes, I know. Thanks."

"Come on," Sam said. Taking Chana's hand, he led her into Laevsky's office.

"My favorite girl is here," Laevsky said as Chana walked over and gave him a kiss on the cheek. Then he turned to Sam. "I heard there was a fight out there tonight. What happened?"

"Yep, there was a fight. Some broad got smacked around by her boyfriend. I punched him a few times to stop him. Then the broad was so grateful that I couldn't get her off me. Chana walked in and saw this girl hanging on me. Now Chana thinks I have been seeing her on the sly. So I brought Chana here to talk to you so that you could verify that I have not been with any other girls."

"I have never seen Sam with anyone but you," Laevsky said. "He's a little dumb, but not that dumb." Laevsky smiled at Chana. "He knows he's damn lucky to have a girl like you."

"I love you, Chana. I don't want anyone else," he said, looking into her eyes.

"Really, Laevsky?" Chana said.

"I'd never lie to you," Laevsky said.

"Oh, Sam, I was foolish to get so angry. I think I am just worn out, with working and all the wedding plans."

He took her in his arms and kissed her. "We'll have time to relax on our honeymoon," Sam said, holding her in his arms.

"I'd tell you to go home, Shatzy, but the craps game is about to start, and I need you to check the players in. Did you verify that they are all clean? No police?"

"Yes, boss."

"Good."

CHAPTER NINE

The players began arriving to join the craps game upstairs. As always when there was a game, the speakeasy became crowded and a little chaotic. While everyone was occupied, Izzy walked over to the bar and stood beside Rose.

"What can I get you?" Joey asked.

"Whiskey," Izzy said. Then when Joey went to pour his drink, he turned to Rose and whispered, "What did Chana ask you?"

"She asked me if I ever saw Sam with that girl before."

"What did you say?"

"I told her no. Because I haven't."

"You, idiot," Izzy said, taking his drink and walking away.

Rose stared after him. She hoped he wasn't too upset with her. *I did what he told me to do. I don't know what I did wrong.* He'd already introduced her to Ben as he'd promised, and Ben had given her a small part. But the last thing she needed was for Izzy to be angry with her. She didn't know him well, but she knew that he was dangerous, and she didn't want to end up on his bad side.

CHAPTER TEN

Manhattan, November 1, 1930

The day of the wedding finally arrived. Fannie went to Chana's apartment early and knocked on the door. "Who is it?"

"Fannie."

"Fannie, come in," Chana said.

"I sent the cake and everything for the sweet table to the Waldorf early this morning. So it's all ready to go for tonight."

"You did it already? What time did you start baking?"

Fannie laughed. "My bakers and I have been working on the wedding for a week. I think you're going to be very pleased. At least I hope so."

Chana hugged Fannie. "I know I will," she said.

"So did you have coffee yet?" Fannie asked.

"Not yet. I just got up."

"Why are you up so late? It's ten o'clock. I know you couldn't see Sam last night. No seeing the groom the night before the wedding." Fannie winked.

"No, we didn't see each other. But I was so nervous and excited that I couldn't sleep. I finally dropped off to sleep at four in the morning."

"I brought a challah. We'll have breakfast, then I have a surprise for you."

"Another surprise? Fannie, you are too good to me."

"What are best friends for?'

Chana put a pot of coffee on the stove. Then they sat down to eat. Chana was too nervous to swallow any food. She quietly sipped a cup of black coffee while Fannie had two thick slices of challah with butter. Once they were finished, Fannie said, "Get dressed. But don't put on any makeup."

"All right, where are we going?"

"You'll see."

Fannie drove them in her car to a huge beauty salon where Fannie had made an appointment and paid in advance for a complete makeover for Chana.

After four hours of having her hair shampooed and set, her fingernails and toenails manicured and polished, and her makeup applied by an expert, Chana was ready for her wedding.

"Look at me, Fannie. You've made me so glamorous."

Fannie smiled. "You were always glamorous. I just thought it would be fun to have the experts perform some magic."

"I love the way I look. Thank you."

"Oh honey, you don't have to thank me. I'm having a ball with this wedding of yours. And, by the way, I love the dress you made for me for tonight."

"I am so glad. I knew that deep orchid would be a good color for you."

"It sure is. And I don't know how you did it, but the design makes me look thinner. Talk about working magic. You are one hell of a designer."

"I am just glad you're happy," Chana said.

"I'll pick you and your parents up at five thirty to leave for the synagogue. Is that all right?"

"Yes, of course. Are you sure you want to drive us? I can probably get a taxi if it's too much trouble."

"Don't be a meshuggeneh, that's crazy. Of course, I am going to drive you."

CHAPTER ELEVEN

When they arrived at the shul, Chana, her mother, and Fannie went into the women's dressing room. Chana's father went into the men's. Chana's mother and Fannie were helping Chana to button the bodice on her gown and to place her veil and headpiece on her head. Once they were finished, Fannie took a tiny red ribbon out of her handbag. She reached inside Chana's dress and tied the ribbon around Chana's bra strap. "You look so beautiful I wanted to be sure to prevent the evil eye."

Chana took Fannie's hand in her own and smiled. "Thank you."

Across the way in the men's dressing room, Sam was already in his tuxedo and was pacing the floor.

"Today's the day, Shatzy," Laevsky said.

Sam nodded.

"You nervous?"

"Sure, a little."

"Not having second thoughts, are you?"

"Never," Sam said. "I just want everything at this wedding to go well. It means so much to Chana."

"Don't you worry. It'll be just fine," Laevsky said. Then taking Sam into a corner where Chana's father couldn't hear them, Laevsky said,

"Listen, I put a couple of armed men outside. They know that I expect them to stay inconspicuous. Now, Shatzy, I know my men. As I've said before, you don't rise to my position if you don't know the men who work for you. At any time, a guy like me can be hit by one of his own if he's not careful. You understand?"

Sam nodded.

"I know my men's strengths and their weaknesses. Now, what I am getting at, here, is that I know Izzy. He can be a good fella, but he can also be treacherous and hotheaded in the right circumstances. So, I figured, considering the way Izzy feels about Chana and that nasty fistfight you had with him, it was a good idea to have some soldiers outside just in case Izzy shows up."

"He wasn't invited," Sam said.

"I realize that, Shatzy. That's why I have the guards outside. Just in case he decides that he wants to do something crazy."

Laevsky patted Sam's arm and walked away. He lit a cigar and looked out the window, watching as the guests began to arrive. *I still have my suspicions about what happened on that run when Harry was killed. But I won't say or do anything. Not yet. I'll watch and wait until I am sure I am right.*

CHAPTER TWELVE

There was a long, white runner on the floor from the entrance of the room to the magnificent, oversized chuppah. White tulle was draped from pew to pew, and each of the pews had an arrangement of flowers. The chuppah was covered in white roses accented with sterling-silver roses that were the palest shade of lavender.

The guests began to arrive; the men in black tuxedos, the women in elegant gowns. They were seated by ushers from the temple. A pianist in a dark gray suit with a matching tie and crisp white shirt took his place at the black grand piano at the front of the room. Once the guests were all seated, the pianist began to play, and the bridal party assembled outside the room. All except Chana, who was waiting in her room for the signal. She didn't want Sam to see her before it was time for her to come down the aisle.

First Sam and Laevsky walked down side by side, followed by Fannie who was already tearing up. Next, Chana's mother made her way to the end of the aisle. And then the pianist stopped and began to play "Here Comes the Bride." Chana walked into the hallway and took her father's arm. When they entered the ceremony room, everyone stood to look. Sam was breathless. He knew Chana was beautiful, but he'd never seen her as radiant as she was tonight. She walked slowly beside her father until they reached Sam. Then Mr. Rubinstein placed Chana's arm on Sam's and walked forward to join his wife, leaving the couple to stand together, as they should for the rest of their lives, before the rabbi in front of the bema. Chana's hands were trembling as she held her long bouquet of roses and orchids.

Everyone was silent as the rabbi began the ceremony with a Hebrew prayer. Sam couldn't take his eyes off Chana. Finally, the rabbi told Sam to slip the ring on Chana's finger. Then she slipped her ring on Sam's. A wine glass was handed to Chana. Fannie helped Chana remove her veil. She took a sip of the sweet red wine and handed the glass back to the rabbi, who then handed it to Sam. He took a sip and looked into Chana's eyes. Once both Sam and Chana had drunk from the glass, the rabbi wrapped the glass in a white cloth and placed it on the floor. Everyone was silent as Sam raised his foot. He stamped hard on the glass and when the guests heard it break, they all yelled "Mazel tov!"

Sam took Chana into his arms and kissed her. Her face was wet with tears. He touched her face and wiped a tear away. Then he whispered in her ear, "From this day forward I'll make sure that you only cry tears of happiness." She smiled at him and they kissed again. And then they began to walk back down the aisle. Once they were in the hallway outside the ceremony room, they started down the receiving line where they would greet their guests.

All the men who worked for Laevsky were in attendance with their wives. As they came through the receiving line, they handed Chana envelopes filled with money as wedding gifts.

Then Sam and Chana left the temple to drive to the Waldorf for the reception. Meanwhile at the synagogue, waiters passed crackers with kosher caviar. Laevsky looked around. He was disappointed that he had not been able to convince the rabbi to allow him to serve liquor. But at least he'd been permitted to bring wine for the ceremony.

However, the reception was a different story. At the Waldorf, Laevsky had paid off the police so that they would overlook it when champagne was served at the party. However, the Waldorf was not aware of the arrangements Laevsky had made. So Laevsky hired men to walk around the room while the guests were dining and discreetly add champagne to their glasses from fourteen-carat gold flasks that they carried in their pockets. Each flash was engraved with Sam and Chana, November 1, 1930.

The band was already playing as the guests trickled in. Chana and Sam were off alone in a room going through their envelopes waiting for the guests to be seated. Chana was shocked at how generous everyone had been to them, but no one was more generous than Morty Laevsky. He gave them one thousand dollars.

"I wonder why Laevsky is so good to us," Chana said. "I mean, he gave us this honeymoon, and now he is giving us all this money."

"He loves you. What can I tell ya?"

"I think there's more to it, Sam," Chana said, tucking the envelopes into her white satin bag.

Once all the guests were seated, the wedding coordinator from the hotel knocked on the door to the room where Chana and Sam were waiting.

"The band is ready for you," she said.

Chana checked her lipstick. It was a little smeared from kissing all the wedding guests. She took a moment to fix it then she said, "Ready, Sam?"

He nodded, and they left the room arm in arm. They waited in the doorway until the bandleader said, "Ladies and gentlemen, for the first time ever, it is my pleasure to introduce to you, Mr. and Mrs. Samuel Barry Schatzman."

Everyone stood up clapping and cheering as Sam and Chana walked into the room. Then the band began to play a slow song. Sam put out his hand, and Chana put her hand in his. He whirled her into his arms, and they began to dance.

"I love you so much," Sam whispered into Chana's hair.

"I love you too."

"Forever," he said.

"Forever."

Laevsky climbed up on the podium with the band. He had a glass of orange juice in his hand to which champagne had been added. "I'd like to make a toast to the bride and groom," he said. "May they live long and healthy lives. And may they have plenty of nachas."

Everyone raised their glasses and drank.

Green salads were served followed by thick slabs of rare prime rib with baked potatoes, wild mushrooms, and carrots. Then the cake was brought out. It was a four-tier cake covered with white-chocolate roses. The bride and groom on top had been fashioned out of fourteen-carat gold. Each of the tables were covered with white tablecloths, and on each table there were plates of cigarettes, chocolate candies, and nuts. Next to the cigarettes was a crystal container with match books that had been engraved in gold writing to read Sam and Chana. While the guests dined, Sam and Chana walked around the room thanking everyone for coming. They were so nervous, neither of them ate a thing. However, they fed each other hunks of Fannie's delicious carrot cake which she made because she knew it was Chana's favorite. As Sam put a piece of cake into Chana's mouth, the photographer snapped his camera, and Sam and Chana laughed.

The party was a wild success. All the mobsters brought flasks of whiskey in their coat pockets, which they added to their glasses of orange juice. So they were drunk within a couple of hours. The band played just the right mixture of lively and soft, sentimental music. Chana danced with Laevsky and with Screwy. She danced with Lenny and Joey. She danced with her father and so many others that she lost count. By the time the sweet table was displayed, Chana was exhausted and her feet hurt. But when she saw the sweet table she began to cry. Fannie was beside her. "What's wrong?" Fannie asked.

"I've never seen anything so beautiful, Fannie. And . . . I never thought that a girl like me . . . a girl from a poor family, would ever have a wedding like this. How can I ever thank you for everything?"

"You already have, kid. You've been my best friend when nobody else wanted to."

CHAPTER THIRTEEN

Meanwhile, Izzy was at home alone fuming. *I've been snubbed again. Everybody is at Shatzy's wedding but me. And I was the fella who taught him everything. If it weren't for me, he would never have made it into the organization. He'd still be baking cakes, working fifty hours, for twelve dollars a week. That's what he deserves. He stole my girl. He won my boss over. Now Laevsky puts him above me.* Izzy was drinking heavily and chain-smoking. *Shatzy gets the girl. Laevsky loves Shatzy, and he gives him an expensive honeymoon. What doesn't Shatzy get? Lucky bastard.* Then Izzy remembered that Sam and Chana were leaving for a two-week honeymoon tomorrow. He picked up the telephone and called an old friend. A fella who was a small-time crook. One who'd never made it into the organization. But Izzy knew that this guy was good at what he did. "Hello, Zed, it's Izzy Reznick. I have a job for you."

"Izzy, it's been a long time," Billy Zedman said.

"Yeah, it has."

"I heard you were working for Laevsky now."

"You heard right," Izzy said.

"I have to say, that's pretty damn impressive. Good for you. I'm not one to take orders, but if I could I'd sure try to work for Laevsky. I hear he's pretty fair."

"Yeah. He's a great boss," Izzy said, not wanting to discuss this any further. Then he added, "Listen, I have a key to an apartment that will be empty after tomorrow. Nobody will be there for the next two weeks. There is plenty of expensive stuff in there. But if you're going to break in, you have to be careful. Really careful. And if you get caught, you gotta make sure you never mention my name. I don't like to threaten, but if you do happen to point a finger at me, I'll make you sorry. I know you have a wife and kids. So . . . enough said."

"What do you want from the job? How much is mine; how much is yours?"

"Nothing. Whatever you take is yours to keep. Just make sure you aren't seen and you don't get caught. And most importantly, no matter what, you never bring me into it."

"Can I pick the key up from you tomorrow night?"

"Sure, but wait a day or two just to be sure that the people that live at this place are gone. I wouldn't want this to get ugly, if you know what I mean." *I don't give a shit if he kills Sam but not Chana. So it's best if he breaks in when they're not there.*

CHAPTER FOURTEEN

It was after one in the morning when Sam and Chana waved goodbye to their wedding guests. They got into Sam's car and drove away slowly.

Sam turned onto a side street and parked. Then he turned to Chana. "Well . . . we did it, didn't we, Mrs. Schatzman."

"We sure did, Sammy," Chana said, ruffling his hair.

"I like the sound of that . . . Mrs. Schatzman," Sam said.

"We're married. It feels so funny to say it out loud," Chana said.

"You're my wife. We are truly one now," Sam said.

She cuddled into his arms. "I think everyone had a good time."

They sat like that for a few minutes. Then Sam said, "Hey, I got a question for you."

"Sure."

"Are you hungry, Mrs. Schatzman?"

"You know what, Mr. Schatzman, I sure am. I haven't eaten a thing today."

"Me neither. Let's go and see if we can find something open," Sam said. He started the car and drove to an all-night diner. It was nothing fancy. Sam and Chana were still wearing their wedding clothes. But they went in. The restaurant was empty except for an old couple who were sitting at a small table in the back holding hands.

There was no waitress. The owner walked over and handed Sam and Chana menus. "Let me guess. You two just got married, and you were so excited at your wedding that you forgot to eat."

"Yep," Sam said. "How'd you know?"

"'Cause when I got married twenty years ago, my wife and I did the same thing. But we didn't go out to eat. We went home and ate everything in the house."

The old couple overheard, and the woman laughed. "We did the same thing, didn't we, Elmer?" she said to the old man.

"Yep. We went home and ate a whole loaf of bread," Elmer said. "That was all we had."

"Well, we don't have any food in the house," Chana said, smiling, "so we came here."

"So what can I get for you two kids? It's on the house," the restaurant owner said.

They both ordered cheese omelets with toast.

When they finished eating, Sam whispered to Chana, "I know the owner said everything was on the house. But he has a small business, and I'm sure he could use the money. How about we leave a note to thank him and a sawbuck. In the note we can say that the money is to pay for the other couple in the restaurant and that the rest is a tip for the owner who waited on us. What do you think?"

"Sure, I love the idea of doing a mitzvah on our wedding night."

And so they did.

CHAPTER FIFTEEN

The following morning Sam packed the car. He was complaining, but only a little, that Chana packed too much. Then they had a quick cup of coffee and sweet rolls at the corner restaurant. And by 9 a.m., they were on the road north to Canada. It was a glorious day. God had painted the hills with leaves of vivid fall colors that had fallen from the trees. It looked like an autumn quilt. The sky was cornflower blue, and the air was crisp and fresh. Sam and Chana sang old familiar songs, trying to harmonize as they drove. By noon, Sam was hungry. So they stopped for lunch in a small town. They walked into a little café with a counter and two tables. A young blonde girl was serving. The cook was a big bald man, wearing a white dirty apron. Both of the private tables were occupied, so Sam and Chana sat at the counter. They ordered hamburgers and french fries. But Sam was suddenly quiet. He was staring at the waitress.

"What's wrong?" Chana asked.

"This place reminds me of Medina."

"And let me guess, the waitress reminds you of Betty?"

"Yeah, how did you know?"

"I can tell by the way you're looking at her."

"I am not looking at her the way you think. I am looking at her, and

I am feeling grateful for you and for how far I have come from my humble beginnings. You know, Betty can't hold a candle to you. Not in her looks, not in her personality. But most of all, not in my heart. You, and you alone, are my bashert. And I am so glad I found you."

She took his hand and kissed it. "You know, Sam. I think it might be nice to live in a small town someday. Everything looks so clean. The people are so friendly to each other. Watch them. They greet each other when they walk in here. It's kind of nice."

"Maybe it is. But I prefer the city. Even with all the dirt and hustlers, it has a special kind of charm."

She patted his hand.

The waitress brought two plates and set them down in front of Sam and Chana. Sam gobbled up his food quickly, and Chana could see that he was discreetly eyeing hers. "Are you still hungry?" she asked.

"I'm all right," Sam said.

"I'm full," Chana said.

"Are you sure?"

"Positive."

Sam pulled Chana's plate over and finished her food. She had to hide her smile. *I know you so well, Sam Schatzman. I knew you were still hungry,* she thought.

CHAPTER SIXTEEN

Niagara Falls, Ontario, Canada, *November 1930*

It was cold and they felt the mist come up from the Falls when they arrived at their hotel that night. It was a clean but small establishment right across the street from the Falls. Quickly, they dropped their luggage off in the room. Then they walked to a café. It was a star-filled night. Sam ordered wine and cheese with crackers.

"I can't believe we can order wine and drink it right here in plain sight," Chana said.

"That's how it was in Germany."

"Do you think the government will ever allow this in America?" Chana asked. "I mean, it wouldn't be good for business for you or for Laevsky if they made drinking legal."

"They've been talking about it. But I'm hoping it's just talk."

CHAPTER SEVENTEEN

Chana woke up early the next day, but Sam was tired from driving so she let him sleep. She longed to open the drapes and look out the window because although they'd seen the Falls the night before, she longed to see them in the daylight. The sound of rushing water penetrated the walls of the small hotel. Just as Chana wondered how long Sam would sleep, he turned over and took her into his arms. "Good morning" he said.

"Good morning. Can you hear the rush of the water?"

"Yep," he said, then he kissed her, and she felt herself melt into his arms.

After they made love, they both got dressed and went out for breakfast. As soon as they left the hotel room, they were both awestruck by the power and beauty of Niagara Falls.

"Would you just look at that. It's magnificent," Chana said.

"Like you," Sam replied.

She laughed. "Let's take the boat that goes under the Falls, today."

"All right. Right after breakfast."

Sam was famished. He ate a full breakfast while Chana sipped a cup of coffee and had two slices of buttered toast. Then they walked down to the dock where they paid to ride the boat under the Falls. It wasn't crowded, but there were several other people in line to board. As they handed the crewman their tickets, he said, "It gets wet out there. Put these on." He gave Sam and Chana yellow, hooded raincoats. They slipped them on.

As the boat made her way toward the Falls, Chana felt her heart race. There was a slight spray of water that dusted her face as the boat moved beneath the Falls. The spray increased as the boat made its way farther in. The powerful roar of the water was astounding. Sam put his arm around Chana. "It's breathtaking, isn't it?"

She nodded. Then when the boat stopped right under the Falls with the water pounding on their rain slickers, Sam turned Chana to face him and he kissed her. "I love you."

"I love you."

CHAPTER EIGHTEEN

The next two weeks were filled with lazy days of lovemaking and eating too much, of wandering through small gift shops, and of long conversations about nothing that lasted well into the night.

Chana could not remember ever having been as happy as she was during those days. She forced herself to put her work out of her mind and to think only of Sam and herself and the beauty of the moment. *If only this honeymoon could last forever*, she thought. But before she knew it, the time had come to return home.

Sam looked sad as he packed to leave. "This was wonderful," he said. "I never took a vacation before. But we have to plan to do this once a year."

"I'd like that," Chana said. But she knew she could not leave her business every year.

They checked out of the hotel. Laevsky had paid for everything.

Sam put his arm around Chana, and she lay her head on his chest as they drove back to Manhattan. They stopped for lunch, and then four hours later, because they knew they didn't have any food in the house. They stopped for dinner before going home.

Chana laughed as she watched Sam eating. "It was only a six-and-half-hour drive, and we had to stop twice to eat. You'd better be careful, Shatzy, or you're going to get fat."

"Will you still love me?"

"Of course. Just don't get too fat, or I'll have to be on top all the time." She giggled.

"And that would be so bad?" he asked.

The waitress dropped off the check. They paid and left. They were on their way home.

Once they arrived home, Sam carried all the suitcases to the door of the apartment while Chana waited. Then she opened the door, and he swept her into his arms and carried her across the threshold. "Welcome home, Mrs. Schatzman," he said as he flipped the light switch.

But instead of falling into bed together, they looked around the room in horror. Their home had been robbed and ransacked. The china dishes in the kitchen lay in broken pieces all over the floor. The silverware was gone. The sofa had been sliced open, and all the stuffing lay scattered around the living room. It was as if the burglar had been looking for something inside the couch. In the bedroom the drawers had been pulled out of the dressers, and their contents were strewn across the bed and floor. Sam's suits were missing from the closet. All of Chana's expensive gowns were gone. The bottles of whiskey he kept in his closet for personal use had been taken. And so was the champagne that he'd purchased and saved for their first night back home from their honeymoon.

Chana put her hand over her mouth to keep from screaming. She glanced over at Sam. Neither of them wanted to say what they were thinking. But then Sam forced himself to ask. "Where did you put the money from the wedding? The money we got as gifts?"

"I put it in my lingerie drawer," Chana said, looking at her lingerie spilling from the drawer and scattered like bird feed over the room. She knew the money was missing even before she searched for it. She wanted to yell at Sam because she'd begged him for months to have a safe installed in the apartment. But he had never gotten around to it. And now everything was gone.

Sam looked through the lingerie frantically. But the envelopes were not there. They had even taken all the money Sam had saved over the years that was hidden under his mattress.

"We're broke," he said in a shocked voice. "We were rich an hour ago, and now we're broke."

Chana nodded.

"What are we going to do? Everything I had saved is gone. All of our gifts are gone," Sam said "We can't call the police. Not with my job. They will ask too many questions."

"Well"—Chana took a deep breath—"we still have each other. You have a good job. I have a good business. We'll be all right. It will take some time, but we'll rebuild."

"Maybe I should call Laevsky and tell him what happened."

"No, it's late. No reason to wake him. What can he do now? Tell him in the morning," Chana said, "but don't let him give you any money to make up for this. I don't want to make him feel like all we want from him is money. He's been kind and so generous with us. We'll fix this problem on our own."

"Yeah, you're right. And I am sure he's going to offer us money when he finds out what happened because that's how he is."

"Not with all the guys, Sam. Just with you. I still have to wonder why," Chana said.

Chana and Sam straightened up the mess in their apartment in silence. And then they got into bed. Neither one of them felt like making love, so they lay in each other's arms and took comfort in the warmth of each other's bodies.

CHAPTER NINETEEN

New York City, *April 1931*

If Chana and Sam had not been so much in love, they would have been devastated by their loss from the robbery. They both worked hard through the winter and were able to pay the rent on the expensive, well-heated apartment. Nothing had really changed in their lives. Sam drove his automobile. Their table was always filled with good food. They went out for dinner and drinks with friends at least twice a week. The only thing missing was the money they would have saved from their wedding gifts. Money for a rainy day. But being young and in love, they couldn't imagine a time when things might not be so good. All they could see was today, and today was glorious.

Chana smiled as she put the candlesticks in the middle of table. She looked around the room. Everything was perfect: the flowers, the candles, the dinner. Sam would be home any minute. She glanced in the mirror. Her makeup was perfect. Not too heavy. She wore a white négligée, with her hair falling about her shoulders.

A key turned in the door. Chana let out a sigh as Sam walked in.

"What's all this?" He was genuinely surprised.

"Dinner," she answered.

He laughed. "It looks beautiful. But not as beautiful as you." He kissed her and took her in his arms. "Is this new?" he asked, looking at the négligée.

"It is. Do you like it?"

"Like it? Sweetheart, I can hardly make it through dinner."

"Well, you're going to have to. I have something to tell you. So go and change. I'll put the food on the table."

Sam went into the bedroom and got undressed while Chana put the brisket and kishka on the table. *His favorite*, she thought, and her heart was filled with tenderness.

"Kishka? It must be some special occasion. Most of the time you forbade me from eating it because it's cornmeal stuffed in a cow's intestine." He laughed.

"I don't forbid you. I just don't usually serve it because it's not my favorite."

"But you are serving it tonight?"

"Yep." She winked at him.

Sam sat down across the table from Chana and watched her serve the food. When she was done, they started eating.

"Don't tell me you're going to make me finish dinner before you tell me the big surprise."

"I am," she said. Chana served herself but she couldn't eat. She was too sick to her stomach and also excited. So she pushed the food around her plate. Then once Sam was done, she took his hand and led him into the living room. She sat down on the sofa and pulled him down beside her. Then she whispered in his ear. "I'm going to have a baby."

He looked stunned. "Are you sure?"

"Yep. I went to the doctor today. I am going to have a baby."

"Oh my God!!" he said. "What can I do for you? I'll clean the kitchen. You sit here and take it easy."

Chana laughed. "Let's clean up together. I'm fine. Women have been having babies since the beginning of time."

"That's true," Sam said. "But those women weren't you. They weren't my woman. My wife." He kissed her. She leaned back, and they began to make love on the sofa. "Is this safe for the baby?" Sam asked.

"Yep, the doctor said it's fine until the last trimester."

Chana could feel that Sam was especially gentle and tender when they made love that night. After they'd finished, they lay in each other's arms. She whispered, "Better get used to making love in our room. Once the baby is here, we are going to have to be a little more discreet."

"Well, if you say so. Then I guess we'd better take advantage of our freedom while we can." He kissed her and they made love again.

After Chana fell asleep on the sofa, Sam got up and quietly cleaned the kitchen. Then he put a blanket over Chana and went into the bedroom to write a letter to Alma to tell her the good news.

CHAPTER TWENTY

Berlin, *Summer 1931*

It had been a year since her father's death. But Alma could not find peace within herself. She was filled with grief over her loss and a terrible burning anger toward her mother. Many nights she awakened, unable to sleep, pounding her fists into her pillow. Finally, she went to her grandmother, who was sitting in the reading room adjacent to the living room, to ask for advice.

"Bubbie, I can't believe my father is gone. It's been a year, and I am still so angry with my mother and how she treated my dad."

"Perhaps you should write her a letter."

"I've tried, Bubbie. But I can't."

"Sure you can. Write everything you feel. Everything. Don't leave anything out. Then when you are done, read it back to yourself, and add anything else that you want to say."

"How can I ever say the things I want to say to my own mother. It would be so disrespectful."

"It's all right, Almalah, because once you have finished the letter, you are going to burn it, and when you do you are going to burn up all of your bad feelings with it. Then you will be able to go forward with your life."

"You think it will work?"

"I know it will," Bubbie said. She took a piece of paper and a pen out of the drawer and handed them to Alma. Then she nodded. "Go, write this in private in your room."

"All right, Bubbie. I'll try."

Alma took the paper and pen and went back up to her room. She sat down at her desk and stared at the blank sheet of paper. Then she began.

Mother,

When dad passed away, I hid in my room for an entire week and sat shiva alone. I wept for the wonderful father that he'd been, and for how much I knew I would miss him. But I also wept because of you. How could you hurt him the way you did? And then how could you not even show up at his funeral? After nineteen years of marriage, he meant nothing to you. Who are you, mom? I don't even know you anymore.

At the funeral, the rabbi tore Sam's lapel and the jacket to my dress because we were in mourning. I wore that jacket every day for a year. Because my heart was still mourning. Thank God Sam was here. I leaned on him and he helped me to make it through that funeral. When I shoveled the dirt on dad's grave, I wanted to die too.

I know I was always a disappointment to you because I looked like Dad. You thought I was the ugliest child you'd ever seen. And you made no secret of it. You told me every day how ugly you thought I was, and you did it in your own sweet way. By calling me your ugly duckling. But you know what, mother? I forgave you because I loved you, and I wanted a mother more than anything in the world. I could forgive you for hurting me, but not for what you did to dad. Right now, the only thing I wish was that I could relieve myself of these feelings of hatred I feel toward you.

At the funeral I met Bubbie Schatzman. She was a sad and strange old woman with her hair covered by a sheitel, a wig. I watched her and my heart went out to her as she stood in the back of the cemetery wringing a handkerchief in her hands. I tried to comfort her, but she wouldn't let me. It's no surprise. She doesn't really know me, does she? You made sure of that. When Sam and I would receive letters from our father's family, you threw them away. I am sure you thought I didn't see that, but I did. Once when I was only eight, I pulled one of those letters out of the garbage. I tried to read it, but I couldn't at the time because it was in Yiddish and I hardly knew how to read English then. However, I remembered your desire to keep us away from anything that had to do with dad. You just thought he was so beneath you. Well, you were wrong.

After the burial Sam and I went to the first shiva we'd ever attended. It was at your parents' home. We had no idea what to do. Bubbie had to help me with everything. She told me to wash my hands with the water that she'd left outside the door. She explained that it was symbolic we washed off the sadness from the cemetery so that death would not enter the house. Then Sam and I were told to walk around in our stocking feet and to sit on wooden boxes that were set up for the mourners. Can you imagine how that made me feel? I was a mourner. My father was dead, and you might as well have been. All the mirrors in the house were covered. I never knew that Jewish people even did that. You never told us. You never told us much, did you, mom?

I watched ten men gather and say kaddish for my father. Sam stood beside them, but he didn't know the prayers. He had never heard them, and he told me secretly that he wished he could say them because it might make him feel better.

Then Sam left for America and Bubbie and I grew even closer than before. She was the mother you should have been. I often talked to her about my memories of my dad. I told her about the time dad tried to take Sam and I fishing. It was a fiasco, but we had so much fun. Dad made us laugh but by the end of the day we realized that we hadn't caught a thing. So on the way home dad stopped at the fish market and bought fish because he had promised you that he would bring it home. He was always so careful not to disappoint you, mom. But no matter what he did, it was never good enough.

*I also told bubbie about the time dad took all of us to the zoo. You were there, complaining about the smell if I recall correctly. The big black bear was walking around his cage making a strange sound. We watched him for several minutes. Then out of nowhere dad began to imitate the bear perfectly. We all laughed until our bellies hurt.
Even you.*

Do you remember the day dad taught me to knead bread? He knew my hands weren't strong enough to actually do the job. But unlike you, dad made me feel useful.

I work at a hospital now. Every time I have a male patient that is around dad's age, I take extra special care of him. I do for that stranger what I was unable to do for my father. And sometimes it makes me feel better.

*Mom, I don't want to hate you. I want to love you. I wish I knew how to make you love me. But I can't. All I can do is try to let go and heal from the past so I can get on with my life.
Alma*

Alma read the letter over to herself. There was nothing more to add. She wept until she had no more tears. Then she took the paper outside and burned it.

CHAPTER TWENTY-ONE

Alma used her job at the hospital to help her cope with her grief. She agreed to take on extra shifts and was always eager to learn. But she found it difficult to make friends with the other girls. They were more outgoing and vivacious. They read fashion magazines and knew who the latest heartthrob male movie idol was. Alma had no interest in fashion or men. So she had nothing to talk to them about. Besides that, she had always been a loner, introverted and quiet. So when the weather permitted, while the others gathered around the lunch table showing off pictures of their latest boyfriends, Alma went outside to sit alone under an elm tree. She didn't mind being alone. It was easier than trying to think of something to say to the other girls. And she loved working at the hospital. It gave her a sense of purpose. Although she was not a doctor, at least she felt she was able to help people who needed her.

Esther was Alma's best friend and strongest supporter. Although Esther agreed with Ted that Alma should get married and have a family. Esther was more concerned with Alma's happiness than her husband was. Because most people in the Jewish sector of Berlin knew of her grandparent's wealth, there were still men who were interested in making a match with Alma regardless of Goldie's tainted reputation. Zede tried his best to make a match. He invited men to come to their house for dinner to meet Alma. But when they came, Alma was purposely standoffish, and they never returned or offered a proposal. She was perfectly happy with her life just the way it was. To go to work each day, and to go shopping and out for lunch with her grandmother on her days off.

The Birnbaums had recently hired another new maid who prepared a packed lunch for Alma to take to work each day. The previous maid had just disappeared one afternoon. Alma had overhead her grandfather saying something to her grandmother about catching the last maid stealing. But Alma didn't listen too closely. She hated to hear bad things about anyone. The new maid was a sweet young German girl. Her name was Marta, and she insisted on packing Alma a heavy and nutritious lunch each day. Since Alma was not a big eater, most of it went to waste. She tried to tell Marta that she didn't need such a large meal, but each day there was enough for three people in her lunch bag.

One day, when the sky was as blue as Wedgwood china, and the clouds were as white as a wedding gown, Alma sat beneath the elm tree looking up at the sky.

"Mind if I join you?" A man who was short and sturdy in stature walked over to her. He wore a white doctor's coat, and a stethoscope hung from his neck. His thick black hair was a mass of curls and he had a small potbelly. The man was only a few inches taller than Alma. She looked up at him. His gentle eyes were the blue-green color of the ocean.

"Oh, you want to sit here? Yes, I mean . . . I suppose so," Alma said. She'd been caught off guard.

He sat down cross-legged on the grass across from her. "I've seen you around the hospital," he said with an accent. "My name is Lorenzo Bellinelli. It's a pleasure to meet you." Then he gave her a wide smile that made his eyes twinkle.

Alma looked down at the ground. "Nice to meet you," she whispered.

"May I ask your name?" he said in German.

"Alma Schatzman." Her accent was definitely not German.

"You are an American, no?" he said in English.

"Yes, and, let me guess, you are an Italian?" she said.

"Now, how can you tell?" he joked. "Could it be my good looks? Or my charming personality?"

"It's your last name and your accent. But may I be so bold as to ask how is it you speak such good English?"

"I have studied languages all my life. That's because I've always loved to travel. So I speak several languages: German, French, English, Latin, and, of course, Italian. You?"

"Just English and a pathetic bit of German. But my German is really derived from my growing up speaking Yiddish."

"Yiddish? You are Jewish, then?"

"Yes," she said proudly.

"I have many Jewish friends and colleagues. Nice people," he said, then continued. "Where are you from in America? I am from Rome. My family is still there."

"Upstate New York. Recently my family moved to the city."

"You can call me Lory. All of my American friends call me Lory."

"Lory it is, then," she said.

"I love Italy. And, of course, I miss home sometimes. I miss my family and, of course, the food. Have you ever been?"

"To Italy? No."

"It's a shame. I say everyone should go to Italy at least once in their lives. But, of course, I'm biased. It's my home."

"So what brings you to Germany?" she asked, wondering why it was so easy to talk to him. It was unusual for her to find it so easy to communicate with anyone.

"I have come here to study for the summer, and I must say, Berlin is quite the city, don't you think?"

"It's a bit wild for my tastes. I stay here because my grandmother is here."

"You miss America?"

"No, not really. There was a lot back there that I was glad to leave behind. My brother is still in America and I miss him. But he is married. He has recently written to tell me that his wife is pregnant, so I doubt he will be coming to Germany any time soon." She looked at him and saw that there was a glow of warmth in his eyes unlike anything she'd ever seen before.

"Perhaps you will go home to America to visit?"

"Perhaps. I would like to go because I have never met my sister-in-law. She and I have exchanged letters though, and she seems very nice."

"When is the baby due?"

"Sam, that's my brother, says he expects Chana to give birth in December."

"Chana, is that your sister-in-law's name?"

"Yes, it is."

"Pretty name."

"It's a Jewish name," she said.

"Are you very religious?" he asked.

"No, my family wasn't when I was growing up."

"I am a nonpracticing Catholic. My mother is incredibly angry about that. She is religious. But not me. I don't go to church or celebrate holidays. But I try to do good things for my fellow man, and I am fairly certain that there is a God. I've seen his presence in my work with very sick patients. Not always, but sometimes he makes an appearance." He smiled.

"Don't you think that maybe what you are seeing is just coincidence? I mean when you think you are seeing God?"

"Oh no. I have seen a family pray and heal a man I was certain was going to die. I have seen a mother pray for her child with a fatal disease, and the disease has miraculously disappeared."

"That's fascinating," Alma said. Then she remembered she had two more cheese sandwiches in her lunch bag. "By the way, would you like a sandwich?" she asked.

"Sure." He grinned. "And . . . by the way, there is something else you should know about me . . . I love to eat."

She smiled and handed him the sandwich.

CHAPTER TWENTY-TWO

The following afternoon Lorenzo appeared a few minutes after Alma had sat down under the tree. He carried a white paper box. "I've brought some cookies," he said. "Now, I have to make a disclaimer. These are German cookies, and they can't compare to Italian pastries. I tried to find an Italian bakery that was open because I would have preferred to bring Italian pastries. Unfortunately, I was not able to. So accept these as a gift of my appreciation for your sandwich yesterday."

She laughed. "You didn't have to do this."

"I know. I am sometimes a silly man. But I always try to be thoughtful. Anyway, I hope you like the cookies. And someday, maybe you will come to visit me in Italy, and I will take you for some truly delicious cookies."

She laughed again. "Thank you. This was very thoughtful, and these are just fine."

He stood balancing on one foot, then the other, looking like he was at a loss for words. "I suppose I should go," he said, but he didn't leave.

"Well, you could go, I suppose," she said, but when she saw his face fall and the disappointment in his eyes, she added, "But . . . just in case you're hungry, I have another sandwich for you."

"I'm always hungry."

She handed him a sandwich. "Good, because I always have plenty of food."

Lory took that invitation to mean that he might come and have lunch with Alma each day. And so he did.

For the rest of the summer, every day that Alma worked, Lory met her under that elm tree at noon. He always brought desserts, and she always had plenty of sandwiches. The first week, she found his constant company intrusive. She was not used to socializing with anyone other than her grandmother. And until she met Lory, she'd spent her lunch hour regrouping after working with the patients all morning.

He liked to talk, to tell jokes that required her to laugh, and he loved to eat. Alma had never had so much attention, and sometimes she found it unnerving. But then one afternoon when she went to sit under the tree, Lorenzo was not there waiting for her. Ten minutes passed, and he still had not arrived. She looked around wondering if she'd somehow offended him. And it surprised her that she was disappointed, and even a little hurt, that he hadn't come. *He's probably found someone more interesting to spend his lunch hour with. I suppose it's for the best because there is nowhere that this friendship between us can go*, she told herself. *He's fun to talk to, and he makes me laugh, but I don't want anything more from him or any other man.* But in spite of herself, she still found herself watching the door to the hospital for Lory to come out. He didn't come. At the end of her lunch hour she packed up her things, feeling strangely sad, biting her lip, and feeling like she wanted to cry. Then she began walking back to the door to the hospital.

"Alma." She heard his voice and stopped cold in her tracks. "Alma." He was running toward her. "I'm so sorry. I had to stay; I couldn't leave. An emergency patient came in. He was in need of an emergency surgery, and our instructor insisted that the class stay and observe it. I tried to pay attention, but all I could think of was you waiting here and wondering where I was."

"Who said I was wondering where you were," she said, angry with

CHAPTER 22 | 69

herself for the feeling of relief that had come over her the moment she saw him.

"You weren't?" He looked at her as if she'd broken his heart.

Alma shrugged; her lip quivered. "I was," she admitted.

"I am sorry. I would never want to make you wait for me or wonder where I was. You have become very important to me. My first priority. I don't know if you realize this or not, but you have." Then he leaned over and kissed her. Alma froze. The lunch bag that she held in her hand fell to the ground.

She pushed away from him. "I'm sorry, Lory. I have to go to work," she said, confused by the mixture of feelings that were shooting through her. Then she picked up the bag she'd dropped and almost tripped as she ran toward the door and then inside the hospital. The rest of the day was a blur. Her feelings frightened her. *Did my pushing him away when he tried to kiss me put an end to his interest in me? I hope not, and yet I know that I am not capable of being in love, and it would be best if he left me alone.*

That night Alma lay awake unable to sleep.

The following day, when she left the building for lunch, she breathed a sigh of relief that Lory was waiting under the tree for her. When he saw her he waved. She walked over and sat down beside him. His face exploded into a smile. "I have a surprise for you," he said in an excited voice.

"A surprise?"

"Can you guess what it is? You will never guess." He laughed. "I'll have to tell you."

"All right." She shrugged and smiled. "Then tell me."

"I found an Italian bakery. And so . . . I brought you pastries from my country today. Here, look." He opened the box.

"That was very sweet of you." She looked into his eyes, genuinely touched that he'd made such an effort for her.

"I am a very sweet man. And I am also, how do you say it in America, very sweet on you, Alma."

She looked away.

"I am afraid I offended you yesterday when I tried to kiss you. Please, you should know that I have the utmost respect for you. I would never want to do anything that made you feel uncomfortable."

"It's not your fault," she said. "It's just me. It's just me. It's just the way I am."

"And . . . Alma . . . I like you just the way you are. I wouldn't want to change anything about you. You see I like you a lot."

"I know," she said, handing him a sandwich. "And I like you too. But . . ."

"There is no but. You like me. I like you. Perhaps we should arrange a day off together, and then we can go for dinner or perhaps lunch if you would prefer. Maybe you would want to walk around the zoo . . . or the park . . . or . . ."

"Lory . . . I can't."

"Why? Why can't you?" he said. And she knew he was nervous because whenever he became uncomfortable, his English suffered, and he sounded like a foreigner. It reminded her of her father who had the same thing happen whenever he got upset. Seeing something that reminded her of her father in Lory made her want to touch Lory's shoulder. It was a bittersweet mixture of missing her dad and feeling close to Lory, almost like he was a part of her family.

"I am Jewish. You are not. My grandmother would be so upset," she protested. But she knew her protest was weak. *Can I tell him the truth? It's so painful to talk about.*

"I'll convert. My mother will be upset. But I will do it for you. I like you, Alma. I don't know how else to put it. I haven't ever really had a girl before in my life. And you are very special to me," he said. She could hear that he'd regained his composure.

"I am not your girl. I am just some girl you have lunch with to pass the time."

"I know you don't believe that. You can't possibly believe that. Alma, you are more important to me than I can ever express."

They sat together in silence for a few minutes. Then he smiled and it broke the tension.

"I don't know about all of this, Lory," she said, looking down at the ground.

"There is nothing to figure out. What we have is timeless. You understand what I am saying to you?"

She looked into his eyes. Tears were forming in hers. A single tear fell down her cheek.

Lory touched her hand. Then he offered her a smile. "Don't cry, beautiful Alma," he said, then he added with a big smile, "Hey, have you ever had a cannoli? Here, taste this." He broke off a piece of the pastry and put it into her mouth. She looked into his eyes, and he smiled. "Good, huh?"

She chewed and swallowed. "Yes, very," she said, nodding. A bit of cream was on the side of her lip. He wiped it away with his thumb. She looked down, but her hand went to her mouth.

"You would love Rome. And, Jewish or not, my mother would love you. You know why?" he said in a soft voice.

She shook her head.

"Because I do."

"You do what?"

"I love you," he said.

She felt another tear slip down her cheek.

"May I kiss you?" he asked.

She nodded.

He placed a gentle, soft kiss on her lips. Her hand went up to her mouth again, and she held it there for a moment. And for that single moment she was the girl she had once been. The sweet, naïve young girl who believed in romance and read books about everlasting love. The girl she had been before those boys had hurt her in Medina.

CHAPTER TWENTY-THREE

When Alma and Lory first started having lunch together, their discussions revolved around the hospital and the patients. But as time passed, they both realized that they shared a deep desire to help people. They both longed to make a difference in the world.

The day after Lory confessed his love for Alma, they sat under the tree looking at the blanket of colorful fall leaves, holding hands. Alma told him about her disappointment at not being allowed to attend medical school. Lory said he understood how she felt and that she had a bright and fascinating mind, but he also said that he agreed with her grandparents. "A girl should be a wife and mother. Motherhood is the most important job in the world," he said.

"I don't think I will ever be a mother," she said quietly.

"You don't like children?"

"I love children. I just don't think I am the marrying kind."

"What is the marrying kind?" he asked.

"I am sorry, but I don't want a husband . . . ever." The thought of getting married frightened her and she became defensive. Alma took her hand away from Lory and wrapped her arms around her chest.

He nodded. "My time here in Germany will be up at the beginning of October. I will be returning to Rome," he said. "I don't want to hurry you. I would never want to make you uncomfortable. But I care for you, Alma. I care deeply for you. Deeply enough that if you want to go to medical school as soon as I could afford it, I would do my best to help you."

She looked away from him. "I don't know what you are trying to say."

"Yes you do. I am asking you to marry me."

"Just like that? Marry you? You are not even Jewish. Even if I wanted to marry you, which I don't, I couldn't because you are not Jewish." She ranted at him angrily.

"I told you that I'll change my religion. I know you said you didn't want me to. But I would if it would make your family happy."

"It's more than that."

He reached over and took her hand. "Talk to me, Alma. Tell me what it is that is that you are afraid of."

She felt a tingle go up from her palm and through her entire arm. She tried to pull her hand away, but he held her firmly but gently. "I don't know how to tell you why. I don't know what to do."

"It's me. You can tell me anything. You should know that by now. No matter what you say to me, I will always love you. And I will never hold anything you tell me against you"

She put her hands over her face. "I still don't know how to tell you."

"Just tell me. Is it that you can't have children? If it is, it's all right. We can adopt a child. Or we can spend our lives helping children who are sick. I don't care. I want to spend my life with you. Together, we can move mountains."

"Lory . . ." She hesitated. Then she cleared her throat and continued. "I was raped. It was so horrible. There was more than one boy. There were several terrible, sadistic boys, monsters, one after another." Her entire body was trembling. "I can't bear the thought of anyone ever touching me like that again." She began to weep. He reached over, and without a word he took her into his arms and held her close to him rocking her like she was a frightened child.

"It's all right," he said. Then he began to sing softly to her in Italian. He stopped for a moment and said, "My mother used to sing this song to me when I was a little boy and I was afraid of the dark. It's a song about not knowing what lies ahead. But overcoming your fears and going forward with your life. I know you are afraid. I understand. But I am here, and I will be with you every step of the way. I'll hold your hand, and I'll sing this song to you to give you strength. If you will let me love you, I'll be your guiding light. I promise you I will never hurt you."

She nuzzled closer into his soft, warm body.

"Will you be my wife?" he asked. "Will you give me a chance to help you to believe in love again?"

"Yes. But . . . there is something else I think you should know."

He continued to hold her in his arms. "Tell me . . . anything."

"Well . . ." She hesitated. "We have never really discussed our parents or our backgrounds. All I know about you is that you were raised Catholic. All you know about me is that I am Jewish, and I have a brother and sister-in-law who are expecting a child."

"All right. I'll tell you more about me. My life is an open book. Especially to you. My father was a construction worker. He died in a terrible accident a few years ago. My mother moved in with my brother and his wife. They have no children as of yet, but we are all hopeful that they will have a child soon." He massaged her head, then continued to speak. "And I have no other siblings. I don't really have much to tell."

"I do, I am afraid. My father died of a heart attack last year. It happened when he came here to Germany to visit. It was devastating."

"I'm sorry."

"Yes, me too. But . . . the reason he had the heart attack is because of my mother." Then she blurted out the entire story of Sam and the blood libel and how her family had lost the bakery. "It drove my mother crazy. She left my father and came back to live here in her hometown of Berlin. I came with her. I thought she would stay for a while and realize that she missed my father and brother and return home to America. But she didn't. She's not the same woman anymore. She doesn't live with my grandparents. She is living with a friend. She's drinking heavily and using heroin or some other kind of dope.

It's like she's gone crazy. I haven't seen her in a long time. But I thought you deserved to know about her."

"I see," he said.

"She has brought shame on our family. My grandparents don't know what to do with her. So, knowing this, I don't know if you still want to marry me. My mother could easily bring shame upon you if you were my husband."

"Don't worry. I am not afraid."

"You don't know her."

"I don't; it's true. But I'll meet her if you would like, and I'll go with you to invite her to our wedding. If that's what you want."

"I don't know what I want. But I would like to know if you are having any second thoughts about marrying me now that you know this."

"Not a one," he said.

CHAPTER TWENTY-FOUR

Esther had made a batch of mandel bread. It was hot from the oven and loaded with nuts. She asked Alma to sit beside her at the dining table and have a piece with a cup of tea.

"I made this. Not the maid!" Esther said proudly. "This was my own mother's recipe. I haven't made it for years."

"It's good, very good," Alma said.

"I am glad you like it."

"Bubbie . . . I have something I have to tell you," Alma said, trying to sound sure of herself. "I have met someone, and I am going to get married."

"Oy, I had no idea," Esther said. "This is the first I am hearing of you having a boyfriend. NU, who is he?"

"Bubbie, I am sorry. You know I want you to be happy. But I am afraid you won't when I tell you about him. His name is Lory. He is a nice boy . . . but . . ."

"Nu? So what are you trying to say?"

"I am sorry, Bubbie. I am so sorry. But he's not Jewish. His name is Lorenzo Bellineli, and his family is from Italy."

"A goy?"

Alma nodded.

"And you love him?" Esther said, putting her cup down, her face turning white.

"I do, Bubbie. I love him."

A few moments passed. Esther silently stirred her tea. Then she smiled and gently caressed Alma's cheek. "What can we do? If this boy is the one you really want. Then, although I am not happy about it, I will accept him. I will because I love you, Alma."

The following day at breakfast, Alma told her grandfather about Lory. He had a different reaction.

Zede Birnbaum was clenching and unclenching his fists. His face was as red as the Nile River when God turned it to blood, but his voice was deep and controlled. "I will not give you a dime nor will I make you a wedding if you marry this goy. So you can tell this Italian gold digger that he is looking in the wrong money pot. There will be nothing from me. Do you understand? Nothing," Zede said.

"I understand, Zede," Alma said.

"I've brought plenty of good Jewish boys home for you as prospective matches, and to each one you said no but to this shegetz you say yes? Why, Alma? To hurt us?"

"I would never want to hurt you or Bubbie. I love you both. It just happened. Lory and I met at the hospital, and he is the first man who I have ever felt this way about. I feel like I could live the rest of my life with him."

"Is this because of your mother? Is this because you are afraid that if you get engaged to a nice Jewish boy from a good family again, they will find out about her again and break it off like the Finkenbergs did?"

"No, Zede. It's not that simple. There is something very special about Lory. He is the kind of man I used to dream about when I was little girl."

"You used to dream of a shegetz from Italy? Are you crazy? I know you aren't the prettiest girl, and that has been a little bit of a deterrent for some of the fellows I've brought home, but, Alma, we can try harder. And if we do, I am sure we can find you a Jewish boy."

"I'm sorry if you are angry with me, but I am going to marry Lory.

We don't want your money, but we would like your blessing. Lory is willing to convert to Judaism if that would help."

"I don't believe in converts. A Jew is born a Jew. Someone who converts is never a real Jew in my estimation. And like I told you, don't expect a wedding or any financial help from me." Zede Birnbaum slammed his fist on the table and walked out.

Alma put her head down. For a few seconds neither Esther nor Alma spoke. Then Esther got up and walked over. She put her hand over Alma's. "I know you didn't do this to hurt us. I know you are a good girl. I understand you, better than you think." She lifted Alma's face gently. "So you will live here in Germany or you are moving to Italy?"

"We will live in Rome because he will finish medical school there. But I will come back to see you often. It is not so far from Italy to Germany."

"That's very true," Esther said. "At least it's a lot closer than America." She smiled. "I was afraid you were going to return home with Sam. I'm glad you didn't. And like you said, Italy isn't far at all."

"You aren't angry with me, Bubbie?"

"How can I be angry with you? You've been the light of my life. Since you came to stay with us, I have had such naches. I love you, Alma. I want you to be happy."

CHAPTER TWENTY-FIVE

That night after Esther went to bed, Alma went up to her room and wrote a letter to Sam in America telling him that she was going to get married. She told him there was to be no wedding; however, he was welcome to attend the civil ceremony. She sealed the envelope. Then she sat down on her bed and thought about her mother. *Even though there will be no wedding party, there will be a marriage. And she is my mother. She has a right to know that I am getting married. Lory has agreed to go with me to speak to her, although I am ashamed of her. Still, I will bring him with me. I know I told him about my mother. But he needs to see her firsthand to see how bad she really is. He should know the truth about everything, even my mother, before he marries me. Poor Lory, I know he loves me, but he has no idea how bad my mother really is. And besides that, I hope he won't be disappointed when I tell him that my grandfather refuses to make us a wedding.*

The following day while Alma and Lory were having lunch, she told him that she'd sent a letter to her brother inviting him and his wife to the wedding. "I also told my grandparents about us," she said.

"And . . . what did they say," he asked.

"My grandmother was upset at first, but she is willing to accept us. I know she wishes you were Jewish. But she is glad I am happy."

"Are you happy?" he asked.

"Yes, I am."

"That is what matters to me. Knowing you're happy is all I need," he said.

"But, Lory, my grandfather was angry. He refuses to make us a wedding. I don't know if he will even come to a civil ceremony."

"All this because I am not Jewish?"

"Yes. It means that much to him. I told you this would happen."

"You told him I would be willing to convert?"

"Yes, I told him. But it won't help."

"I'm so sorry he feels that way. I think maybe it's about time I meet him. Maybe once he meets me and sees just how much I love you, he will change his mind."

"I wouldn't count on it. He's a stubborn old goat sometimes."

"The least I can do is try, right?"

"Yes."

"I know this has all been very hard for you. Would you like me to convert, Alma?"

"Not at all. I don't want to change anything about you," she said. "You're perfect just the way you are."

CHAPTER TWENTY-SIX

Three weeks later, Alma received a letter from Sam wishing her the very best, but that he and Chana would not be able to make it to Germany to attend the ceremony because Chana was too far along in her pregnancy to travel. He promised that they would try to come to Germany and visit the following year.

Alma wasn't disappointed. She'd expected as much. A long sea voyage wasn't the best idea for a pregnant woman.

Arrangements had been made for Alma and Lory to take a Sunday off from work so he could have lunch at her home where he would meet her grandparents. Then after lunch they planned to go to Leni's apartment to tell her mother about their plans to marry.

Lory arrived early. He brought a cake from a kosher bakery. When he handed it to her at the door, he whispered, "I made sure it was kosher. I hope it's all right."

"It's perfect," she said. Although Alma's grandparents had never kept kosher, she had to smile at Lory's thoughtfulness.

The table was set beautifully with gold flatware and cream-colored china with a gold design around the perimeter. Frau Birnbaum showed Lory to his seat beside Alma. Herr Birnbaum took his seat at the head of the table. Then Frau Birnbaum turned to the maid and said, "You may begin serving, Marta."

Dinner was delicious. There was a brisket of beef that was so tender it could be cut with a fork. And crispy potato latkes that had been fried to a perfect golden brown, then drizzled with applesauce. A huge platter of fresh, buttered green beans and a hearty German bread completed the meal. However, there was an awkward silence in the room.

"This food is wonderful," Lory said.

"I'm glad you like it," Esther answered.

Zede cleared his throat and looked at Lory. "You want to marry my granddaughter?" he said, shaking his head. Then he stared at Lory and added, "I think you should know that I don't approve. You must realize that you are from a different country. You are of a different religion. You and Alma are not for each other. And I want you to know that if you go ahead with this foolhardiness, I will not make you a wedding party. Nor will you receive any money from me . . . ever. So if you happened to have had your eye on my fortune, you can cast your glance at some other girl."

"Sir, with all due respect, I have no interest in your money. I am in love with your granddaughter. I plan to marry her with or without your approval. You needn't worry about her; I am in medical school. I will earn a good salary, and I will take good care of her. She will always come first in my life."

"Hmmm, and when are you scheduled to complete your schooling?"

"I will be finished with all my tests and licensing in January. That is only a few months from now. Then I will be a doctor. If Alma would like, I will have her help me in my practice. Together, we will dedicate our lives to helping those in need because that is what we have both aspired to do since we were children."

Alma cast an admiring glance at Lory. *Sometimes he makes me so proud of him*, she thought.

"So when do you want to get married?" Esther asked.

"I have to return home to Italy at the end of October. I would like to marry before I have to go, so Alma could go with me."

"That's less than a full month," Zede said. "Is there something I should know? Is there some reason you feel a need to rush like this?" Then he studied Alma. "You're not expecting, are you?"

Alma shook her head.

"No reason other than that I have to go home to finish my education. It would make me happy to have Alma by my side. She is not expecting. I have treated your granddaughter with the utmost respect."

"Would you still marry him if I said I would not attend the ceremony, Alma?" her zede asked. "Do I mean so little to you that you would marry him regardless?"

Alma chewed her lip. Then she said, "Zede, I love you and believe me, I would never do anything to shame you or to hurt you. But I am in love with Lory, and whether you decide to show up or not, I am getting married to him at the end of October."

"I will not stand for anyone speaking to me so impertinently in my own home," Zede said. He stood up, slammed his fist on the table and walked out of the room.

Alma put down her fork. She tried to keep the tears from falling down her cheeks, but she was unable to stop them.

"Would you like me to leave?" Lory asked.

Alma shook her head. "No. It's all right. I'm sorry, Bubbie. But we should get going. We are going to talk to my mother. I want to invite her to the courthouse to see me get married."

"Your mother? Vey iz mir. Maybe you should save that for another day? You think it's a good idea to go and see her right now? After you're so upset from your zede?"

"Probably not, but I have to Bubbie. I have to."

Esther went over to Alma. She sat down beside her and patted Alma's hand. "I suppose you have to do what you feel is right. You want maybe I should ask Hans to drive you?"

"No, Lory and I will take the bus."

"Are you sure?"

Alma nodded.

Esther stood up and kissed Alma on the forehead. Then she said, "And don't you worry about your zede. He's just hurt because he feels powerless to control you. But you don't know him like I do." She winked. "He's mad now, but he'll be at the wedding. You'll see."

"You really think he'll come?"

"Of course he'll come, Almalah. He is a hard man; I won't deny that, but your zede is no fool, and I know he wouldn't miss his granddaughter's wedding for the world."

CHAPTER TWENTY-SEVEN

Alma and Lory got off the bus and then followed the directions Esther had given them to Leni's apartment. The area where she lived was very different than the wealthy neighborhood where the Birnbaums' home was. The apartments were older and more run down. There were pharmacies that advertised sedatives and stimulants right in their windows. Half-torn political posters hung from the sides of buildings beside provocative advertisements for seedy nightclubs. And although the Jewish neighborhood where Alma lived in New York was poor, the two areas were very different. Here, in Berlin, there were no raggedy-clothed children running through the streets. This place had a seedier feel to it. There were pornographic book and magazine stores and peep shows around every corner. For the most part the streets were empty. During the day everyone slept, but this part of the city came alive at night.

"This is it," Lory said, reading the address on the side of the building. "Are you sure you want to go in?"

"I have to, Lory," Alma said, taking his hand. He gave her hand a gentle squeeze for support, and they walked inside the building. They still held hands as they headed up the stairs. Walking down the hall to Leni's apartment, Alma noticed little notes on several of the apartment doors. One read "Tall blonde female. Dominatrix who adores submissives."

Another read "Young man. I am twenty but I look fifteen. If you like young boys, knock."

"For a good time, just knock."

Alma turned to Lory. "What is all this?"

"Prostitutes," he answered. "They advertise themselves this way, I suppose."

"You've seen this before?"

"Yes, I have."

"You went to a prostitute?"

He shook his head. "You want to know the truth?"

"Of course. I always want you to tell me the truth."

"I went with some friends in Italy when I was young. We all paid the girl. But when it was my turn and she took off her clothes, I was repulsed. So I left."

"Really, why?"

"Disease. I have been studying it since forever. Even when I was just a boy, I was interested in medicine. Here is this naked girl laying on a bed, and all I can think of is syphilis." He laughed.

She laughed in spite of the tension she was feeling. "I understand because I know you."

"I think maybe I am not normal. My fear overcame my hormones and I ran. Besides that, for me I would rather make my first time with someone I truly love, like you."

"You're a virgin?" She stood still and looked at him shocked.

"Actually, yes."

"That's unusual for a man."

"I suppose. Do you still love me?"

"Even more." She smiled.

They walked a few feet and then stood side by side at the door to Leni's apartment. Alma took a deep breath and knocked. Several moments passed. "I don't think anyone is home," she said.

"We can come back another time."

They were just about to leave when the door creaked open. A woman wearing a silk kimono, with what appeared to be blood splattered all over her neck, opened the door. There was black mascara smeared all around her eyes, giving her the appearance of a human racoon. "Who are you two? And what do you want?" she said, holding her head as if she had a miserable headache.

Alma could not take her eyes off of the blood on the woman's neck.

"What are you staring at?"

"I'm sorry. I didn't mean to stare," Alma said. "Actually, my name is Alma. You must be Leni."

"I am Leni. What do you want?" Then she tilted her head for a moment. "Alma. I know that name. You're Goldie's kid, right?"

"Yes. That's right. I am here to see my mother."

"Oh, come on in." Leni laughed.

Lory and Alma walked into a room filled with clothes strewn across every available surface. On the table was a spoon that had a burn mark and a hypodermic needle beside it, and next to that was a dirty rubber cord. Two empty bottles that said "Absinthe" lay on the floor discarded.

"You keep staring at my neck," Leni said. "It's nothing. It's not real. It's just fake blood. Don't look so shocked, dear. Why don't you two sit down."

Lory moved a pile of clothing from a small section of the sofa and motioned for Alma to sit. "Is my mother here?" Alma asked, "I need to speak to her."

"Oh yeah, I almost forgot why you came. My mind isn't what it used to be." Leni giggled. "Sorry. That's right. You came to see Goldie." She took a cigarette butt out of the ashtray and lit it. "I'm all out again. I can't keep 'em very long. As soon as I get a pack, I enjoy them so much that I smoke like a fiend. Then before I know it, these butts are all I have left." Leni indicated the cigarette butt.

"My mother," Alma said, her voice hoarse. "My mother. Is she here?"

"No. I thought I told you. Goldie is down the street at the Chinaman."

"You mean the Chinese restaurant?"

"No, silly. I mean the opium den. It's right down the street. It's in the basement of Wong's Chinese food."

"Opium den?"

"You'll find it. Just go into the restaurant and tell the fella at the counter that you want to go downstairs. He'll take you to the den."

Alma thought she might vomit or faint. She wasn't sure which. But then Lory's hand was on her arm helping her up, and somehow she could draw strength from his touch.

They left the apartment and the building as fast as they could. Then they walked for a few steps before Alma leaned against the brick that surrounded a small general store and bent over at the waist.

"It's all right. Breathe deep," Lory said. "Take as much time as you need." He gently rubbed her back, then added, "Are you sure you want to go to this place?"

"I have to see her. I've come this far," she said, sucking in a deep breath.

"I understand. And I'm ready to be at your side. Let's go."

When they told the host at the Chinese restaurant that they wanted to go downstairs, he called out in Chinese, and an old Chinese woman came to show them the way. They followed the old woman down a narrow flight of stairs without a banister. At the bottom, a door opened to a private room that smelled like fish and rotten vegetables. Lory glanced at Alma. "Are you all right?" he asked.

She nodded.

"Go on. Go on. Hurry, hurry. I have work to do, can't stand around here all day," the old woman said, holding the door open. Alma and Lory entered.

People lay on cots and sofas in the dimly lit opium den. Some were asleep; others were naked and tangled up in one another. At first Alma didn't see her mother. But when she spotted Goldie naked in the corner with a half-dressed man laying beside her, she gasped. "That's her," she said to Lory, and even though she'd been expecting this, the reality of it left her appalled. Lory took off his suit jacket as they walked over to Goldie. He placed it over Goldie without asking. She looked up at them both. Her eyes were glassy, and she looked dazed. But then she squinted and something registered. Her mouth flew open. "Alma? Am I dreaming or is that you?"

"It's me, Mom," Alma said, feeling bitter bile rise in her throat.

Goldie pulled Lory's jacket closer around her. "What are you doing here?"

"I came to find you."

Goldie rubbed her eyes. "Get off me," she said, pushing the man away from her and sitting up. "I wish you hadn't come here, honey," she said, not meeting Alma's eyes. Then she added in a sad voice, "Oh Alma, my poor sweet Alma. This is no place for you. You see, I don't come here too often. But . . . after your father, I was so sad. I was just so sad . . ." then Goldie started crying. She wiped her eyes and nose with the corner of Lory's jacket. "Yeah, I really was sad. I felt so guilty and I just couldn't cope. Ya know? So, to make it better, sometimes I came here to see the China man. And the opium worked. It helped me forget. And that made it better. But I promise you, honey. I really am trying to get myself straightened out. I'm gonna quit the opium and all the other stuff too. I will; you'll see. I know that I made a lot of mistakes. Don't make mistakes like I did . . ." Goldie was slurring her words and rambling.

"I didn't come here to hear a confession," Alma said, cutting her mother off. Her tone of voice was curt. "I came to tell you that Lory and I are getting married at the courthouse on October 28th. You are welcome to come if you would like. If not, I understand. But I thought it was only right to extend the invitation."

"You were always such a good girl." Goldie smiled. "Not a pretty girl." She shook her head. Then she studied her daughter. "Are you happy? Because if you're not, don't marry him. It will ruin your life. Believe me, I know. I married your father and I shouldn't have, I knew . . ."

"I'm very happy, Mother," Alma cut in again. "I have to go."

"I'll be there. What time is the wedding?"

Alma looked at Lory. They hadn't set a time yet. "You want to get married at, say, eleven in the morning, then maybe we can take Bubbie out for lunch?" Alma asked.

"Yes," Lory said.

"Eleven a.m. on October 28th."

"I'll be there, Alma. At the courthouse, right? See, I remembered."

Goldie smiled. "And you'll see, by then, I'll be all straightened out." Then she turned to Lory and offered him his jacket.

"It's all right," Lory said. "You go ahead and keep it."

Alma turned and left the room with Lory walking behind her. When they got outside. She turned to Lory. "You sure you still want to go through with the marriage?" she asked. "I've heard insanity can be genetic."

"I'm not scared. And yes, I want to go through with it."

CHAPTER TWENTY-EIGHT

On October 28th, at 11 a.m. in the courthouse in downtown Berlin, Alma and Lory were wed. Goldie never came. But as Esther promised, she and Zede Birnbaum were there. And after the ceremony, Zede took everyone out for a nice lunch. Then he handed Lory an envelope. "A little wedding gift," he said, "and maybe a little apology too."

"Not necessary. I told you before I am not here for your money," Lory said.

"I know. And I believe you. That's why I am giving you this," Zede said, then he continued. "Take it. It will help the two of you to start your lives together."

"Thank you, sir," Lory said, putting the envelope into the breast pocket of his suit jacket. "You are very kind."

"You are now my grandson," Ted said. "You can even call me Zede."

"All right. Zede, it is," Lory said.

In all of the excitement, Lory forgot about the envelope. Until that night when he took off his suit jacket and it fell to the floor.

"What's this?" Alma asked.

"It's a gift from your grandfather," he said, picking up the envelope.

"Open it."

Lory opened it and counted out ten thousand marks. "Oh!" he said, shocked. "That's very generous of him."

"My zede came through after all," Alma said with tears in her eyes. "He is a hard man, just like Bubbie said. But he loves me."

CHAPTER TWENTY-NINE

That afternoon Alma and Lory moved into his small apartment located across the street from the hospital. They had both already left their positions and had finished packing to leave for Italy. They were scheduled to leave the following Monday.

"My mother never came," Alma said to Lory as they ate a light dinner under an umbrella at an outdoor café.

"I know. I wasn't going to mention it."

"I guess I knew she wouldn't."

"She is your mother. I understand that you will always love her. But you must accept her as she is and not expect anything from her. As long as you continue to hope she will change, she will have the power to hurt you. Once you let those dreams go, you will be able to live without her love."

"You're very wise." Alma smiled at Lory. "But it's easier said than done."

"Believe me. I realize this."

They walked hand in hand back to Lory's apartment. "You're scared," he said as he turned the key in the lock.

She nodded. "How can you tell? I thought I was doing a good job of hiding it."

Lory picked Alma up into his arms and carried her over the threshold. She laughed.

"I saw this in a movie once?" he said.

"I think I saw the same film. But I can't remember the name of it."

He smiled and then took her chin in his thumb and forefinger and lifted her head, so their eyes met. "You're trembling," he said in a whisper, then added, "Don't be afraid. I promise you. I won't hurt you. If, at any time you want to stop, we will. All you have to do is say the word. You have all the control. I won't force anything."

He placed a gentle kiss on her lips.

"Why are you so willing to put up with all of this for me?" she asked.

"Because a truly good woman is worth all the effort in the world. And if it takes you time to be able to consummate our marriage, it's all right. You're worth waiting for."

They walked hand in hand to the bedroom.

Lory undressed Alma slowly, stopping every few minutes to kiss her eyelids or her hands. Once she was naked, she stood shivering. He took the blanket from the bed and wrapped her in it. "I love you, Alma. And I am going to do my very best to erase that terrible thing that happened to you, from your mind. Just give yourself over to me, and let me work my magic."

"Magic?" she said skeptically.

"Yes, the magic of love. Don't you know that there is real magic in love? It has the magic to heal."

"Oh really? I had no idea," she said, trying to laugh at what she thought was a joke.

"You doubt it? Just let me show you."

Lory was as patient and gentle as he'd promised he would be. At first Alma was timid, but by the end of the night she was fully and completely Lory's loving and devoted wife not only in the eyes of the law but also in the eyes of God.

CHAPTER THIRTY

Chana had gone through a difficult pregnancy. But it was almost over now. As she looked back on it, she wasn't sure if she'd have any more children. For the first three months she'd been terribly sick, unable to keep any food down. She'd gone to work because she had to. But she found that it was best not to try to eat anything. Still she was nauseated and tired.

As she entered her second trimester, Chana was able to eat. But she was still very tired. Her skin lacked its regular glow, and her hair had lost its shine. None of her clothes fit. So she'd made herself a few tent-like dresses. But her belly was still growing. Whenever she looked in the mirror, she felt depressed. *Everyone said that a woman is most beautiful when she's pregnant. Well, I can certainly see that's a lie. I just hope I can get back to myself when this is over.* But then in her eighteenth week of pregnancy, something miraculous happened. For the first time, she felt the baby move inside her. She and Sam had just gone to sleep, and then it happened. A feeling of wonder came over her. For the first time she felt a strong connection to her unborn baby. *There is a child inside of me. There is a living, breathing human being inside of me who was created through the love Sam and I share.* Chana reached over and nudged Sam.

"Is it time?" he asked.

"No, silly. I have another three months. But give me your hand."

He turned over still half asleep and gave her his hand. She placed it on her belly. When he felt the baby stir, Sam exclaimed, "Oh!"

"That's our baby," Chana said.

Sam wrapped Chana in his arms and held her close. "I love you so much. God has been so good to us."

A single tear ran down her cheek. "I know that women have been having babies since the beginning of time. But this is different because it's ours."

"I know, Chana. I know," Sam said.

By her third trimester, Chana was ready to give birth even though she was a little afraid of what it would be like. Her body ached. She was still exhausted. But now she was only able to sleep for a few hours at a time because her bladder was constantly full, and the baby would kick or elbow her, and she had to run to the bathroom.

The baby was a week early. The pains started when Chana was at work. They were slight at first, but she knew that the child was coming. She was excited but also nervous. Her father saw her leaning over her worktable. "I'll call Sam," he said.

"No, no, wait. I have a fitting in a half hour. I want to try to take the fitting before I go to the hospital."

"I don't think that's a good idea. I'll explain everything to your customer when she comes. Right now, I'll call Sam."

CHAPTER THIRTY-ONE

Sam worked nights so he was at home. He'd just finished reading the newspaper when the phone rang. Since Chana was so close to her due date, he'd made sure to stay close to the phone.

"Sam, it's Jake. Chana is going into labor."

Sam didn't say a word. He hung up the phone and got dressed quickly. Then he ran downstairs, got in his car, and drove to Chana's store. Her customer had arrived early. She was a young woman who had given birth to two children, so she was helping Chana to stay calm.

"I'm here, sweetheart," Sam said, putting his arms around Chana and helping her to the car. "You'll be all right." Sam's heart was pounding. Even though he'd expected her to go into labor, the reality of it was scary. *Please God, don't let anything go wrong*, he thought. Sam gave Chana a smile. He wanted her to feel confident and not to see how worried he was.

Once they arrived at the hospital, Chana was surrounded by nurses and doctors, and then she was whisked away in a whirlwind of white uniforms. Sam was instructed to go the waiting room. He did as he was told, but he paced the floor. The door to the delivery room was closed to him. He could feel that Chana needed him and wanted to break that door down so he could be beside his wife. Hours passed. Another expectant father joined him. The man was a talker.

"Is this your first?" he asked Sam.

"Yes," Sam said. He didn't want to be bothered. He was sweating and anxious.

"Mine too," the other fellow said. "By the way, my name is Mark Kleinberg."

"Sam Schatzman," Sam said.

"Nice to meet you."

Sam nodded.

"What do you for a living?" Mark asked.

Sam didn't answer. He had enough.

"You all right?" Mark asked.

"I'm sorry. I don't feel like talking."

Mark looked hurt, but Sam didn't care. *I know he is offended, but at least that shut him up.*

Finally, after what seemed like forever but was in reality only five hours, a nurse came out of the delivery room. "Mr. Schatzman," she said.

Sam jumped to his feet. "I am Sam Schatzman," he said.

"Congratulations. You have a little girl."

"How is my wife?"

"Both your wife and your daughter are doing just fine," the nurse said, smiling. "You'll be able to go in and see them in a few minutes. Wait here, I'll be right back."

CHAPTER THIRTY-TWO

Chana had been moved from the delivery room to a hospital room before Sam was allowed to see her. When he entered and looked at her with her red hair fanned out across the white pillowcase and the tiny baby in her arms, he gasped. "You are so beautiful," he said. "You take my breath away."

She smiled. "This is Ida Ruth . . . your daughter."

"My daughter," he said in awe as he looked at the tiny bundle in Chana's arms. "She looks just like you."

"You think so? I think it's too soon to tell," Chana said, smiling.

"I love you so much," he said. Then he took Ida's hand out of the blanket.

"I love you too."

"Look at this hand," he said. "It's so tiny."

"I know." She smiled. "Let me show you her feet . . . and just wait until you see her tiny, perfect ears."

CHAPTER THIRTY-THREE

Chana was tired. "They don't call it labor for nothing," she said, smiling at Sam. "Having a baby is hard work."

"Do you want to get some rest? I have to go home and set up the nursery, but I'll be back tonight."

"I'll bet every Jewish father curses the crazy Jewish superstition about not setting up anything for the baby before it's born. You poor thing, after being up all night in the waiting room, you have to leave the hospital and then go and buy a crib and everything else we need for the baby. Then you must be sure that it's all set up and ready when we come home. I wish I had been able to help you set everything up before I gave birth."

"And risk the evil eye?" He smiled and winked at her.

"You make a joke. But we were both a little afraid of the evil eye, so we followed the tradition now, didn't we?"

He laughed. "Yep. We sure did. We'd like to believe we're modern and we're beyond all those old bubbe-meises. But we just weren't ready to tempt fate, now, were we?"

She laughed. "My bubbie used to call it insurance. She used to say, you follow the traditions even if you think they're crazy. Just in case."

"Get some rest, sweetheart. I'll be back tonight. It's my turn to labor."

CHAPTER THIRTY-FOUR

When Chana brought Ida home from the hospital, the first thing she did was tie a red ribbon around the baby's crib to ward off a kenahora, the evil eye.

Chana took two weeks off to take care of Ida. Then she returned to work, taking the baby with her into the store most days. Reluctantly, her mother came in to help. Since she was breastfeeding, Chana couldn't leave Ida at home with Sam while she was at work. And since Sam worked nights, Chana was alone with the baby. But she could see her figure returning to normal, slowly but surely. And her skin and hair had regained their previous luster.

CHAPTER THIRTY-FIVE

Italy, January 1932

When Alma and Lory arrived in Rome, they rented an apartment that was a few buildings away from the apartment where his brother Giorgio lived with his wife and their mother.

Moving to Italy had not been as easy for Alma as she had originally anticipated. First off, she did not speak the language, so everything that was said had to be translated by Lory. Her mother-in-law was demanding, and sometimes, it seemed, she was a little critical. She had her ways of doing things, and she was certain they were the only way. "I change the sheets on the beds every other day, and I iron them. Lory is used to this," Lory's mother said, leaving Lory reluctant to translate. But Alma wasn't one to fight. So even though her mother-in-law could be difficult, Alma accepted her as she was. Her brother-in-law was shy around her and not very talkative.

But she was glad to find a friend in Bria, her sister-in-law. Bria spoke broken English, making their communications strained but not impossible. When they went to the market together Bria helped Alma shop. Bria taught Alma to prepare the big Sunday family dinners, which they prepared together under the constant direction of their mother-in-law. If Bria had not been there to make Alma laugh, she might have resented her mother-in-law. But Bria made light of the whole situation, and everything seemed to fall into place. Lory was the kindest and most loving husband she could ever have hoped for. So if overlooking his mother's overbearing personality was all she had to endure, Alma felt she could manage.

On January 15th, a letter arrived. It had been redirected from Berlin to Rome by her grandmother. She knew because she recognized the handwriting. It read:

Dear Sister,
I am assuming that you are married, and you are now Mrs. Lory Bellinelli. Mazel Tov, almalah!!! My baby sister, a wife! I can't even imagine. I can still see you as a small child playing with your dolls. But the truth is I am so happy for you.

I have wonderful news! You are an aunt! Ida Ruth Schatzman came into the world on the first of January weighing seven pounds and six ounces. She is our beautiful blessing for the new year. As you can see by her name, I named her for dad. Ida for Irving. Her middle name is Ruth for Chana's aunt Rachel who passed away last year. The baby is such a joy to us. I can't express how it feels to look at her tiny fingers and toes and to know that with the help of God, Chana and I created this marvelous creature. The miracle of having a child is just beyond explaining.

I can't wait for you to meet Chana. She is so looking forward to meeting you too. Perhaps in the summer when the weather is better for travel you and Lory can come here to America. If you want, I will send passage. I have something I have been meaning to tell you. The other night I was sitting in my chair watching Chana nurse the baby, and I thought about how happy I am and how everything happened just perfectly. When you withheld that information from me about Betty it caused me to get off the boat. Then I needed to find work before I went

back to Medina, which in turn caused me to meet Chana. And Chana turned out to be my bashert. God is truly wonderful in the way he orchestrates things. Don't you think?
Love, your devoted brother,
Sam

CHAPTER THIRTY-SIX

Berlin Germany, August 1932

A scorching hot day late in the afternoon Goldie stretched across the sofa and sipped her glass of chilled absinthe. Sweat formed on her upper lip. There was a swift knock on the door. Leni gave Goldie a look of annoyance. "It's too early for company," she said. But she got up and opened the door.

"Oh, it's you, Felix. Well, you might as well come in," Leni announced. Leni found Felix to be boring with his constant chatter about politics. He was a devoted member of the SA and a real hater of Jews. And although she'd promised Goldie she would never tell Felix that she and Goldie were Jewish, she'd considered breaking that promise in the hope that Felix would be repulsed and disappear from their lives. The only thing stopping her was that she and Goldie had been posing as non-Jews for so long that she didn't want their other friends to find out the truth.

"Goldie," he said, "I brought some sausages and sauerkraut and some good German beer. Felix said as he pushed empty bottles and dirty dishes out of the way so he could put the food and beer on the countertop in the kitchen. "Nobody, and I mean nobody makes beer like we do here in the fatherland." He stopped for a minute and glanced over at Goldie. "You should eat. You are getting so thin, I feel soon you are going to fade away to nothing. I will be looking around and saying, 'Goldie, Goldie? Where is Goldie.' And I won't see you because you will have vanished from not eating." Felix laughed heartily at his own joke. Then he took a sausage and a bottle of beer and sat down.

Goldie looked up and offered him a weak smile. "I'm not hungry."

"You'll eat anyway. To please me, yes?"

"I suppose." She groaned. Then she added under her breath, "If you weren't so damn good in bed, I'd get rid of you."

Felix heard her and let out a belly laugh. "But I am good in bed. After all, how could I not be good in bed? I am one of the superior race. As are you . . . and because you are, you should have more respect for yourself and your health," Felix commanded. "You drink too much of that green stuff. And you don't eat."

"Yes, yes. All right. I'll eat. A sausage, but please, no sauerkraut."

"It's good for you."

"I can't. It's too early in the day to eat something like that. If I try, I'll vomit."

He handed her a sausage Then he sat down at the table. She noted that he was getting fat. His belly hung over his belt.

"It's not early in the day; it's after three in the afternoon." He shook his head. "You girls are like vampires: sleeping all day, carousing all night."

"The word vampire is not funny, Felix. I know you've heard about that horrible man they call the Vampire of Düsseldorf," Leni said.

"Yes, I've heard. Another murderer associated with that Lustmord. They find dead bodies all the time here in Berlin. You girls play a dangerous game running around all night, playing around with strangers," Felix said.

"So why don't you marry her, make a decent German woman out of her?" Leni teased, indicating Goldie.

"Who said I wanted to get married? I don't. I am not ready yet. But that doesn't mean you girls should be acting so carelessly. Sexual sadists are everywhere. I worry about you, Goldie."

"Oh, come on, Felix, you can't tell me you don't like our little S&M games," Goldie said.

"That's not the point. I just wish you wouldn't be doing these things with other men. It could cost you."

"We said from the beginning that we were not going to be committed to anything. I don't want you telling me who I can be with," she said.

"If you don't want to marry her, then how dare you tell her she can't be with other men," Leni said.

"I don't want to get married, Leni. So please shut your mouth," Goldie said.

"I know you don't. I was just kidding. You're awfully testy today."

Goldie turned away from both of them and grunted, wrapping her arms around her chest. "I don't need a man telling me what I can and can't do. I had nineteen terrible years of that, and I won't take it from a casual lover," Goldie said.

Leni didn't listen. She had too much to say to be silenced. She glared at Felix and said, "You know only one in a million of these men who like to play domination games is a killer. I turn tricks with them all the time. They pay well. They pay much better than other johns. So why not? They don't really hurt me. They just tie me up and—"

Felix interrupted, "When you are tied up, you are helpless. How do you know you can trust these men not to take things too far? You don't know, do you?"

"I'm very tired of this conversation," Goldie said. "I don't care what you think I should or shouldn't do, Felix. And if you are going to insist on trying to control me, you can leave right now." She looked at him, and then calming herself, she added. "Look, I like you. I like the gifts you bring. And there is no denying that you are a marvel in bed. But I won't tolerate this from you or anyone else. So if you're going to continue, you can get out right now," Goldie said.

"I'm sorry for offending you, my dear. Will you forgive me?" Felix said, taking a swig of beer."

"You don't even sound remotely sincere," Goldie said.

"I truly am sorry. I just want to help you. I don't want you to get hurt. I promise you I will try to keep my opinions to myself. Forgive me?"

She shook her head, then she said, "All right. But please . . . don't do it again."

"Of course," he said. His voice was a little too flippant for her taste. She would have liked for him to be more afraid of losing her. Lately, he seemed more interested in his political party than he was in her. And this bothered her. Then she remembered why she'd started this affair with Felix in the first place. It was to get back at Luisa. She was certain that being a member of this political group meant a lot to Luisa. After all, Goldie remembered how they were in school when no one ever befriended Luisa. The other students made fun of her because she would come to school with dirty elbows and knees. She wasn't very pretty, and she always smelled like sauerkraut. And she looked like a rat. The boys shunned her. Every day at lunchtime, Luisa could be seen sitting alone. She walked to and from school alone. Even the other outcasts wanted nothing to do with her. So Goldie thought this was probably the first time Luisa had ever found acceptance in her life, and if Goldie could find a way to discredit Luisa, she would, because it would make her feel vindicated after the way Luisa treated her.

Goldie stood up. She arched her back and stretched like a cat. Then she slowly sauntered over to Felix. Putting her hand on his shoulder, she leaned down and kissed him on the neck and blew softly in his ear. Felix began to breathe heavily. It was as if she'd lit a flame inside of him reigniting any waning interest. A quick glance down at his crotch told her that she had his full attention. She sat down beside him pressing her body against his and put her hand on his thigh. If she'd placed her hand a little higher it would have been considered indecent. "By the way, Felix," she said fetchingly, "do you know of a girl by the name of Luisa Eisenreich? I believe she is a part of your SA group."

"Luisa Eisenreich?" Leni said, "Why the hell would you bring her up?"

"Mind your own business, Leni," Goldie snapped. She was glaring at Leni, warning her to be quiet. *Even if Luisa tells him I am Jewish, he'd never believe her. Look at me, I look like the perfect Aryan woman.* She smiled slyly.

"Yes, I know who she is. A heavyset girl with brown hair? Yes?"

"Yep, that's her."

"Do you know who her superiors are?" Goldie asked.

"Not really. I was never really friendly with her. I do remember that she, along with a group of other girls from the SA, went off to study nursing. I haven't seen her in a long time. Why do you ask?"

"Just wondered. If she returns, will you let me know?" Goldie asked. She was kneading his upper thigh with her hand.

"Of course. Anything for you, my love." He put his arms around her and pulled her close to him.

"Take off that uniform," Goldie said. "You know I don't like it when you wear the uniform when you come here to see me."

"I just finished attending a SA meeting."

"Hence the uniform. Of course. I should have realized it. You are here awfully early in the day. You usually come at night after you have taken that thing off."

"While I was at the meeting all I could think about was you, Goldie."

"Oh really?" she said, smiling slyly.

"And as far as what I said before, I am only having your best interest at heart. You can't chastise a man for caring about you, can you now, Goldie?"

"I am still a little upset with you, Felix," Goldie said, but then she took a deep breath, and a smile came over her face. "But I forgive you. Let me know if you hear anything about Luisa."

"You know I will," he said. "I brought you some money toward your rent."

He'd helped them with the rent in the past.

"You are so kind," Goldie said. "Let's go in the bedroom so you can get rid of that uniform."

"I like my uniform," Felix protested weakly. "But, of course, I would be happy to remove it."

"Please don't be offended, Felix, but I hate uniforms too," Leni said as she smoked a cigarette. "They make a man look like he is part of a herd, like a sheep. Instead of an individual."

"It's all in the eye of the beholder, my dear," Felix said, annoyed with Leni. "You would be lucky to find a man who is a member of the SA who would be interested in you," he added with a hint of cruelty.

"And it doesn't hurt that you give our little Goldie money for her little addiction to snow," Leni chided him.

"Someone is jealous," Felix said, winking. Then he added testily, "The rent money I just gave Goldie will be helpful to you as well. So I suggest you shut your mouth."

"Come, let's go to the bedroom so you can change your clothes," Goldie said.

"I'd follow you anywhere." Felix laughed.

After they finished in the bedroom, they returned to the living room because Felix wanted to finish his food. Leni was reading a magazine. The same catty argument between Leni and Felix began again right where they had left off.

"You are a follower. And I don't care about your money. I don't want it, and I don't need it," Leni said.

"But when Goldie pays your rent with the money I give her, you live here, so you benefit. If you hate me so much, why don't you just move out?"

"To hell with you, Felix. This was my flat in the first place. Goldie moved in with me. Why should I leave?"

"All right. Enough of this, you two." Goldie lit another cigarette. "So tell me about your meeting, Felix."

He sat down on the sofa in his white underwear and men's sleeveless white undershirt. Then he took a bite of his sausage, and with a full mouth he said, "I don't like that Adolf Hitler. I don't think he knows enough to govern our fatherland, and he is certainly not as qualified as Röhm. But he is so damn forceful, and some of the men are afraid of him. I've said this before: that Hitler could be trouble."

"But he is weak in comparison to Röhm. Yes? I am sure everything will be all right," Goldie said as she repeated the things he had told her previously. She'd never paid attention to the politics in Berlin. There were far too many political groups with confusing agendas. There were communists screaming in the streets, and then there were other groups like the one Felix was so attached to. Sometimes the different political factions got into bar fights like little children.

Felix had come to see her after many of these bar fights. When he arrived after a good fight, he would be on fire, and the sex would be outrageous. He would rant and rave about hating Jews and creating a superior race and other such nonsense. And she would pretend to be interested. But if anyone asked Goldie, she would tell them that she doubted things in Germany would ever really change. After Hindenburg, she was quite certain that another man would take office who was just like him. The poor economy was obvious to everyone. But these small groups of political rebels were never going to fix anything nor would they ever be in charge.

"Hitler doesn't have as many followers as Röhm. But the ones he has are ruthless."

"Well, I wouldn't trouble yourself too much over this Hitler fellow," Goldie said.

"He is dividing the party. There are those of us who know Röhm is the rightful leader, and we would follow him to the ends of the world. But then there are the upstarts who think Hitler has the right ideas."

"Yes, yes, I know. You've mentioned all of this before, love," she said, taking a cigarette out of her jeweled case. "And, quite frankly, I have a headache."

He ignored her plea for him to stop talking. "This Hitler fellow infuriates me. Do you know what he is doing? He is accusing all the men in the SA of being homosexuals."

"Well, you just let him come and talk to me," Goldie said, taking a puff of her cigarette and then giving him a quick wink. "I'll tell him that you like women. And I can certainly attest to that. In fact . . . why don't we just go into my bedroom, and you can massage my neck and then prove to me how much you like having sex with women."

Leni let out a laugh. "Goldie, you are so conniving."

Goldie stretched her body as she stood up, then she crooked her finger at Felix. "Come on. You're done eating. Let's go back to bed," she said. Her robe opened slightly, and he could see one of her breasts. His eyes grew soft with desire, and for the moment he forgot about Adolf Hitler.

CHAPTER THIRTY-SEVEN

Manhattan, May 1, 1932

Chana was listening to Louis Armstrong play "All of Me" on the radio. She sang along as she rocked Ida in her arms. "All of me. Why not take all of me? Can't you see, I'm no good without you..."

The music stopped and the announcer broke in with an emergency announcement.

On March 1, 1932 the young son of the famous aviator Charles Lindbergh was kidnapped. The child had only been a few months shy of his second birthday when he was taken from his crib in his own home. There was much speculation about who might have been responsible for the abduction. Ransom notes were received and paid. But the baby was not returned.

Today we regret to inform you that, tragically, the child was found dead.

I heard that Charlie Lindbergh had ties to the mob, because Al Capone offered to help find the child, Chana thought. *I also heard that Lindbergh might be anti-American. I wonder if he was a secret spy for the Nazis working to help Hitler gain power in America. I know he's openly praised the German führer.* Chana looked down at her own child asleep in her arms. *A baby stolen from his own home, from his own bed, and murdered.*

Chana felt a chill, and she squeezed Ida tightly to her breast.

CHAPTER THIRTY-EIGHT

Adolf Hitler had never been a popular fellow. It seemed that everything he tried to accomplish failed. His early childhood consisted of an abusive father who beat him and terrified him, and a doting mother who did her best to comfort him. Later, as a young adult, he applied for art school. It was his dream to become an artist, but he was rejected. He was told his work was mediocre. He wandered the streets of Austria homeless and penniless until he found some degree of self-worth in the Bavarian Army in WW1. Although he was only an infantryman, he felt important, and this fueled his desire for power.

After the Great War, in 1919, he joined a little-known political group called the German Workers' Party. It was there that he found his calling. The German Workers' Party believed the reason why the good German man suffered centered around the Jews. The war was the fault of the Jews, hyper-inflation too. Now Hitler could tell himself that he had not failed due to his own inadequacies, of course. It was the Jews. The Jews were the reason he'd never succeeded at anything he desired. He became fanatical about the party. In 1923 he was arrested for trying to take over the government in Munich in an event that would come to be called the Beer Hall Putsch. While serving time in prison he wrote a book called *Mein Kampf*, or translated, *My Struggle*, which would later serve as a manifesto for the terrifying Nazi regime.

CHAPTER THIRTY-NINE

August 1932

Late one afternoon, Hitler was having a few beers at a local tavern with a few of his close his friends: Joseph Goebbels, a brilliant but diabolical little man who had been born with a clubfoot, and Heinrich Himmler, a chicken farmer with an obsession with the occult. They had spent the last hour discussing the incompetence of Ernst Röhm, the leader of the SA, the organization of which they were all members. Himmler was a ruthless, cruel man. And Goebbels, grateful to have finally found a friend in Adolf, had ideas on how to use propaganda to help him to rise to power. These and a handful of others, who were the outcasts in the SA, became Hitler's inside men.

"There is far too much homosexuality in the SA. It is embarrassing to see the way Röhm tolerates outward displays of perversion. A good number of the men in the SA are blatant homosexuals, and that gives the rest of us a bad name," Himmler said.

"Röhm is a queer himself," Goebbels said.

"Yes, I know. Everyone knows. So how can they take us seriously? He is far from the perfect example of an Aryan man," Himmler said.

"I couldn't agree more," Hitler said, taking a swig of his dark, thick beer.

"Too bad we can't start a rumor about him, something that would smear his name," Goebbels offered.

"Don't worry, I have a plan, a better plan," Hitler said. "Hindenburg trusts me. He likes me. You two don't need to worry. When the time comes, you will be with me at the top." Hitler smiled. "I have a secret to tell you both. Are you ready?"

Himmler and Goebbels nodded.

"Last night I met with a famous psychic. It cost me a small fortune. But it was worth it. His name is Erik Jan Hanussen. Have you ever heard of him?"

"I've heard of him," Himmler said, "but he's a Jew, isn't he?"

"Yes, he's a stinking Jew. That's why it cost me a fortune. You know how the Jews are; they take advantage of everyone. And I didn't say I like him. I know what he is. However, I went to see him because I had a feeling that he had a message for me. Do you want to know what he told me?" Hitler said, his left eye and short mustache twitching slightly.

They both nodded.

"He said that my rise to power is inevitable," Hitler declared. "You know the Jews are all demons. I've said that many times before. And he probably got his message straight from the devil. I don't care where he got it. I know it's true."

"Yes, and I believe it's true," Goebbels said.

"So, even though I don't like him, I think Hanussen is right. I believe him," Hitler said.

"You will rise to power. I know it," Himmler said. "I've always known it."

"Let's make a toast to our future. A toast to the power we will have when we take over the SA and get rid of Rhom and his followers," Goebbels said.

"Yes, let's toast to that. A new day is coming," Himmler said.

"Prost!" Hitler said, raising his glass. "To the fatherland."

"Prost!" the other two answered. "To the future of our great country."

CHAPTER FORTY

December 1932

Goldie was getting ready for her date with Felix. She'd washed her hair and set it in pin curls. Once she was sure it was dry, she removed the clips from her hair. With a comb, she carefully styled her hair in perfect finger waves. Then she applied rouge and lipstick. The final touch was several coats of black mascara. Goldie blew herself a kiss in the mirror.

She'd been dating Felix for several months but not exclusively. He was member of some political group called the SA. She never paid much attention to his political rantings, although he had made it clear that his political party hated Jews. That made Goldie snicker because both she and her roommate and best friend, Leni, were Jewish. They'd both decided Felix need never know. After all, it had become rather chic to join radical political parties in Berlin these days. And neither Goldie nor Leni took the anti-Jewish sentiment seriously.

Goldie went to her closet to look through her dresses to decide what to wear. Her clothes had acquired such memories since she'd come to Berlin. She took out the dress she'd been wearing when she and Leni had first met Felix. It had been on a night when his SA group was having some sort of rally. *Leni and I were coming out of a nightclub when we got caught in the middle of that violent fight between the SA and some communist group. The streets were filled with angry rioters who were throwing punches at each other. There were so many people and nowhere to go. We were trapped in the middle of the crowd. I'd almost gotten hurt. But then out of nowhere, Felix appeared. I have to admit that he wasn't exactly handsome. But he rescued us. How gallant he is, I thought, as he led us through an alleyway to safety. That had been the beginning of our little affair. Although he is far too poor for me to ever consider marrying him, I love the attention he pays me. After spending the last nineteen years working beside Irving in the bakery, I am quite done with working men. If I ever marry again, the man will have to be independently wealthy. And even then, he would have to be a very special man for me to consider giving up my newfound freedom. It took me nineteen years to get away from the last husband. Why would I ever want another one? Even so, what makes Felix so much fun to date is that he is wildly attracted to me and so darn easy to manipulate. I love the way it feels to have such power over him. And to add to all of that, Felix is very good in bed. Not like Irving. I could fall asleep when Irving made love to me.* Then she looked at the dress again. *Nope, not that dress,* she thought, shaking her head. *He's seen that one before. And I love the way he responds when I wear something new and sexy.*

She rifled through the closet. *I wish my mother and I were on better terms. If we were, I could probably convince her that I am in desperate need of a new wardrobe.* Then her eyes fell upon the robe she'd been wearing the day Irving died. She felt the bile rise in her throat. *I've never worn that robe again because I could never get the bloodstains out of it, but I can't throw it away. It's Irving's blood, and it's all that is left of him.* Suddenly she was overcome with guilt about her husband dying of a heart attack because Felix had pushed him when he refused to leave Goldie's apartment. And she knew that it was because Irving had come all the way from America to take her home with him. *But what about what I wanted? Doesn't that count for anything? My father caused all of this. He sent for Irving. He thought Irving would be able to control me. He didn't know my husband. If Irving had not gone and died the way he did, I would have to admit that since I returned to Berlin and moved in with Leni, I've been the happiest I have been in a long time.*

CHAPTER 40 | 127

On the one hand she was glad to be free of Irving. But she wished he had not died. Their lives had been boring, and when she was married to him she felt as if the light of her spirit was dimming every day. But because they lived in a small town she always felt as if she had to keep up the appearance of being a good wife and mother. In the Jewish section of that town in Upstate New York, women behaved properly, and the men were boring and respectful. Although she couldn't say she really missed Irving, she would have chosen things to have ended differently for him. His dying had made a real mess of things. Her adult son, Sam, resented her. And although she hadn't heard from her teenage daughter, Alma, since she missed Alma's wedding, Goldie was certain that Alma blamed her too.

It would have all worked out so much better if Irving had finally gotten over his obsession with me and found another woman in America. A woman who would have actually loved him and been satisfied being married to a baker who had recently lost his bakery. If the fates had been kinder, Irving and his new wife might have rebuilt their lives together. After all, Irving was not the only man to have suffered a huge financial loss in the depression. But he couldn't get over Goldie. He adored her. So when her father had sent for him, Irving and Sam had taken a boat to Berlin to convince Goldie to come home. When she saw Irving, she felt her skin crawl. Her hatred for him was so strong that she said hurtful things. But it was time that he realized he needed to leave her alone forever because she'd never loved him, not when they were doing well, and not later.

Bringing herself back to the present, she looked at the clock and realized Felix would be arriving any moment. She grabbed a red-beaded dress and put it on, and right as she zipped the zipper, there was a knock at the door.

CHAPTER FORTY-ONE

Felix arrived at the apartment to pick Goldie up at eight that evening. He was always exactly on time. She opened the door to find him waiting with a bunch of flowers.

"Hello," he said, handing the flowers to her. "You look gorgeous as usual."

She smiled. "Where are we going?"

"It's a surprise," he said.

"Oh, Felix. Last time you surprised me we wound up at a beer garden with a bunch of the men from your group."

"You didn't like it? I thought you did. They were all enthralled with you. And . . . who wouldn't be."

"Were you jealous?"

"Not really. I enjoyed the envy in their eyes."

She let out a laugh. "So are we going to another beer garden?"

"Not tonight. Tonight we are going to have a quiet dinner. Just the two of us."

She smiled. But she thought she might prefer the beer garden.

They took the bus into town where they went to a reasonably priced restaurant. They were seated in the back.

"Would you like me to order for you?" he asked.

"No, thank you. I can order for myself."

The waiter took their orders. And then he came back with a beer for Felix and a glass of wine for Goldie. After he left the table, Goldie turned to Felix. "Felix . . ." Goldie said fetchingly as she squeezed his thigh under the table.

"Yes."

"I have a favor to ask of you."

He put down his beer and gazed into her eyes. "What is it?"

"Leni and I are short on money for the rent this month. Can you help us?"

"Again, Goldie? I gave you money the last two months. I am short this month," he said. Then seeing the disappointment in her eyes, he added with a smile, "You are going to see why I am short of cash in just a few minutes."

"You bought me a gift?" she asked. Even though she and Leni needed the money for rent, Goldie couldn't resist a present.

"In a way, yes."

"That's so exciting. What did you get me?" She sounded thrilled like a child.

"You'll see."

After dinner Felix took a tiny box out of his pocket. "I have something I want to ask you."

She glanced at the box, and her stomach lurched. This was not a gift she wanted.

"I was wondering if you would marry me," he said, opening the box. There was a ring with a tiny diamond, inside.

Goldie turned away. She took a sip of the wine on the table and wished she had something stronger. "I wish they served absinthe here," she said. Then she called out, "Waiter . . . a glass of schnapps."

Goldie was so disappointed, that when the glass of schnapps came, she downed it in a single swig. Then she turned to Felix and said, "I'm sorry. I told you I don't ever want to get married again. I wish you hadn't spoiled our evening like this."

"But . . ."

"I said I can't."

When she looked at him, she saw the hurt in his eyes.

CHAPTER 41

"So you are saying no?"

"That's right. I am saying no." Goldie was angry. She looked at the tiny diamond. She looked at Felix, and she shook her head. "You knew I never wanted this," she said.

He drummed his fingers on the table for several seconds. His face turned red. Then he said bitterly. "It's probably for the best. You're not the right kind of girl for any man to marry. You are a good-time girl, Goldie. That's all you are. You're only good for one thing. You would never make a proper German hausfrau."

He called the waiter over and paid the check. Then without looking at Goldie again, Felix got up, put on his coat, and walked out of the restaurant, leaving Goldie to get home on her own.

As Felix walked to the bus stop, he cursed himself for the strong feelings he had for Goldie. He knew he wasn't done with her. She had poisoned him for any thoughts of another woman. Whenever they were apart, he was driven to go and see her again. It felt like she had a spell on him.

CHAPTER FORTY-TWO

December 1932

Leni returned to the apartment in the wee hours of the morning with a proposal for Goldie. She found Goldie asleep on the sofa. Goldie still wore the dress she had worn earlier. Gently she shook her shoulder.

"I have a really good offer for the two of us," Leni said. "You know we are short on the rent again this month. I haven't sold a painting. You haven't brought any money in either. Instead, you have been spending so much time with Felix that you haven't done any posing for artists or turned a trick. I went behind your back, and I asked Felix for the money. He said he's short on cash."

"You asked Felix for money? How dare you?" Goldie said, shaking herself awake.

"I couldn't help it. He was here when the landlord came by and I didn't have the rent. He heard the landlord tell me that we had to leave if we didn't pay by the end of the month. So, since he heard it anyway, I just asked him. He said he can't help us this time."

"Oh damn," Goldie said, sitting up and taking a cigarette out of its case. "So what kind of an offer did you get?"

"This artist wants two girls to pose together for a Lustmord painting. It pays very well. A thousand marks. That will cover our rent and leave some over for fun. What do you say?"

"Sure, but when?"

"Later today. Not too early. He knows we don't like mornings. But he needs us to come as early as we can because he wants to use as much of the daylight as he can. I understand that. I need the light when I am working too."

"All right. How soon do we need to go?"

"He says he would like us there by eleven."

"Eleven in the morning? Oh, that certainly is early. But I'll get up," Goldie said. "I'll set an alarm for ten," she said, getting up and taking the old alarm clock off the shelf. "I am going to shower before we go."

"Yes, so am I. It should be easy to get into the shower down the hall. Most of the tenants in this building are night owls like us. So there should be no line for the shower in the morning."

At ten, the alarm clock went off. "I hate that thing," Goldie said. Then she got up and went into Leni's room. Leni was sprawled out naked on the bed with her mouth open, snoring.

"It's ten o'clock," Goldie said, shaking Leni's arm.

"That came around fast, didn't it?" Leni said. "It felt like I just closed my eyes."

They went into the living room to gather their things for the shower.

Goldie snorted a line of snow to help her wake up. Then she offered one to Leni who gladly accepted. They both took a quick shower and got dressed.

At half past ten, Goldie and Leni boarded a bus that would take them to the address that Leni had for the art studio, where they were to pose that day. It was freezing outside when they got off the bus. As they were walking, Goldie shivered and pulled her scarf tighter around her neck. She hated winter. She always had bad feelings in the winter. The gray skies, the chilly air, the icy streets, all gave her a feeling of impending doom. And today was no exception. *If only I would have refused to go on this job with Leni,* she thought. *I could be warm and comfortable in my bed instead of braving these icy winds. But, of course, then how would we pay the rent?*

They found the street address. It was a flophouse hotel.

"This is his art studio?" Goldie asked skeptically.

"Yes, plenty of artists have apartments that don't have good lighting. Maybe the room he's renting has a lot of windows."

"Perhaps," Goldie said, shaking her head. "But this place looks like a real dump."

"Yes, and I am sure it is. But he's an artist. He's not concerned with the place, only the light and the subject matter. Now stop complaining. We are making nice money for an afternoon of posing. We don't even have to turn a trick. That is unless he is handsome." Leni winked at Goldie.

"Yes, he might just be handsome," Goldie said.

They went to the front desk where a man with open sores all over his face sat biting his nails.

"Excuse me," Leni said, "I'm looking for a man. His name is Rudolf Hickman."

The man behind the desk pushed his greasy hair out of his eyes with the tip of his finger. Then he looked up at Leni. "Who are you? I don't want no trouble here in this place. This Hickman fellow, does he know you're coming?"

"Yes, he's an artist. We're his models."

The man behind the desk leaned over and looked at Leni and Goldie. "Yeah, makes sense. The two of you look like models. He's in room three-ten."

"Thanks," Leni said, blowing the man a kiss. Then she whispered to Goldie, "He was repulsive."

"That's for sure," Goldie said, and they both giggled.

At the top of a creaky staircase they followed the numbers until they arrived at three-ten. Then Leni knocked.

"Come in," a voice called out. "It's open. I've been expecting you."

"Welcome, ladies. I'm Rudolf Hickman. You can call me Rudy." He was handsome, very handsome, rugged with a scruffy shadow of a beard and dark, brooding eyes. His dark hair fell over his forehead. "I have some interesting poses planned for today." He smiled, and his white teeth caught the light from the single bulb that hung overhead.

Goldie noticed there was no natural light in the room. In fact, it was dimly lit, if anything, and she wondered why he would choose this room to do his painting. But she said nothing because before she could even ask any questions, Rudolf presented Leni with a wad of bills. "Here is the payment I promised you," he said, smiling. "Both of you are beautiful. This painting should be just perfect."

"Thank you," Leni said after she counted the money. "It's all here."

"Of course, it is." He nodded. "Now, take off all of your clothes. Here is a bottle of fake blood. Use it sparingly or it won't be realistic."

Goldie shrugged and removed her dress. Leni did the same. Then they removed the rest of their clothing and poured the red liquid down their bodies.

"Kneel," Rudolf said. Both girls complied with his request. Then he took a rope and bound their hands behind their backs and their feet together.

"This is very uncomfortable," Leni said. "I've done these kinds of poses before, and they aren't usually this bad. This rope is very scratchy, and you've tied it so tight."

"I'm terribly sorry. Please be patient. I'll be quick," he said. Next, he took a long stick and put it between each girl's lips, taping it on either side with a strong tape.

Goldie grunted, then gagged. She shook her head. If she could have spoken, she would have said, "Let's forget the whole thing. I don't like the way this feels." But she couldn't speak. The stick was gagging her.

"I'm sorry that the stick is bothering you, but you must try not to vomit," Rudolf said. "It looks perfect. Very realistic. I am aiming for realism."

Goldie nodded but she felt like crying. *How long is this going to take? My back hurts; my knees are killing me, and this stick is choking me. I don't care about the money. I just want to leave.* She groaned as loudly as she could, hoping he would take the stick out of her mouth and ask her what she wanted. He didn't.

Without speaking, Rudolf looked down at the colors and began to mix his paint. His eyes were focused. His brow was furrowed with intent. Then he began to paint furiously, making wild strokes on the canvas. "It's not realistic enough," he muttered more to himself than to the women. "I'm not achieving what I set out to achieve." He picked up a knife and walked over to Leni. With slow precision, he sliced a thin line in her chest. Blood came to the surface. "Better," he said. Leni was making whimpering noises and shaking her head frantically. But Rudolf wasn't paying any attention. Instead, he took the knife and cut deeper into Leni's breast. Her entire body shook. Blood was pouring like a river from the wound. Rudolf nodded. "Yes," he said, and his eyes grew wide as he raised the knife and sliced off one and then both of Leni's breasts. Leni fell forward into a pool of her own blood. Rudolf turned her over so that he could see her face. Her eyes were wide open with fear. She was bleeding out all over the old dirty wood floor. Goldie wanted to scream. Leni was dying. Leni's entire body was writhing in agony, a stream of urine drizzled down her legs. Then she stopped moving and lay perfectly still: her long, dark hair matted with blood, her white skin contrasting against the rich red river that surrounded her.

Goldie had never felt as terrified as she did at that moment. It was hard to believe that Leni was dead, and she was tied up and at the mercy of a madman. Tears spilled down her cheeks. *He killed Leni. He is going to kill me. Please don't hurt me*, she longed to say. She wanted to scream, to scream, and scream as loudly and as long as she could. But she was unable to speak. *Please . . .*

Rudolf's eyes were glazed over. His face was distorted. He stared at Goldie with an intense gaze. Goldie trembled and tried to unbind herself. But it was no use. She felt the knife penetrate her flesh right between her ribs. Then she passed out.

CHAPTER FORTY-THREE

Goldie awakened alone. She was in terrible pain, but she was no longer tied up. The room was dark. Her legs and arms were spread. It was wet all around her, and even though she couldn't see, she knew it was blood. She tried to stand, but she was terribly weak. She tried to scream, but the stick was still in her mouth. She reached up and pulled the tape off her mouth. The stick fell. Goldie tried to scream, but her voice was too weak to be heard. With all the strength she had, she crawled to the door. Then she got on her knees and opened it, crawling out into the hallway. But that was as far as she was able to go. She fell forward and lay there on the cold floor. A few minutes later a woman walked by. When she saw Goldie, she let out a scream. That brought the man at the desk upstairs. He almost fell over when he saw Goldie. He had to hold on to the doorknob of the room to steady himself. Then he went into the room and turned on the lights. He saw Leni, and the floor, and walls covered in blood. He vomited. Then he ran downstairs and called the police.

Goldie was unconscious when she was taken to the local hospital. The police found identification for her in her handbag and notified her parents, who came as soon as they could. For two weeks Goldie lay unconscious. She was pale and thin. The doctor told her parents that she'd lost a lot of blood. Her body was scarred from the knife wounds. Goldie was knocking on death's door. Her mother refused to leave her, not even to eat. She came as soon as visiting hours began and stayed until the nurses insisted she go home when visiting hours ended. Esther was sick with guilt.

"Will she survive?' Esther Birnbaum asked the doctor.

"I don't know. She's lost a lot of blood. We are doing all we can."

Each evening when the factory closed, Ted Birnbaum, with a heavy heart, made his way to the hospital. The events that took place leading to Goldie's attempted murder were all over the newspapers. Goldie's wild and out-of-control lifestyle became public knowledge. The sensationalism of it gave birth to even more outrages and untrue rumors. Reporters attacked Ted at every turn, overwhelming him with questions, but he refused any interviews.

When he got to the hospital, he would always find Esther sitting beside Goldie's bed. One night he found her weeping. He handed her the handkerchief in his breast pocket and sat down beside her.

"I feel guilty. This is all my fault. If I had been a better mother this would never have happened. If we had not insisted she marry Irving, maybe she wouldn't have gone so crazy. I don't know. I don't know what to think," Esther said, throwing her hands in the air.

You can't blame yourself. She was always looking for trouble even when she was just a child," he said, shaking his head. "I did the best I could for her."

"I don't like to talk badly about the dead. But that Leni was her downfall. From the day she met that girl, Goldie changed," Esther said.

"Sometimes a friend can be a bad influence. But there is no point in discussing Leni now. That's all over. All we can do is hope Goldie makes it through. She is young and strong. So she has a chance," Ted said.

Goldie stirred in her bed, and her eyes opened slowly. "Where am I? Mama? Papa? Is that your voices I hear, or am I dreaming?"

"It's us, Goldalah," Esther Birnbaum said, tears running down her cheeks as she stood up and took Goldie's hand in hers. She was gently kissing the palm.

"Is Leni here? Is she all right? Where am I?" Goldie was confused.

"You're in the hospital," Esther said as calmly as she could. Gently, she stroked Goldie's hair. "I'm sorry. Your friend has passed away."

"Leni is dead?"

Esther nodded. "Yes, I'm so sorry."

"I'm not. She was no good for you. Look what happened to you. This was all because of her," Ted said, his voice raised.

"Shaaa," Esther said, patting her husband's forearm. "Goldie has been through enough. Let her be. Yeah?"

Ted nodded and grew quiet. But his face was still crimson with anger.

"I'm going to let the nurse know you're awake," Esther said. "I'll be back in a second. All right?"

"Yes," Goldie said, her voice barely a whisper.

Esther kept her promise. She left the room but returned very quickly with a nurse at her side.

"You gave us all quite a scare," the nurse said, touching Goldie's forehead. "You don't feel feverish. That's a good sign. I'm going to let the doctor know that you're awake. I'm sure he'll be here to see you first thing in the morning."

Esther begged the nurses to allow her and Ted to stay an extra half hour after visiting hours ended. They agreed.

In the morning Esther arrived before the doctor made his rounds. Goldie was sitting up in bed, still weak but looking more alive than she had in a long time. Esther handed her daughter the box of cookies she brought. Goldie laid the cookies on the bed without opening them. Then as Esther settled down in the chair beside the bed, a police officer entered the room.

The police officer said, "Goldie Birnbaum Schatzman, is that you?"

Goldie nodded.

"How are you feeling?" the officer asked.

"I'm very tired. And . . . very sad."

"Yes, I can imagine. Your friend was murdered right in front of you. And you were hurt badly too. Now, can you tell me what you remember about the day that this happened. And what can you tell me about the man who did this to you?"

"His name is Rudolf Hickman. He's an artist. Leni and I were posing for a Lustmord painting for him. He offered us a lot of money, so we did it. We couldn't afford to pay our rent otherwise."

Esther gasped. "You needed money, so you did this? Oy vey, didn't you realize how dangerous something like this could be?" she said, holding her head.

"Mother, you know that if I would have come to you for money, you and Papa would never have given it to me. You would have demanded that I come home. And I never want to come home again."

"Oy, Goldie, you should have given us a chance to help you."

"You would have never helped me and Leni stay in our apartment. You know that." Goldie snorted, glaring at her mother. Then she turned to the police officer and said, "Rudolf Hickman met Leni the night before we did the posing. He gave Leni an address, which turned out to be in this lousy hotel room. We went anyway for the money. When we got there, he told us to take off our clothes. He tied us up. And then everything went bad, very bad." She put her head in her hands and started to cry. Tears covered her cheeks, spilling onto the blanket, and her nose was running. "I can still see Leni's face when he cut off her breasts. Oh, it was so horrible. So horrible. There was no stopping him. I couldn't beg him to stop because he gagged me with this stick. I was so scared. There was blood all over the room, all over Leni, and all over me. He went crazy." Goldie was unable to speak because she was sobbing, deep gulping sobs. "Leni was my best friend. Now she's dead. Dead. I can't believe it happened like this. I never thought that something like this could happen." Esther gathered her daughter into her arms.

A nurse who must have heard Goldie weeping came into the room and told the policeman that he would have to leave. "She's had enough. You can come back another time."

The police officer nodded.

"I'm going to give her a sedative. Once she's asleep, the doctor would like to speak with you, Frau Birnbaum. He's in the office down the hall," the nurse said to Esther.

"Very well. My husband is on his way here. He should be arriving any minute," Esther said. "Is it all right if he goes to speak to the doctor with me?"

"Of course."

Esther stayed until Goldie calmed down and fell asleep. Ted arrived a few minutes later, and the two of them went down the hall to speak with the doctor.

"Will she be all right?" Goldie's father asked the doctor.

"Aren't you Theodore Birnbaum, the owner of the big factory?" a girl who was filling papers in the doctor's office asked.

"Yes," Ted Birnbaum said, giving her a frown.

"That will be all," the doctor said to the girl. "Leave us. I would like to speak to Herr and Frau Birnbaum alone."

"Yes, Doctor," the girl said, then she left, closing the door softly behind her.

"In answer to your question, Herr Birnbaum, your daughter will be all right physically. But I believe that she is a very troubled young woman. I spoke with her when I came in to make some rounds late last night. And I am sorry to have to tell you that I can see that she has some very severe mental problems." The doctor could see that Goldie's parents were not shocked by his diagnosis, so he continued. "I am afraid that it might be in your best interest to consider sending her to a facility for those with mental illness, where she would get help instead of allowing her to go back out on the streets. When next time things go bad, she might not be as lucky."

Esther Birnbaum's shoulders slumped. She looked at her husband. He nodded. "I think the doctor is right. It would be best for Goldie to go to a hospital, where they could treat her," he said. "The truth is, you're right; we were lucky this time. We can't risk anything like this ever happening again."

"A mental hospital?" Esther said. "Our daughter, our only child, locked away like an animal in a crazy house?"

"Would it be better if she were found dead?" Ted asked.

Esther shook her head.

And so arrangements were made for Goldie to be transported to a mental hospital as soon as she recovered. It was a private hospital that the doctor highly recommended.

CHAPTER FORTY-FOUR

Felix Straus was appalled and sickened when he read the news about what had happened to Goldie and Leni. The papers said that Leni had been killed, but Goldie survived. He knew from the newspaper articles that Goldie was in the hospital, so he waited several weeks before returning to the apartment to search for her. But when he arrived, he knocked on the door and found that the apartment had been rented out to new tenants. He would have wallowed more deeply in sadness from the loss had Röhm not brightened his mood by giving him an unexpected promotion. Felix was now one of Röhm's personal bodyguards. And that made him feel important.

He thought of Goldie often. He remembered the long, wonderful nights of wild sex, but the papers had mentioned something that had shocked him. When he and Goldie were seeing each other, he'd had no idea that she was a member of the Birnbaum clan. Everyone in Berlin knew of the Birnbaums. And everyone knew that they were Jews. Jews who, Felix was sure, had become rich by stealing from the Germans. Felix's family, especially his mother, had always envied their wealth. Felix remembered a day when he and his mother had been walking to a bus stop. They saw a black car stop across the street. A woman wearing a heavy fur coat got out. She looked elegant next to his own mother, who wore a used wool coat that she'd purchased secondhand. "You see that woman?" his mother had whispered to Felix. "That's Esther Birnbaum. Her husband owns that ready-to-wear factory that you walk past every day on your way to school. You know where I mean? The big building."

"Yes, I know where it is," Felix said, then he added, "She looks like a queen."

"She's a Jew. A good-for-nothing Jew," his mother said as she spit on the ground.

From that day on he took notice of the factory each day when he was on his way to school, and he thought of the woman in the fur coat and how lucky that she was to be so rich even if she was a Jew. But all that ended when he was thirteen and was forced to get his first job to help his family pay the bills.

Felix and his family knew poverty. He might have been a different man had education not been denied to him. But as things were, he grew up hating everyone who was rich but hating and distrusting Jews even more.

Now, as he thought about Goldie, he remembered how she had made him feel inadequate when she'd refused to marry him. How he had hated her for that. But she was so beautiful. Even now, he could close his eyes and see her stretched across the bed naked, her golden hair catching the light from the candles she'd lit. Her skin was soft and white like a baby's skin. Felix would never admit it to anyone else, but he was still mad about her, and if he had the chance to see her again, he would take it without hesitation. But now he understood why she had such a hold on him. He'd been right all along; she'd cast a spell on him. Jews were known to consort with the devil. And from the strong pull Goldie had on him, he was certain she'd made some sort of a pact. But even now, with all that he knew, he would lie with her if he could regardless of the danger.

CHAPTER FORTY-FIVE

January 30, 1933

On January 30, 1933, to the chagrin of Ernst Röhm and his staunch followers in the SA, Adolf Hitler was appointed chancellor of Germany. And then in February of that same year, *Der Stürmer*, the propaganda newspaper created by Hitler's close friend Joseph Goebbels, became the official paper of the Nazi party. The motto of *Der Stürmer* was "Jews are our misfortune."

CHAPTER FORTY-SIX

Spring 1933

Esther Birnbaum had just returned from a visit with her daughter, Goldie, at the mental institution. As always, Goldie begged to come home. She promised she would behave. But Esther knew better.

These monthly visits left Esther feeling exhausted and defeated. Goldie seemed better, but she still could not be trusted. So many times in the past, Esther had seen Goldie act as if she had changed. Esther would put her trust in Goldie, but it was only a matter of time before Goldie would be back on the same dangerous path again. Esther had spoken to Goldie's doctors explaining the friendship between Goldie and Leni. But even with Leni gone, the doctors at the institute felt that Goldie was not stable enough to go back out into the world.

Esther could not see any end to this. Goldie would probably spend the rest of her days in the institution. Esther put her hand on her lower back. She'd begun having back pains the last couple of weeks. She sank down onto the sofa and put her hands over her face. *If she had only felt safe coming to me and her father for money to pay the rent, that terrible thing that happened to her with that monster would never have happened. And still he roams the streets. Who knows if they'll ever find him?*

Then tears burned the corners of Esther's eyes. *But I can't lie to myself: Goldie was right when she said her father and I would never have given her the money to live with Leni. We would have wanted her to come home and straighten out her life. So the truth is that this is all my fault. All my fault.*

"I brought you the mail, Frau Birnbaum." It was Christa, the new maid Esther had hired the week before.

"Thank you," Esther said, looking at the pile of letters on the table in front of her.

She sorted through the mail in search of a letter from Alma, who wrote every week. But there was nothing today.

There was a knock on the door. Esther was fairly certain it was her nosy neighbor, Harriet Dorfman, who came at the same time every day hoping to be invited in for a nice snack. *I don't want to see her today. But I am sure she knows I'm home. She's always looking out her window. She probably saw me get out of the car.* Esther sighed.

"Frau Birnbaum, Frau Dorfman is here to see you," the maid said.

"Show her in please, Christa."

"Esther, how are you? You have been away for a couple of days. I came by, but you were out of town visiting Goldie."

"Harriet, do come in," Esther said. *Perhaps spending time with Harriet and listening to her nonsense will be a good distraction for me.*

"How are you? How is Goldie? Doing better, I hope."

"She is doing much better. Thank you," Esther said, wishing the entire neighborhood wasn't privy to Goldie's unfortunate situation.

"Nu, so look at this." Harriet handed Esther two newspapers.

Esther looked at them. "These are Nazi newspapers," Esther said.

"Yes. I read them because I like to stay informed."

The first one was the *Völkischer Beobachter*. The second was *Der Angriff*.

"These papers are notorious for having all kinds of propaganda against the Jews. Why would you, a Jewish woman, want to read them." Esther shook her head.

"Like I said, to stay informed. That Adolf Hitler is going to be a problem for us Jews. You mark my words. I am telling you. I can see it coming. A pogrom maybe," Harriet said. "Look, the papers say he is burning books at the university. What kind of an animal burns books?"

"A pogrom? In Germany? Nonsense," Esther said. The last thing Esther wanted to do after her grueling visit with Goldie was discuss politics and the growing hatred of the Jews in Germany. "Ted says not to worry too much about this Hitler fellow; his popularity won't last. The German people are too smart to follow such a radical. He says Hitler really has no power; he's nothing but a pawn. President Hindenburg is the one who is really in control."

"Yes, perhaps. But Hitler is gaining in popularity every day. I am worried."

"Don't worry, Harriet. Everything will be fine."

"My two grandchildren are attending the university in Munich. I hope that all of this hating of Jews won't affect them."

"I'm sure they are all right," Esther said, wishing that she told the maid to tell Harriet she was asleep. But now that Harriet was here, Esther couldn't send her away without offering her some refreshment. After all, she was raised properly, and a lady always behaved properly no matter what she felt inside. "Would you like something to eat, or a cup of tea perhaps?"

"I would love that. Do you have any of those lovely little poppyseed cakes. I just adore them."

Esther called for Christa.

"Christa, can you prepare a platter ofcakes and a pot of tea for us? And once it's ready, we'll take it in here, please."

"Yes ma'am," the pretty young blonde maid said.

"Thank you."

"I always enjoy coming to see you, Esther. You have such a lovely home."

Esther managed a smile, but she thought, *at least if she's busy eating, she'll stop talking so much.*

CHAPTER FORTY-SEVEN

Manhattan, New York City, Early in December 1933

Chana was dressing Ida for another day at her mother's apartment. She hated leaving her baby and often considered bringing Ida to the store with her. In the spring when the weather was nice, she'd taken Ida to work with her every so often. But during the winter she felt that the cobbler's shop was too drafty for the baby. Besides, she had women coming in for fittings all day. The line of clothing she had created was taking off with the younger generation of women. It consisted of Chana's own designs which were stylish, made to fit, and not too expensive. So every morning she would drop the baby off with her mother. Then her father would climb in the car and he and Chana would drive into work together. Just as Chana pinned Ida's diaper, Sam walked into the room, stretching his back.

"How are my beautiful girls?" Sam said, kissing Chana and then touching Ida's cheek.

"Da, Da, Da," Ida rambled. "Da, Da, Da."

"Amazing. I take care of our little ingrate and what are her first words? Not Mama, but Dada," Chana joked.

"Ida adores you, and so do I," Sam said.

"I know." Chana smiled.

"Sweetheart, it's so damn cold outside. You don't really need to work. I can take care of us. I wish you would sell the business and stay at home with the baby. She needs *you*, not your mother. *You*."

"We go through this at least once a week, Sam. I'm not selling. I love having my own business, my own income. I feel like I am doing something with my life."

"Fixing shoes and belts and designing cheap dresses?"

She glared at him. "That was not nice. I run a business that serves a purpose in our community."

"I'm sorry. You know I didn't mean it. But I would love to travel with you once the weather is better. We could go to Italy, and you could meet my sister and her husband. Alma would love you and the baby. How about this—you don't have to sell the store. We don't need the money. Why don't you think about giving it to your dad? He has been doing so well since he started working there."

"Yes, he has, and do you know why? I'll tell you. It's because I am there with him. If he were alone, I am afraid he'd turn right back to drinking. He's an alcoholic, Sam."

"Yes, yes," Sam said "I can't argue with you. I love you too much, so you'll always win. Maybe you have a few minutes for me to show you just how much I love you before you go off and conquer the world again today." He caressed her breast.

She laughed. "Tonight," she said, then added, "I have a fitting at nine, and it's now after eight. By the time I drive to my parents' house and then drive to the store, I'll be lucky to make it on time."

"I give up. You win," he said. "I'll have to suffer in silence until you get home. But when you get home, my love . . ."

She giggled. He kissed her. Then kissed her neck. She pushed him away gently. "Tonight," she whispered. Then she added, "Are you going into work today?"

"No, there's nothing happening. I don't need to." Sam watched his wife and thought about how much he loved his family. He was glad he'd purchased a car for Chana for her birthday in July. Before that, he'd been driving them every morning.

Chana buttoned the fuzzy pink sweater she put on Ida. Then she lifted the baby and slipped each arm carefully into a warm white coat.

"She looks like a little polar bear. Only my wife buys a white coat for a one-year-old child." He laughed. "How long do you think that coat is going to stay clean?"

"I don't care. If she stains it, I'll get her another coat."

"Chana," he said.

"It's nice to earn money, Sam. I can give my daughter the things I never had."

"I know. I understand you. I was just teasing you when I said that nobody would buy a white coat for a one-year-old."

"Well, maybe not. But . . . you are not exactly correct. Ida won't be one for another month." Chana winked at him as she was slipping her own black cashmere coat on. Then she lifted the baby into her arms.

"I love you. I'll see you later." Sam kissed Chana on the lips and planted a kiss on Ida's forehead.

He opened the door for his wife and then closed it behind her. Once they were gone, Sam went into the kitchen to brew a pot of coffee when the phone rang. He picked it up. "Shatzy?" It was Lenny.

"Yeah, it's me," Sam said.

"The boss wants you to come in as soon as you can. He needs to talk to you."

"Sure. I'll be there in a half hour." Sam looked at the clock. It was a little after eight in the morning. Laevsky never called anyone in for a meeting this early. Something had to be wrong.

CHAPTER FORTY-EIGHT

Sam walked into the empty speakeasy and headed right for Laevsky's office in the back. He knocked on the door. Screwy, Laevsky's partner, opened it. Sam looked around the room. At least fifteen men were scattered there with glasses of whiskey in their hands. Laevsky was seated behind his desk. "You want a drink?" Laevsky asked Sam.

"No, it's too early in the morning for me," Sam said. "I never drink before noon."

"Sissy," Izzy whispered under his breath.

Sam gave Izzy a dirty look. They hadn't spoken since Sam and Izzy had a fistfight at the speakeasy. There was bad blood between Sam and Izzy, and the rest of the gang was aware of it. And although Sam would have liked to punch Izzy in the face, he knew better than to start trouble in Laevsky's office. Especially on a day like this.

Laevsky lit a cigar, and the smell filled the room. "All right," he said. "I brought all of you here today because I have some bad news. There has been a lot of talk about the end of Prohibition. So this is not coming as a shock. We've known it was only a matter of time. But I have a friend who told me that the papers coming out tomorrow morning will announce that the end of Prohibition will begin at seven tomorrow night. This sure is going to put a hurt on our incomes. So if we are going to stay alive, the only thing we can do is branch out into other areas of business.

I got ideas about what we're going to do, what we are going to need to change, and how we are going to do it all. Now, I know that you boys have been loyal to me, and I always reward loyalty. So you fellas don't need to be worried about your futures. I am going to keep all of you on. And if things go as I plan, nobody here is going to starve. Over the next week or so, I am going to talk to each one of you alone. When we talk, I'll tell you where you will fit in to our new business plan. Anyway, I just wanted to let you know about Prohibition ending before you saw it in the papers. I'll be in contact with each one of you, so we can arrange for a private meeting," Laevsky said. "That's all for now. You boys can leave. I'll be in touch."

The men started to walk out the door. Then Laevsky called out, "Izzy. Let the other fellas go. You stay back. I want to talk to you."

Izzy felt his eye twitch. He tried to control it as he watched the others leave. *What if Laevsky has found out that I was responsible for the robbery and Harry's death. If Laevsky has discovered the truth, I can kiss my time on earth goodbye. Laevsky would consider disloyalty like this to be unforgivable. There would be nothing I could say or do that would save my life.* Izzy felt sweat trickle down the back of his shirt. *Stay calm*, he told himself. *Don't show the boss you're scared. He's very perceptive. He might not know anything at all. So don't show him you have anything to hide.*

"Izzy. It's been a while since you and I have spent any time talking," Laevsky said. "So how have you been?"

"All right, boss," Izzy said as calmly as he could.

"Found a girl of your own yet?" Laevsky asked.

"I have a few on the line." Izzy could hear that his voice was higher pitched than usual, and he cursed himself for it. *I don't have any interest in other girls, and everyone knows it. Everyone knows I am still in love with Sam's wife. Why would Laevsky humiliate me this way?*

"Well, that's good. I think it would be good for you to find a wife and settle down. I always say that I know my men. And you're the kind of fella who would thrive as a husband and father. You'd make a good family man," Laevsky said as he lit a cigar. Then he added, "But I didn't ask you to stay to talk about your personal life. I asked you to stay to talk about business."

He's watching me. He's watching to see if I'll break. If I'll reveal anything or show any fear. "So what is it, boss?" Izzy tried to sound casual.

"I kept you behind because I want to talk to you about a special job for you. As I said earlier, when everyone was here, I am going to have to reassign all of you men to new jobs. If we are going to stay alive, we are going to have to diversify. This legalization of liquor could be our downfall if we don't watch out. So I want you to go to all of the local restaurants and the taverns which will be springing up everywhere. Find out how much the owners are paying for their liquor. I don't care who they have been buying it from. But let them know that you are with the organization and you mean business. That way they'll be sure to not try to lie to you. Then I want you to tell them in a nice way that we'll sell them the same liquor that they have been buying, at the same price they have been paying. Make sure they know that they will have no choice but to buy from us. Be nice at first, but if they give you any argument, clamp down and tell them that if we find out that they buy from anyone else, we'll make them sorry they did. Do you understand me?"

"Yes," Izzy said. He breathed a sigh of relief. *It's not the greatest job. But I can do it. And at least he doesn't know about the robbery and Harry and Sam.*

"When you go to see these people, make sure that you stay in our neighborhood. Don't venture out to bars in other areas. And make sure that you stay away from the Italians. A boss has to know what his men are capable of in order to survive in my line of work, and so I am putting you on this job because I know how ruthless you can be when you have to be."

"When do you want me to start?" Izzy said.

"Give the fellas who own these places a chance to get themselves established. They're going through a change too. Last week they owned speakeasies. Next week, they'll own legal taverns. I'd say give them two or three weeks. Then go in and talk to them. Talk nice at first. Don't muscle them unless you have to."

"Will do, boss," Izzy said.

Izzy got up and started to leave, but just as he reached for the doorknob, Laevsky said, "And, by the way . . . make sure I don't ever hear that you had anything to do with that robbery."

Izzy felt his face flush. He felt his hand tremble. Then he rushed out the door. *He knows*, Izzy thought.

CHAPTER FORTY-NINE

S am walked out of the speakeasy and got into his car. He lit a cigarette and then started the automobile. *Laevsky says he'll have new jobs for us. I have to believe him because if he doesn't, I don't know where else I can turn. I sure don't want Chana supporting me, and I sure don't want to go to work as a baker for some bakery. I'd never earn the kind of money I have been earning. I know I should be glad that Chana has her own business. It is good to have something to fall back on. But I am not glad. I'm not the kind of man who can be dependent on his wife. I hate it that she's working more than she's home. That's not the way it should be. I want her home so she can be a full-time mother to Ida. And a full-time wife to me. No matter what happens, I must earn enough money to support my family. I must. That's what a man is meant to do.*

Sam drove by the window of Chana's shoe repair shop and looked inside. He caught a glimpse of her, and his heart swelled. *Not because she's my wife, but she is the most beautiful woman I've ever seen. Not to mention, the kindest.*

He pulled the car over to the curb and parked. Then he got out and went into the store. When Sam opened the door, the bell chimed. Chana and her father looked up. "Sam, what are you doing here?" Jake Rubinstein said.

"Came to see my beautiful wife."

Chana looked at him skeptically. "Is something wrong?"

"Why would anything have to be wrong? I just wanted to see if you'd like to have an early lunch with me," Sam said to Chana.

"It's very early, Sam. It's not even eleven yet. But sure. I'd love to go and have something to eat with you. Let me get my coat. Watch the store, will you, Papa? I don't have another fitting until this afternoon. So, don't worry, I'll be back before then."

"Of course," Mr. Rubenstein said.

Sam took Chana's arm, and they walked a few doors down to the deli. Once inside, they took a small table in the back and sat down.

"What can I get you?" the waitress said.

"Two coffees to start." Sam smiled.

They sat in silence for a few minutes, then Sam forced a smile and said, "You want something to eat?"

"No," Chana said. Then she added, "Talk to me, Sam. I know that look on your face. Something is wrong."

She always knows. From the beginning of their relationship, Chana had been his strength. Even though he hated to admit it, especially to himself. She had helped him solve every problem. And now, when he was feeling uncertain about his future, without even thinking about it, he'd driven right to her store. "Alcohol is going to be legal. That will put me out of work," he blurted. Then he put his head in his hands and added, "I just got back from a meeting at Laevsky's office. He says he is going to have work for me. But who knows if that will really happen? His empire was built on the sale of illegal liquor. What can he possibly do now?"

Chana sipped her coffee. Then she reached across the table and took Sam's hand. "Ohhh, your hand is freezing," she said and put it up against her cheek. He tried to smile, but his brow was lined with worry. Chana kissed his palm. Then she looked into his eyes. "You and I are husband and wife. That means that no matter what happens, we will find a way to get through it together."

"I don't want you supporting me," he said stubbornly. "You're my wife. It's my job to take care of you and Ida."

CHAPTER 49 | 163

"So would it be so terrible if you came to work with me at the store?"

"Yes, it would be terrible. You would be my boss. I would be working for you?"

"You are as much an owner of that store as I am, Sam. You're my husband; what's mine is yours."

"I don't know, Chana. Maybe I'll have to go to work someplace. But where? What can I do?"

"Someplace? You're used to earning a lot of money, Sam. Who do you think can pay you that kind of money? Fannie at the bakery? No. The only place you could earn that kind of money is in your own business. And that would mean coming to work at the shoe store with me."

"Don't be sarcastic."

"Well, if you could just hear yourself. You want to go to work at some menial job instead of joining me at our family business, where you would be in charge of things. And . . . the harder that we work, the more we'll earn. Together."

He nodded. "We'll see," he said, but the last thing he wanted to do was go to work in Chana's store.

They sat in silence holding hands across the table for several minutes. Then she whispered, "Sam."

"Yeah?"

"Remember . . . for better or for worse. For richer or for poorer. Till death do us part."

He nodded.

CHAPTER FIFTY

Laevsky didn't keep Sam waiting for very long. Lenny called a little before three that same afternoon. "The boss wants to see you. Can you be here in half an hour?"

"I'll be there," Sam said, relieved to have received a call.

Laevsky and Screwy were sitting in the office when Sam arrived. "Bad news this morning, huh?" Screwy said.

"That's for sure," Sam responded.

"Bad news, yes. But we are going to survive, and we won't do it by dwelling on what was in the past. Now, I am a businessman. When a money source dries up, I find another one. That's the only way to stay above water," Laevsky said. "Shatzy, you have been a good employee. You've proved yourself to be loyal and trustworthy. So I am going to put you right under Screwy in charge of a prostitution ring."

"Prostitution?" Sam said. He was worried about how Chana would feel about this.

"Yes. But first I need a little favor. Something to prove to me that you're worthy."

Sam sucked in a deep breath. "What do you need, boss?"

"I need you to collect some money for me from a jerk who has been making it his business to avoid paying what he owes me. He came to me in desperate need of cash, and I was kind enough to lend him the money he asked for. Now, he doesn't pay, and he avoids me. I am only being fair, and I'm not asking for anything that is not mine. He knew he had a month to repay the loan. It's been two months now. The time has come to take action and show this idiot that Laevsky doesn't sit around and let some clown get away without paying what he owes."

"So you want me to go and talk to him?" Sam said.

"Yeah, and if talking don't work. I want you to use a little muscle."

"You want me to beat him up?" Sam asked.

"Do what you have to do to get my money. Here's his name." Laevsky pushed a piece of paper across his desk to Sam. The name written on it was Luigi Calabrese. "Bastard owes me five hundred dollars."

"He's an Italian? Why didn't he go to the Italians for help? Why did he come to us?" Sam asked.

"Why? I'll tell you why. He knew when he borrowed the money that he wasn't going to pay it back. The gonif, the thief, thought he could get away with it with the Jews. He figured if he tried this crap with the Italians, they'd kill him," Screwy said.

"If we put the squeeze on an Italian, the Italian gangs are going to be all over us. Depending on if he has any friends, this could cause a war," Sam said.

"The fella's a nobody. He owns a grocery store. The Italians don't care about him," Screwy said.

"I don't give a damn what the Italians say. I want you to go and get my money. You have to understand that this is not really about the money. But this kind of disrespect makes us look weak to the Italians. We can't look weak. If we do, they'll come right into our neighborhood and take whatever they want," Laevsky said.

"You know, I don't get into fights very often," Sam said.

"Izzy would disagree with you on that. You beat the shit out of him over that thing with your girl," Screwy said. "I think you can take care of yourself."

"She's my wife now," Sam said, perturbed at the reference to Chana.

"No disrespect, Shatzy. But I know that you can fight if you have to. You broke Izzy's jaw."

"Yeah, but these are the Italians. They are bigger than us. And besides, when I got into that brawl with Izzy, I was so angry I couldn't think straight. I know I am not going to feel that way about some Italian grocer," Sam said.

"Ehhh, I don't want to hear it. You do what I tell you to do. Go and get my money. Show this fella that he made a big mistake thinking that he could push the Jews around," Laevsky said.

"But Laevsky—"

Laevsky cut Sam off midsentence. "I'm the boss. And you'll do what I tell you, or you'll be back to baking lousy rugelach again for twelve dollars a week."

Sam looked at Screwy, who nodded. "I'll be there to help you if you need me," Screwy said. "Just say the word, and you won't have to go alone."

Screwy is nuts, Sam thought. *He's erratic and can't be trusted. I can't believe that Laevsky is asking me to do this. But it's either do what Laevsky asks or take charity from my wife.* "I'll do my best, boss," Sam said.

"Do better than your best, Shatzy. There's no room for failure. In other words, get the job done."

Sam left Laevsky's office feeling worse than when he'd arrived. He hated fighting. And until now, he'd made a point of staying away from the Italians. They made their own rules and were ruthless to outsiders. The last thing he wanted was to start trouble with them. If he did, they'd hunt him down for sure.

Every other day he could hardly wait for Chana and the baby to come home. But today he was glad to have some time alone to think things through. *If I muscle this Italian fella, one of two things will happen. Either the Italians won't care, or they'll be mad that the Jews were making loans in their neighborhood, and they'll send their men to seek revenge on me. I can't have some angry hoodlums coming after me. I have a wife and child to think of.* He agonized over what to do until Chana came home.

She walked in and kissed him, then put Ida down on the changing table. "She's been crying since I picked her up. I think she has a fever."

Sam jumped to his feet, forgetting his own problems, and ran over to the baby. Gently, he placed his lips on her brow. Her face was hot. "She's burning up," he said. "I'm going to take her to the doctor." He grabbed the baby, and with Chana following behind him, they drove to the doctor's office with Ida in Chana's arms, screaming. Sam temporarily forgot all about Laevsky and the job he wanted him to do. It was not uncommon for a young child to die of fever. Chana was trembling as the doctor examined Ida.

"When did you say she will be a year old?" he asked.

"January first."

"Sometimes babies run high fevers," the doctor said, "but I am going suggest that we put her in the hospital so that we can keep an eye on her until her fever comes down."

Chana looked at Sam, who nodded. "If you think it's best," Chana said to the doctor.

"Yes, she'll get the best care there. And as long as you can afford it, I would put her in the hospital."

"Then that's what we'll do," Sam said. Chana's business was earning money. She had enjoyed some success as a dress designer, and the shoe repair shop earned a living. But it was a meager income compared to what he'd been earning before. He wished that they had not spent foolishly. *We should have saved more when we had the chance. Chana was always giving money to charities. And at the time I didn't mind, but now I wish we had that money stashed away somewhere. For some reason I thought that I was always going have plenty. I couldn't ever foresee us lacking for anything.* If he didn't do what Laevsky asked or find other work that paid as much as his previous job, they were going to have to move out of their fancy apartment. However, since they'd been married, they had been putting money away to purchase a home. If their apartment had not been burglarized while they were on their honeymoon, they would have had plenty of money. But as fate would have it, they had lost everything and had to start from scratch. Still, they had worked hard, and now they had a small savings. They weren't as vigilant as they should have been. He thought about all the money he had wasted. A hospital stay was expensive. But if they had to deplete their savings, there was no question they would. Even though he didn't have his old job to rely on, he would not risk Ida's life because of finances.

Ida was admitted into the hospital. Sam and Chana stayed with her while the nurses bathed her with alcohol to bring down her fever.

"She looks so small and helpless, doesn't she?" Chana said.

Sam nodded and took her hand in his. "She'll be all right. You'll see. God won't take her. He won't do this to us."

"We've done bad things, Sam. Maybe he will," Chana said, terrified.

"We have to believe that he won't."

CHAPTER FIFTY-ONE

Izzy knew that if it weren't for Screwy, Laevsky would have gotten rid of him long ago. But Screwy and Izzy were old friends, and Screwy always stood up for Izzy. So when Screwy called Izzy and asked him to meet him for coffee, Izzy went immediately. They met at a small coffee shop across the bridge in Brooklyn where they would not be seen.

"What's going on?" Izzy said as soon as Screwy sat down.

Screwy didn't answer. He lit a cigarette and ordered a cup of black coffee. When the coffee arrived, he poured a shot of whiskey into his cup from a flask in his breast pocket. Then he sat back and looked Izzy in the eye. "Listen. I like you. We were kids together. We have a history. Now I don't want to know nothin' about what you may or may not have done. But I have some information for you. I heard that Laevsky asked Shatzy to make a collection from an Italian business owner. I don't think you want Shatzy pokin' around the Italians. What I am trying to tell you is that if you got somethin' you need to cover up, you better do it now. Do you know what I mean?"

"Yeah, I know what you mean. Do you know the store owner's name who Shatzy is supposed to collect from?"

"Sure. Here. It's on this paper." Screwy put a small piece paper on the table.

Izzy took the paper, then he said, "Thanks for the tip. I owe you."

"Sure," Screwy said. Then he winked, took a sip of his coffee, and tossed down a five-dollar bill. "See you later, Izzy. And . . . needless to say, this conversation never happened."

Izzy nodded.

CHAPTER FIFTY-TWO

Izzy left the restaurant and took a drive over to Little Italy to see the grocery store owner. When he arrived, he waited until all the customers were gone and no one was around except the store owner and himself. Then Izzy locked the door behind him and asked for the five hundred dollars. The store owner claimed he didn't have it. Izzy took a knife out of his pocket, and within a second, he cut off the man's ear. The grocery store owner screamed as his ear fell to the floor.

"You want me to cut off the other one? And when I am done, I'll cut off your balls."

The store owner put his hands in the air. "Wait. Wait, please. Don't hurt me." He started walking to the back of the store with his hands still up and blood dripping down his shirt. He opened the safe in the office and took out five hundred dollars.

Slowly, Izzy counted the pile of money. The store owner was holding his head. "You want all of it? Here, take it all. Just don't hurt me."

"I only want what you owe us," Izzy said. And once he was done counting. He put the money in his pocket. Then he looked the shop owner in the eyes and said, "You better keep your mouth shut about what happened here. Or not only will you be missing your ears and your balls. But you'll be missing your wife and kids too." Then Izzy left.

CHAPTER FIFTY-THREE

Izzy returned home and called Screwy. "Listen, I got Laevksy's money from the Italian," he said.

"Bring it to me. I'm at my apartment," Screwy answered.

Izzy drove over to Screwy's apartment. He handed him the money.

"There's a bloodstain on this," Screwy said.

Izzy nodded.

"Is he dead?"

"No."

"All right. I'll take it from here," Screwy said.

After Izzy left, Screwy put the money in an envelope. On the front, he wrote with his left hand, disguising his handwriting, "The money owed to you from the Italian grocer."

The following morning, Screwy got up before dawn and drove to the speakeasy. He put the envelope on Laevksy's desk and left.

CHAPTER FIFTY-FOUR

Two days passed. At first, Ida continually let out high-pitched screams, which was unnerving. Then the baby gripped her left ear with both hands. But on the third day she stopped screaming and lay quiet, which was even worse. Then finally after Chana and Sam had spent four days without sleeping for more than an hour at a time, or eating a full meal, the doctor said that Ida's fever had broken.

"Will she be all right?" Chana begged the doctor to give her the answer she prayed for.

"Only time will tell."

Chana didn't go into work. Her father ran the business. And for an entire week she and Sam stayed at Ida's side. During this time, Sam forgot his meeting with Laevsky.

Every day Ida got a little stronger, and by the end of the week she was sitting up and smiling.

"Everything looks good. She can go home tomorrow," the doctor said.

Sam and Chana squeezed each other's hands.

The following day, they brought Ida home and put her in her crib. She slept.

Once the baby was sleeping soundly, Chana prepared a light meal for her and Sam. As they sat across from each other in silence eating omelets, the phone rang. As soon as Sam heard the ring, he remembered the job he was supposed to do for Laevsky, and fear shot through him. Chana went to answer the phone, but Sam raced ahead of her. "I got it," he said. Then cradling the receiver in his hand, he went as far away from Chana as the cord would allow. "Yeah, hello," Sam said breathlessly.

"You can forget about that money, Shatzy." It was Screwy.

"Listen, I'm sorry it took me so long. My kid was in the hospital. For a while we didn't know if she was gonna make it. We just brought her home. Damn, I really am sorry. I'll take care of it today."

"I said forget it. And don't mention it to the boss. He's pretty hot under the collar about the whole thing. He thinks you didn't take the job seriously. The best thing to do is never bring it up."

"All right. Whatever you say," Sam promised, sweat forming on his brow.

When he walked back into the kitchen, Chana was staring at him. "What was that about?" she asked.

Sam looked away from her knowing she would see the fear in his eyes. But she was too quick for him.

"Sam, tell me what's going on. Please. Let me help you. Is this about alcohol becoming legal?"

"Yes, in a way," he said.

"Go on . . . tell me all of it. Everything. We'll fix it together," Chana said.

He looked into her eyes, then he pulled her into his arms. They sat down on the sofa. Chana curled up in his lap, and he told her everything. Then he added, "I think Laevksy's mad at me. I'm worried."

She nodded. "All right. It will be all right," she said, then she went on. "I'm going to see Laevsky today. I'll talk to him."

"Screwy said to forget the whole thing. But I am sure Laevksy wants his money."

"I know and he'll get it. I am going to withdraw all the money we have left in our account and pay him with it."

"The hospital bill cost us but good," Sam said. "Damn, I wish we still had that money from the wedding. I hope the bastard who robbed us chokes on it. Now all we have is five hundred dollars. That's it. That's everything."

"No, that's not everything we have, Sam. It's only money. We've made and lost money before. But we'll be all right because we have each other, and we have our little Ida. And as long as we have that, we have everything we need." Chana kissed him.

An hour later Sam watched Chana leave the apartment. *She looks like a movie star in that tight red dress and high heels,* he thought. *It really bothers me that my wife is fighting my battles for me. I am ashamed that I am weak, like my dad. I loved my father with all my heart, but I always knew he was weak. Mom hated him for that. And I sure am lucky that Chana doesn't hate me for it. But I can't help it, I hate myself.*

CHAPTER FIFTY-FIVE

Chana went to the bank and made the withdrawal. Then she stopped at a deli in town and picked up a dozen salt bagels and a pot of cream cheese for Laevsky. It was a short drive from there to the speakeasy. Chana parked the car, walked down the alleyway to the private entrance, and knocked. Lenny answered.

"Doll, what are you doing here during the day. The place isn't open yet."

"Can I come in?" Chana asked.

"Yeah, sure. Damn, you look like one hot tomato. Every time I see you, you get prettier. How is that husband of yours treating you?"

She walked inside. She didn't answer Lenny's question. "I'm here to see Laevsky. Is he in?" she asked.

"I don't know if he's gonna want to see you. He's been in a lousy mood since all this started with the end of Prohibition."

"Tell him I'm here. Or should I just go back and tell him myself?"

Lenny looked at Chana. *She sure is a stunner*, he thought. "Yeah, good idea. Go on back. When he sees you, it might just cheer him up."

Chana knocked on the door of Laevsky's office.

"Yeah?" Laevsky answered.

"It's Chana. Sam's wife."

"Come in."

She walked inside. Laevsky was sitting behind his desk smoking a cigar. "NU, so to what do I owe this honor?" he asked, his eyes twinkling.

"Hi, Laevsky. How have you been?" she said, putting the bag from the deli down on his desk and then kissing his cheek. "I came here because I am desperate. I need to speak with you on my husband's behalf," Chana said sweetly as she wrung her hands together.

"Sure, doll. Go on, I'm all ears."

"I know about the changes in the liquor laws. I suppose everyone does by now," she said, "and I realize that the legalization of alcohol has put a damper on your business. But . . ." She hesitated, looking down at her hands and batting her long, dark eyelashes. "Well . . . I just don't know how to ask this of you."

"You need a favor. You ask. Either I say yes or I say no."

Chana forced herself to smile. She hesitated for a moment and then looked directly into Laevsky's eyes. Once she could see that he was receptive to what she was about to say, Chana said in a soft voice, "So, as you can see, Laevsky, Sam needs to continue working for you. I know I'm asking a lot, and I would be forever indebted to you." Then she looked down at the desk and added, "How do I say this . . . please, Laevsky, don't put my husband to work in the prostitution ring. Sam told me that you wanted him to work with Screwy on that. Now, I know you know my Sam is loyal, and I agree with you that he is. But if those whores get ahold of him, they might be able to turn his head, especially as I get older. I'm begging you to help me. Please don't put my Sam in a job where he is tempted by other women all the time. Sam and I have a little girl. She needs her father. I need my husband."

"A girl like you should be worried about other women? You shouldn't; not one of them could hold a candle to you. You are the most stunning woman I've ever seen. But if you want, I could put him in a lesser-paying job. Maybe as one of my collection men."

"My Sam isn't a tough guy. He wants to be, but he isn't. I know him better than anyone. He can only fight when his heart is in it. He doesn't have what it takes to put the squeeze on someone. He'll go soft if the fella starts to beg. He'll take pity on him. I can promise you that."

CHAPTER 55 | 183

"Yeah, I know he's soft," Laevsky said. "You see, I already figured as much. But still, I like him. You know why? Because Shatzy has a quality that some of the other boys in the organization lack. You know what that is? He's loyal and he can be trusted. I don't have to watch my back with him. Shatzy's loyal to a fault. Now I'm not saying that he doesn't do stupid things sometimes. Because he certainly does. But I know he'd never steal from me, and I know he'd never turn on me."

"So then you'll keep him on? Even though he doesn't have the killer instinct?"

"I don't know why you would want me to keep him in the organization. It's a dangerous job. Why don't you take him into your shoe store, and the two of you can build that business together. It sure is a lot safer than what we are doing."

"I know that, Laevsky. And don't kid yourself; I've thought about it. I've even begged Sam to come and work with me. But he won't hear of it. Sam could never be happy working at a job where he was just earning a living. He's used to making a lot of money since he has been with you. He would probably have been willing to accept a working man's salary before he started working for you. But now . . . no. And besides all that, if somehow, I could convince him, it would be no good anyway because he would always feel like I owned the business and he was working for me. It would destroy our marriage."

"You sure are in love with him. A girl like you who coulda had her choice of fellas. You picked that one." He sighed. "Well, I guess if you go for looks, I gotta admit, Shatzy is no lightweight in the looks department. Do you have some money put away? Times might be a little hard until we get up and running again."

"We did. But we recently had an upset. Our daughter got very sick, and we had to pay for a large hospital bill," Chana said. Then she looked down at the floor. "I have something else I must tell you, Laevsky. But you have to promise me that if I tell you, you won't fire my Sam. If you do, he'll never forgive me. I'm begging you, Laevsky. I don't want to keep anything from you. It wouldn't be right."

"Go on, Chana . . . tell me what you want to tell me."

She took a deep breath. Then she said, "After we paid the hospital bill, we had a little money left in the account. I took it out this morning, so I could pay you the money that Sam was supposed to collect from that Italian fella. I knew you wanted your money and I don't blame you. So I was going to lie to you and tell you that Sam put the muscle on him and that he got the money. But I can't lie to you, and Sam said he didn't want me to lie either. The truth is this money is from our account. It's all here, all five hundred dollars." Chana took the envelope out of her handbag and placed it on Laevsky's desk.

What the hell is she talking about? Shatzy already dropped off the money, didn't he? Laevsky paused for a moment and looked away to hide the shock in his face. Then in a controlled voice, he said, "You were going to pay the debt for some Italian grocer in order to protect Sam? Your husband sure is one lucky fella." He shook his head. Then he pushed the envelope with the money inside back at her. I don't want your money."

"You have always been so kind to me," Chana said, putting the envelope back in her purse.

Morty Laevsky leaned back in his chair and studied Chana for several moments Then a smile spread over his face. "I've always had a soft spot for you, doll. But you already know that. That's why you came to see me today instead of sending Sam." He hesitated for a moment. Then he lit a cigar and took a puff. "All right, Shatzy's off the hook. And as far as putting him to work in prostitution, well, I won't do that. How about I give Shatzy an easy job working in gambling?"

Chana's face lit up. "Thank you so much, Laevsky. I will never forget your kindness today." She stood and walked behind the desk. Then she planted another kiss on his cheek.

"Damn, if you don't smell like fresh lilacs," he said. "You are one hell of a girl, Chana. And every time I see you, I wish I was twenty years younger."

After Chana left, Laevsky took the envelope out of his desk drawer and studied the handwriting. Then he glanced at the bills and saw the bloodstains. *I don't like it when I don't know what is going on in business. I don't like it at all. I can't put my finger on it, but something is not kosher.*

CHAPTER FIFTY-SIX

When Chana returned home, she told Sam what had happened with Laevsky. He was ashamed that his wife had to fix his problem, but he was also secretly relieved. "Gambling won't be as bad as prostitution. I don't know what you'll be doing, but I assume you'll be setting up games, and you might even be in charge of the men on the streets who run numbers," Chana said.

"You are the best thing that ever happened to me," Sam said, taking Chana into his arms. "The baby is sleeping," he whispered in her ear. Then he lifted her into his arms carried her to the bedroom.

Two days later, Lenny called. "Laevsky wants you to start work today. Come into the office, and he'll give you your instructions. I heard he switched you out with Izzy. It looks like Izzy's going to work the prostitution ring and do some special collection work for me; you're going to be in gambling."

When Sam arrived back at the apartment building that evening, he was optimistic about the future. The job would require him to work every night. He would not have as much free time as he did when he was running alcohol. But at least he didn't have to muscle anyone. He wouldn't have minded running a bunch of pimps, but he knew that if he'd taken that job, it would have made Chana unhappy. This job would work our just fine. He'd set up craps and poker games. He'd be in charge of collecting from the fellas who ran numbers. It didn't seem difficult at all.

Sam collected the mail before going upstairs to his apartment and found a letter from Alma waiting for him. The apartment was quiet. Chana and the baby were not home yet. So he opened the letter and read.

Dear Sam,
It's been a while since my last letter. I'm sorry. We had a tragedy here. Lory's mother passed away suddenly in her sleep last month. He took it hard. And I felt so bad for him. I know how difficult it is to lose a parent. When dad died, I felt as if a part of me was gone forever. Anyway, I don't want to dwell on the sadness. I have some good news too. Lory has completed his training, and he is now a full-fledged doctor! I am so proud of him. And I have even more good news, I have started nurse's training. I love it. I know I always dreamed of being a doctor, but this is almost as good. Every day is a blessing. I am very happy in my marriage and in my work.

How are you? How is Chana and the baby? You never told me what you are doing for work these days. I hope you are doing all right financially. Lory and I don't have a lot of money saved, but we'll help you two if you need it.

I am stunned by the beauty of this country. Italy is magnificent. Unfortunately, Mussolini runs it with an iron fist. The government controls everything here. There is a group of thugs called the black shirts who are under Mussolini's direction. And they punish anyone who says a word to oppose him. It is not like it is in America where it is all right to voice an opinion. I miss having that kind of freedom. When I tell Lory about the freedoms we had in America, he says he wonders if we shouldn't try to get out of Italy. But the problem with leaving is that we have good jobs here and a nice place to live. It's difficult to leave all of that behind. But there was an incident that still leaves me shuddering. It happened a few months ago. One of Lory's coworkers, another doctor, announced that he was a communist. He stood in the lunchroom at the hospital and declared it out loud so everyone could hear. The next day he disappeared. We have not seen or heard from him since. Lory and I are careful about what we say. We never share our views about anything. It's not safe. I've even heard that the mail is censored. Although I can't say for sure.

I've sent you pictures of Lory and myself. Please send any pictures you might have of Chana and the baby. I can't wait to meet them both. I hope it will be soon.
Love always your devoted sister,
Alma

HE FOLDED the letter and put it on the desk in the living room. Then he poured himself a glass of brandy and waited for Chana to come home. *Life is good*, he thought.

CHAPTER FIFTY-SEVEN

Germany, June 30, 1934

The Night of the Long Knives: Operation Hummingbird
Röhm's SA had grown into a powerful army of over a million men, and Felix Strauss felt proud to be so highly regarded by Röhm. He knew Röhm was not well liked by the German people because of violent street demonstrations of the SA or, as they were commonly called, the Brownshirts. He'd participated in plenty of the violent demonstrations. They were mostly exhibitions of force against the rich and the Jews. Each time he and his colleagues beat up on an unsuspecting Jewish businessman or sexually attacked a young Jewish girl, Felix forced himself to suppress the fond memories he carried of Goldie. She was both rich and Jewish, and somehow she had been his friend. But he knew that she'd also been very corrupt. She'd been involved in things no good German woman would ever become involved in. Even if she had been pure Aryan, she would never have made any man a good hausfrau. She was promiscuous and perverted. And that was, he told himself, because she was a rich Jew.

He put thoughts of Goldie out of his mind and focused on his promising future. Tomorrow was going to be a good day; he was not expected to get into any street fights. He was on holiday with Röhm and several other members of the SA. It was to be a day of relaxation, good food, and plenty of beer. They were staying at the Kurhaus Hanslbauer hotel in the lovely and quaint Bavarian town of Bad Wiessee. He knew that he had been chosen as one of Röhm's bodyguards because he knew how to look the other way when Röhm engaged in his homosexual escapades. Felix had no interest in other men sexually, but he knew that many of the SA did and he didn't care. His fascination with the SA lay in its promise that soon all the wealth of Germany would be taken away from the rich Jews who had stolen it and redistributed to the German people. Once the wealth of the country was restored to its rightful owners, girls like Goldie would not feel superior to men like him.

He, Röhm, and the other SA members had arrived earlier that evening. After they checked into the hotel, they'd had an extravagant dinner followed by a night of heavy drinking and carousing. Felix used discretion, as he always did, when he kept watch over Röhm who had slipped into the shadows with some handsome young fellow. And now, Röhm had that young man in his bed.

It was very late, but Felix was unable to sleep. He lay in bed listening to the breathing of Röhm's other bodyguards who shared the room. Someone was snoring lightly. Felix's drunkenness was wearing off and his head was already aching. He reached over to the night table and took a pill out of the drawer and washed it down with some beer that someone had left in a glass on the top of the table. Then he lay back down. In a few minutes he fell asleep. It was a strange and fitful sleep. He dreamed he saw Goldie. Hitler's bodyguards, the SS, were carrying her away. She was screaming his name. "Felix, Felix, help me!" He shook awake. The dream had unnerved him. He was nauseated and needed a glass of water. Dawn was breaking. If anything, his headache was worse than before he'd fallen asleep. Still in his underwear, he got up and quietly left the room. Feeling as if he might vomit, Felix, walked down the hall to the bathroom.

Outside, several long black limousines pulled up in front of the hotel. Hitler and Goebbels, accompanied by several other armed men from the SS walked inside the hotel lobby. They went to the front desk where they got the room number for Ernst Röhm from the trembling wife of the proprietor. After she gave them Röhm's room number, she watched as Hitler and his entourage climbed eighteen stairs to the first floor where the room was located. The SS drew their guns and then kicked open the door to Röhm's room.

At that moment Felix was coming out of the bathroom. He heard a commotion coming from the rooms. He ran toward the sound because it was his job to protect his leader Ernst Röhm. When he entered the room, he was pushed at gunpoint to stand next to Röhm and his young lover, both of whom were naked. The five other men from the SA who had been staying in Röhm's room were lined up at gunpoint too.

"Röhm, you are arrested," Hitler yelled.

"Adi?" Röhm said, using the nick name he'd always used when addressing Adolf Hitler. "Why?"

Felix knew that Röhm had always regarded Hitler as a friend. After all, Röhm had been instrumental in helping Hitler rise to power.

"You are arrested." Hitler said again.

"Yes, mein führer," Röhm said, his eyes wide open. He covered his private parts with his hand. He was clearly stunned.

"You are disgusting. You should be ashamed of yourself. Put on your clothes," one of the SS officers said to Röhm. "The rest of you, get dressed too."

Felix grabbed his brown uniform and began to get dressed. Everyone's attention was on Röhm, so Felix had a chance to grab his pistol. However, he wasn't quick enough. One of the SS men saw him and shot him immediately. As he lay dying, he watched the rest of the men from the SA being led away by the armed SS, and he knew that although he would not be there to see it, the power had just shifted and history had just been made.

CHAPTER FIFTY-EIGHT

Ernst Röhm was imprisoned on the night of June 30, 1934. The following morning, a guard entered his cell, and handed Röhm a pistol.

"The führer has sent this to you. He wishes to give you the option to take your own life," the guard said.

Röhm stared into the guard's eyes. He did not pick up the pistol. Instead, he said, "If I am to be killed, let Adolf do it himself."

The guard took the gun. Then he nodded and left Röhm alone in the cell.

Ernst Röhm was executed later that morning.

CHAPTER FIFTY-NINE

From June 30 through July 2 in the year 1934, all of the top members of the SA were murdered by the SS. This bloodbath would come to be known as the Night of the Long Knives, or Operation Hummingbird.

Once Röhm and all the leaders of the SA were dead, Hitler had no one left to oppose him within his political party. He had now gained absolute power.

CHAPTER SIXTY

Germany, The beginning of August, 1934

President Hindenburg lay dying of lung cancer. Meanwhile, Adolf Hitler, the chancellor of Germany, was busy drawing up papers that would change the way Germany was governed. In those papers it was clearly stated that if the president were to pass away, the position of chancellor and president would then be joined into one position. Germany would have one, and only one leader. This leader would be referred to as the führer, and his name would be Adolf Hitler.

The day after the papers were signed, President Hindenburg died. And although many people in Germany didn't realize it at the time, their beloved fatherland was about to plummet down a dark and downward spiral.

CHAPTER SIXTY-ONE

America, 1936

On April 3, 1936, Richard Hauptmann, a German-born carpenter who lived in New Jersey, was executed for the murder of the Lindbergh baby. He was offered life in prison if he would admit to committing the kidnapping and killing of the child. But Hauptmann refused. He maintained his innocence until his death.

From 1936 to 1938 Charles Lindbergh made six visits to Nazi Germany. Hitler knew that Lindbergh had been awarded the Medal of Honor in America for flying across the Atlantic from New York to Paris alone in 1927. And he admired Lindbergh for this feat. On October 18, 1938, with Hitler's approval, Reichsmarschall Hermann Goring awarded Lindbergh the Service Cross of the German Eagle with star. Lindbergh graciously accepted.

CHAPTER SIXTY-TWO

Rome, Italy, 1937

Alma finished her course in nursing, and she loved it. Her work was so fulfilling that she found she was not disappointed at not having become a doctor. Lory spent his time curing patients, while she spent her time nurturing them. He was so busy that he never got to know the patients the way she did. There were times she believed that her patients felt closer to her than they did to their own families. Often when she sat at the bedside of someone who was desperately ill, they shared their deepest fears and dreams with her. It was true that when one of her patients passed away, she would hurt as if they were her own flesh and blood. But the rewards she felt when someone left the hospital healed was worth every bit of struggle.

She and Lory made a good team. They were very much alike. Both of them avoided subjects that caused controversy. She was quieter and more reserved. He was more fun loving and extroverted. But somehow they complemented each other. They shared a small close-knit group of friends who were also work colleagues. And on Saturday nights those who were not working went out for a light dinner and a few drinks. Every day of her life since she met Lory, Alma felt blessed. She was grateful to Lory for his patience, which had helped her get over her fear of making love. He was a kind and gentle man, but most of all he was understanding.

All of their friends said they envied them because they were such a happy couple. And they were, but Alma wanted to have a child. They tried very hard to conceive, but each month Alma would feel defeated when her period arrived. They'd gone to see specialists, where they'd both endured a battery of tests. But when the results came in, the doctors could not tell them why Alma did not get pregnant. They couldn't find a legitimate, physical reason. Alma blamed herself and constantly apologized to Lory. Each time she would say she was sorry, Lory would always hold her tightly and tell her that didn't matter to him if they ever had children or not. But it mattered to her. Alma would have loved to have a child of her own. Alma wanted the opportunity to love a child with all her heart and to be the kind of mother she'd always wished Goldie would have been.

When Alma and Lory's friends had parties or dinners at their homes instead of in restaurants, they were able to talk freely. It was too dangerous to ever speak against the government in a public place. If the wrong person overheard, the consequences could be horrific. But at home, among their small group of friends, they could speak openly. Mussolini recently had allied Italy with Germany. Most of their friends were concerned about this new pact. But others felt that if Germany and Italy were allies, at least they would not be going to war.

Alma didn't mind the union for a different reason. For a personal reason. She felt that as long as Germany and Italy were allies, she would be able to return home easily to visit her beloved bubbie. And although she and Lory recently returned from a wonderful visit to Berlin, Alma was ready to go back. Her zede had finally accepted Lory as part of the family. He had stopped making snide remarks about Lory being after his money. In fact, he even congratulated Lory on becoming a doctor. Then, as a surprise graduation gift, her bubbie and zede gave Lory a stethoscope. It made Alma feel so proud and happy to know that her grandparents liked her husband.

The only part of her trip to Germany that had left her feeling miserable was the visit with her mother at the mental institution. It was a short but uncomfortable visit because Goldie was so heavily medicated that she hardly knew her own daughter. Esther had to keep shaking Goldie's arm, so she wouldn't fall asleep, and repeating, "This is your Alma. Your daughter is here, Goldie." And Goldie would nod her head and say, "Yes, yes. That's right." But Alma could see in her mother's blank stare that she was only half present.

One night soon after she and Lory returned to Italy, Alma came home from work at the hospital to find Lory waiting for her. This was highly unusual. Her shift usually ended at least a full hour before his, giving her plenty of time to prepare their dinner.

"Why are you home?" she asked. Then she saw his pale face and frightened eyes. "What is it? Are you all right? Are you feeling ill?" she said, her voice panicked.

"Yes, please don't worry. I'm fine," he said. He was drinking a glass of red wine, which he put down on the table. Alma saw that his hands were trembling.

"Something is wrong. Please tell me what it is, Lory."

Lory cleared his throat. "Angelo was working in the children's ward today. He was taken outside in the middle of his shift. Everyone ran to the window to see why. We watched as he was beaten to death outside the hospital," Lory said. Angelo was a doctor who had been a good friend of theirs.

"By who? Why?"

"Thugs. Blackshirts. I saw it happen. I am so ashamed of myself. I was too much of a coward to go out and help him."

"Blackshirts?" she said. She trembled. Everyone knew of the Blackshirts. They were Mussolini's henchmen. "Why were the Blackshirts at the hospital, and why did they do this to Angelo?"

"You know Angelo. He has a big mouth. He was always talking badly about the government."

"I knew he was a communist. But I thought he only told his good friends, like us."

"Yes, he did at first. But then he got bolder and started telling people what he thought of Mussolini and Hitler. And he obviously told the wrong person," Lory said, shaking his head.

"Oh my God." Alma put her arms around her husband. "Poor Lucinda. She has a little boy to raise, and now she's lost her husband."

"I can't forgive myself for just standing there not moving. It was like I was glued to the ground. I couldn't make my feet move. I was so afraid of Mussolini's men that I was unable to help our friend. How could I be so weak? I am a coward. I just stood there, paralyzed by fear." His whole body was shaking. Alma squeezed him tighter.

"If you had gone outside and tried to help him you wouldn't have been able to do him any good. But instead of one widow weeping tonight, there would have been two. They would have killed you too, Lory. And I can't bear to think of life without you. So I thank God that you didn't do anything," she said.

He nodded. "I would never want you to weep for me."

"Then keep to yourself, Lory. Don't make any waves. Don't stand up for anyone. Just be quiet and do your work. I love you, and I don't ever want to lose you."

CHAPTER SIXTY-THREE

Austria, 1938

On March 12, 1938, crowds of Austrians filled the streets. They cheered and welcomed the German troops as they marched proudly into Austria, Hitler's birthplace. And so began the Anschluss or the annexing of Austria into Nazi Germany.

Then a month later, a law was passed requiring all Jews under Nazi rule to register and report all of their assets to the government.

CHAPTER SIXTY-FOUR

Berlin, July 1938

Four years earlier when Hitler had taken power, Ted Birnbaum had hoped that things might change for the better. He was aware of Hitler's dislike for Jews. But he knew that most political leaders were not fond of Jewish people. It was common for Jews to be scorned throughout history. This dislike of the Jewish people had caused problems, but Ted highly doubted that there would be anything as primitive as a pogrom in a country as civilized as Germany. And since Hitler constantly said he wanted to bring order to Germany, Ted hoped that the demonstrations and abuse of Jews in the streets by the Brownshirts might come to an end.

When Röhm was alive, the sight of a group of Brownshirts was terrifying to anyone who was Jewish. It grew more and more common to see three or four Brownshirts beating someone to death on the sidewalk in front of a shop or a restaurant. People on the streets looked the other way as they rushed by. They would be silent for a few moments until they were away from the violent scene. Then they resumed living as if they had never witnessed the atrocity. No one seemed to care. And if they did, they were too afraid to get involved.

Then Hitler had taken power, and there was a glimmer of hope that this violence in the streets would end. It didn't. For all of Hitler's talk about bringing law and order to the city, nothing had changed. If anything, it had gotten worse. And each day, it was becoming more and more dangerous to be a Jew in Berlin. Ted tried to convince himself that this nightmare would pass. That Hitler was too radical, and soon a new government would take control. A more civilized government.

Ted tried to look on the bright side. He had even been in favor of the decision Hitler made last May to outlaw perverse art. Ted had always hated the sexually exploitive art of the Weimar period. After all, Goldie had almost been killed posing for one of those crazy artists. *Who but a very sick mind would want to paint women who had been brutally murdered?* Ted asked himself. However, Hitler had not only outlawed the sexually explicit art, he'd outlawed many other things too, like books and music. Not all of them were sexually deviant. Many were wonderful classics.

And these things Ted did not agree with. In fact, this censorship worried him. He had talked with his friend and attorney, Michal Mendelson, about his concerns. Mendelson assured him there was nothing to be alarmed about, but when Ted and Esther were forced to register and report their assets to the government, Ted felt a strong sense of unease.

It was common knowledge that Hitler and the SS hated the Jews. Esther would talk to her lady friends from the women's group at the synagogue and come home with fear in her eyes. She would warn Ted that she didn't trust this new Nazi government. She would beg him to consider leaving Germany and moving to Italy or America. "Italy," he told her, "with Mussolini, it is just as bad. And besides how can we leave everything we have here in Germany? Our business is here. Our families are buried in the Jewish cemeteries here. My father built this factory with his own two hands, with the sweat of his brow. Berlin is our home, Esther. We are not young. How could we ever think about starting over someplace else? Most governments don't care for Jews. This Nazi government is no different. But all of this will pass. It always does. You'll see. Please don't worry yourself," he said, patting her

CHAPTER 64 | 209

hand. Secretly, though, he felt a nagging sense of worry. But he assured himself. *I won't deny that I am uncomfortable with all the hatred of Jews here in Berlin. But I am far too wealthy and much too highly respected among my non-Jewish neighbors and business associates for the government to bother me or Esther.*

Ted had been trying to walk every night after dinner. But one afternoon when he was coming down the stairs at the factory, he twisted his ankle. And since July was extremely hot that year, Ted had begun making excuses to avoid exercise. Even after his ankle healed, he did not return to his evening walks. And slowly but surely, he'd put on almost twenty pounds. It had become difficult to breathe and sometimes he had pain in his chest.

Esther was worried sick about him and begged him to go and see Dr. Kleinstein. After a month of nagging, he finally agreed. Esther insisted on going with him. Dr. Kleinstein said that Ted was out of shape and desperately in need of an exercise and diet regimen. He warned Ted that if he didn't stop overeating and start walking again, he would probably have a stroke or heart attack. Ted was unnerved by this news and determined to better his health. So he listened as the doctor instructed Esther to have special bland food prepared for him. Esther followed Dr. Kleinstein's instructions to the letter. And although Ted ate the food he was served, he hated it. Then each night after dinner Ted forced himself to take a walk.

Most nights he walked the tree-lined streets of his own wealthy neighborhood. But on other nights, he would have Hans drive him into town where he could look in the windows of the shops as he strolled along. Sometimes he would stop and have a beer or two even though the doctor had said that it would be in his best interest to give up alcohol. On these nights he would go to one of the Jewish cafés where he would order the dark, thick German beer he loved. Then as he sat at an outside table, he would engage in discussions with the locals, most of who were the Jewish business owners who'd come to have dinner after they closed their stores.

They were small-business owners not nearly as prominent as Ted Birnbaum. So he never told them his name because he was afraid they would feel uncomfortable around him, and he enjoyed their candid conversations. Lately, the discussions had grown more heated. The local people were worried about the Nazis and what effect the Nazis would have on their businesses. Ted just listened. He wasn't concerned. He felt that his business was far too big to be impacted. Besides, he stayed out of politics. He was too busy trying to run a factory to get involved.

CHAPTER SIXTY-FIVE

Even with the occasional beer, by early November, Ted had lost the fifteen pounds. He was feeling more fit and more energetic. Esther was happy. Sometimes Ted was distracted and impatient because he was caught up with business matters. During those times, he failed to show her affection. However, in truth, he adored his doting wife. They'd spent over forty years together. There'd been plenty of good times. But there had also been rough times when he and Esther had disagreements that sent Esther running into the bedroom crying. Strangely enough when the doctor had warned him that he could become very ill, it was not himself that was his greatest concern, it was Esther.

Anyone who met Ted Birnbaum would have said he was a cold and calculating man. He could be ruthless in business and overly demanding of his employees. But, in truth, he was like a crab. His exterior was a hard shell, but inside he was soft and vulnerable, though his vulnerability was only extended to those he loved. And so he'd followed the doctor's orders as best he could, not so much for himself but for his Esther.

It was a lovely evening, just before sunset, filled with the fragrance of autumn. The trees had shed their leaves, painting the ground in brilliant colors. The cook had prepared another dinner of plain roasted chicken and roasted potatoes for him. Esther went on the same diet as her husband, so he would never have to see the food he loved and could not eat. And since Ted was prohibited the use of salt, Esther did not use it either. They ate quietly. Then Ted got an idea: "Would you like to come walking with me?" he asked.

She smiled at him. "Is that an invitation?"

"It is."

"Then, of course, I would."

"How about we have Hans drop us off in town. Then we take a little walk through the shops. I know how you love to window-shop."

"I do," she said. "It sounds like fun."

I'm getting soft in my old age. I don't always tell her how I feel. But I should tell her more often how much I love her. I can't drink in front of her. She would get hysterical and tell me that the doctor said no alcohol. My sweet Esther. She's such a worrier. So I will forgo my beer tonight just so I can spend time with her. Just so she feels loved. He smiled to himself.

The Birnbaums got out of the car in the center of town. Before Hans drove away, Ted leaned into the car and said, "Pick us up right here in two hours, Hans."

"Yes sir," Hans said.

Then Ted took a few Reichsmarks out of his pocket and handed them to Hans. "Why don't you go and have beer or two while you're waiting?"

"Thank you, sir. That's very kind of you."

"Enjoy," Ted said, smiling. Then Esther linked her arm in his, and the two of them began to walk together.

"Two hours? That's a long walk."

"I thought perhaps you might like to stop for a cup of tea afterward."

She nodded. "Yes, that would be nice."

There was a soft breeze that rustled the leaves as they looked into the windows of the stores.

"Do you remember when we were young, and you used to beg me to go into town with you to go window-shopping, but I was too busy with the factory?" Ted said, his voice soft with nostalgia.

"Of course. I remember everything."

"I made so many mistakes." He sighed.

"What kinds of mistakes. You never made any mistakes? You are a wonderful businessman. A fabulous husband and provider," she said, squeezing his arm reassuringly.

"But I missed out on so much of our lives. I've often wondered if Goldie would have turned out differently if I had been around more when she was growing up."

"You can't blame yourself for Goldie's poor choices. You were busy taking care of the business. And that is how you took care of us. We never wanted for anything, Ted. And that was because of you."

"When I was a child, my father was never home; he was always working. And I grew up believing that I must do the same thing because this is what fathers did. But I didn't need to; we already had plenty of money..."

"I don't feel that you had anything to do with Goldie going down the wrong path. I believe Goldie's problems started when she became friends with that Leni. Leni was a wild one. Her parents gave her no supervision. She did whatever she wanted, and Goldie admired her. I tried to break up that friendship, but no matter how hard I tried, those two just gravitated to each other like magnets."

"And look what happened to Leni."

"Poor thing," Esther said.

"I don't pity her. She ruined my daughter's life."

"She's dead. Forgive her. She can't do any harm now." Esther stroked her husband's hand.

"You have always been able to forgive, Esther. I've always admired that in you. It's a gift."

She smiled. "I never knew you felt that way."

"I never told you, I guess. I am becoming tender in my old age."

"I like it," she said.

CHAPTER SIXTY-SIX

They continued walking hand in hand. Esther felt like a young girl falling in love for the first time. She looked up at Ted. "This has been a very special evening," she said.

He smiled.

"Look at that tree," she said wistfully. "It hasn't shed its leaves yet, and they look like a golden halo against the darkening sky. Don't you think so?"

He nodded.

"My hair was golden like that tree when I was young. Everyone used to say it looked like a halo. Goldie has the same hair color," Esther said.

"You are even more beautiful now than you were when you were a just a young girl."

"Do you remember our wedding day?" she asked.

"Of course. How could I forget? My father said you were pretty. But when I saw you, I was overcome by how beautiful you were. And still are."

"Really? You were so confident."

"It was an act. I was terrified."

She laughed. "Me too."

They heard shouting, shattering of glass, and a loud commotion coming from somewhere down the street.

"What's happening?" Esther asked.

Before Ted had a chance to say a word, a loud boom sounded, shaking the ground. Someone yelled, "The synagogue is on fire."

Ted and Esther turned to see flames shooting out of the building as black smoke filled the sky.

Then a mob of angry young men carrying burning torches came running through the streets. They threw rocks through the windows of the stores as they called out, "Filthy Jews," "Jewish swine," "Worthless vermin."

Esther grabbed Ted's arm and pulled him into a thin alleyway between two stores where they hid. But from their hiding place they could hear the boys singing, "When Jewish blood squirts from the knife..."

Esther gasped. She didn't say a word, but she looked up at Ted. Then she pointed across the street where three Brownshirts were kicking a man who lay bleeding on the sidewalk.

"I must go and help him," Ted said. "What is this? What is going on here?" Ted whispered more to himself than to Esther.

"It looks like a pogrom," she said.

"We'll stay here in this alleyway until it's time to meet Hans."

They sat down on the ground and huddled in the shadows as the mob grew bolder and more destructive. Ted continuously checked his watch. Finally, two hours had passed. "Hans will be waiting," he said "We have to run as fast as we can back to meet him. Can you do it?"

"I haven't run in years," Esther said, "but I'll do my best."

"Are you ready?" he asked.

"What if Hans isn't there?" she asked.

"He'll be there. He is one of the finest men I know. He'll be there."

She nodded.

"Are you ready?" Ted asked again.

"Yes."

Ted held on to the building and struggled until he got back up onto his feet. Then he helped Esther to stand up. Taking Esther's hand, they ran through the chaos-ridden streets to meet Hans. Esther tripped and fell, tearing her skirt and skinning her knee. But Ted lifted her back up with one hand. It was hard for Ted to breathe. But the two of them kept running hand in hand until they saw Hans pull up to the curb in the automobile. Hans didn't get out to open the door. Ted flung it open instead. Esther was trembling as she climbed inside the back seat of the car. Ted followed her. Then Hans sped away.

"Are you both all right?" Hans asked as he drove.

"Yes, we're all right," Ted said.

When they arrived back home, they found several windows had been broken. The maid told them groups of young men had called out terrible things as they hurled rocks through the windows. But, she said, when they came to the door trying to force their way in, Hans had held them off at gunpoint.

Ted called Hans into his office. "You were here when all this happened? I told you to go and have a beer. Why did you come back to the house?"

"I preferred to save the money you gave me. My wife is going to have a baby, and we need every extra penny we can get our hands on. I couldn't go to a tavern and have a beer knowing that I could put that money away for our future," Hans said honestly.

"Well, I'm glad you were here. I didn't know you were expecting," Ted said. Then he went into the drawer of his desk and took out a pile of bills. He handed the money to Hans. "This is to say thank you," Ted said.

"I won't say I don't need it," Hans said, "but I was only doing my job."

"Still, you protected our home, and for that you deserve a reward."

"Thank you, sir," Hans said.

Neither Ted nor Esther slept that night. There was noise and commotion outside, but perhaps because of Hans no one came to the Birnbaum house.

Ted and Esther lay wrapped in each other's arms not knowing what the future held.

"Do you think we should leave Germany?" Esther whispered.

"No, we can't leave. Our home is in Berlin. My father built that factory. He did it with sweat and blood. Now we have a thriving business, and that business is right here in Germany. Everyone we know lives within a few miles of us. Both my brother and I fought in the Great War. My brother died for Germany. We have as much right to be here as anyone else."

She was silent now as she listened to the screaming coming from outside.

CHAPTER SIXTY-SEVEN

Berlin, January 1939

Esther received a letter.

Herr and Frau Birnbaum,
This letter is to inform you that the facility where your daughter was being treated has closed. However, we are happy to announce that Goldie has been transferred to a government-run facility in Sonnenstein, where she will be receiving a new treatment that has shown great promise in offering a cure to others who share her condition.

Unfortunately, you will not be able to visit her for a while as we feel that visitors are not conducive to the patient's recovery. I am sure you will understand as I know that you want what is the best for your daughter. I will send updates on her condition by mail.
Director Herman Paul Nitsche

Esther read the letter, then she carefully folded it with trembling hands. *This is good news*, she tried to tell herself. The sick feeling in the pit of her stomach warned her otherwise. *I have to believe that this is for the best even though I can't see Goldie. Maybe the government has really found some way to help people who are out of control. And they've established hospitals to help people like Goldie. After all, she wasn't making any progress at the other place. It was expensive, but, more importantly, it was not doing anything to help her get well. Every time I asked the doctors what their plans were to help her recover, they said that they were doing the best they could. But all they really did was keep her quiet and sedated with drugs. Here, at this new hospital, perhaps she really will be cured. God willing, she will soon be well enough to return home.*

Esther sat down and wrote a short letter to Sam and a longer one to Alma telling them that she thought they should know that Goldie had been transferred to another hospital.

CHAPTER SIXTY-EIGHT

Laevsky had always had a hand in the gambling industry. But once Sam came on board, together they increased the number of games and gaming locations. Money began to flow, and Sam began to feel relaxed again. Since he worked nights, he made sure he was home and available when Ida woke each morning. Chana had been so busy building her shop that she had missed so many of the important moments in Ida's life. These moments held special places within Sam's heart. Sometimes, even now, he would look at his beautiful daughter as she was growing up and remember her first smile. Or the time she stood up and let go of the sofa and walked into his arms. *My Ida's first steps*, he thought.

It was Sam who dropped Ida off on her first day of school. He remembered how worried he'd been until the time came to pick her up. Then, in his mind's eye, he could see her running toward him with her strawberry-blonde hair blowing in the wind. She handed him a picture that she drew and said, "Look, Daddy, I made this for you." And although, at first, he'd resented the responsibility of caring for his child, as time passed, he found that he treasured this special bond he shared with his daughter.

Every Sunday after Chana left for work, Sam and Ida planned their day over pancakes or waffles. Sundays were special days when Sam and Ida always did something memorable. On rainy afternoons they went to the museums. On sunny days they picnicked at the park or went to the zoo.

Ida told Sam everything she thought and felt. And every time she shared a secret with him, like how she felt about a teacher or how she wished her mother was around more, he felt his heart swell with love and pain.

CHAPTER SIXTY-NINE

New York City, February 1, 1939

Laevsky told Lenny to call Sam and his work partner, Yankel Aaronson, in for a meeting. "Have them come by this afternoon."

"Yes, boss," Lenny said.

Sam and Yankel got along well. Sam had learned from his falling out with Izzy, not to get too close to anyone he worked with. So when he was reassigned as Yankel's partner, he kept their relationship on a strictly business level. They worked at night arranging poker, blackjack, and craps games. They were also in charge of collecting money for Laevsky from the street boys who were running numbers. It was an easy job.

Sam was home during the day. And since he was at home, and Chana left early in the morning, Chana had asked him if he would drive Ida to school. He had agreed, and at first he didn't mind it. But as time passed it became more of a burden than a joy. Sometimes he didn't get home until the wee hours of the morning. He would try to stay awake but end up falling asleep on the sofa. Ida would gently nudge him. And he would get up and take her to school. But when he returned home, he was unable to fall asleep.

Sam tried to convince Chana to give up the store, to stay home, and be a full-time wife and mother. But she was insistent on keeping her shop. She had developed a clothing line that appealed to young women who wanted to wear the latest fashions but couldn't afford the couture prices. Her business was booming. Her father had not only taken over the shoe repairs, he'd also started making custom shoes for hard-to-fit customers. Chana kept her prices very reasonable, and the clients couldn't get enough. Sam was happy for Chana. She seemed to really enjoy her success. But he wished she would sell the business because he wanted her to be with him more. She worked all day; he worked all night. They hardly saw each other.

Sam couldn't tell Chana, but he resented doing a woman's work. Chana should be driving their daughter around. Not him. One morning he had just returned from work when Chana was getting ready to leave. She carefully selected a red hat, a red belt, and red shoes to complement her well-fitted black dress. *Taking care of our daughter should be Chana's job, not mine. If the fellas I work with ever found out that I can't go to sleep right after work because I have to drive my kid to school, they would laugh me off the planet*, Sam thought angrily.

"I want you home instead of going to the store every day," Sam said. "I earn plenty of money. We don't need your money, Chana."

"You tell me this at least once a week, every week, Sam. For years already, I haven't changed my mind. I don't plan on it. You can't possibly understand what this shop means to me. Before Mr. Goldsmith left me this business, I never had anything that I could call my own. For the first time in my life I have a degree of success that I could never have imagined before."

"But you also have a husband and child who love you and need you, Chana. Ida is seven years old. Before you know it she will be a teenager. She's going to need her mother to explain things to her."

Chana stopped what she was doing and looked into his eyes. "I love you both with all my heart, Sam. But I won't sell the business. I can't. It means too much to me."

"Give the place to your father, then. Let him hire a dressmaker to take over your end."

"Sam! I am the designer. I've built a client base. I don't want to do that. I won't. I am sorry but I won't," she said. "Can't you just drive Ida to school without complaining for once."

"No, Chana. I want you to be home. I want to give you the world. I don't want you to work."

"I am so glad that you feel that way. It means more to me than I can ever express. But I am going to keep my shop, Sam. You can ask me a hundred times, but I am sorry, I am not going to change my mind," she said, and then she picked up her handbag and left for work.

Sam could hear Ida in her room getting dressed when the phone rang.

Sam picked up the receiver. "Yeah?" he said gruffly.

"Shatzy, it's Lenny. The boss wants to see you."

"All right. I'll be there as soon as I can."

Sam called out to Ida. "Ida, honey, you need to get dressed quickly. We have to leave a little early today."

"But, Dad, don't you remember? We have to pick Tilly up on our way. Her and I are doing our presentation together today."

"Presentation? What kind of presentation? I need you to hurry up and get ready. I have to go into the office."

"The presentation on the planets, Dad."

"Yeah, all right. Just please hurry."

Ida was ready within a few minutes. She took a bagel out of the pantry and ate in the car as they drove to Tilly's house. When they got there, Sam honked the horn. Tilly looked out the window. She was still in her nightgown.

"Go to the door and tell her to hurry up," Sam said impatiently.

Ida walked up to the door. She knocked. Tilly opened the door, and Ida went inside. They both came out almost a half hour later. Sam was livid. He had to contain his anger, or he would have struck his daughter. They drove to the school in silence. When they got out, Ida peeked her head back in and said, "I'm sorry, Dad."

Sam nodded, and as soon as Ida closed the door he sped away.

After Prohibition had been repealed, Laevsky kept the speakeasy.

But now it was a restaurant and bar with a sign over the front door that said, "Laevsky's best food and spirits in Manhattan." The place had been renovated into a modern steak and seafood house with white lace tablecloths. It was only open for customers at night. But during the day, Laevsky conducted his business in the office that he still had in the back of the restaurant.

Sam opened the front door to the restaurant. Lenny was sitting at the bar. "Shatzy, Yankel is here. Everyone is in the office; they're waiting for you," he said.

"Thanks," Sam answered. But as he walked back to the office, he was angry with Chana. It should be her responsibility to take care of the child, not his. He shouldn't have had to be late to an important meeting with his boss because of some stupid school project. Chana should have been at home.

"Took your nice sweet time getting here, Shatzy?" Laevsky said.

"I'm sorry, boss. I had to take care of some things for my wife."

Laevsky nodded. "Your wife is a big success around town, huh?"

Sam shrugged.

"I don't like it that you show disrespect by being late. But since it was for Chana, I can excuse you this time. Anyway, give Chana my congratulations. Beautiful girl that one is." Laevsky smiled. Then he turned his attention to the business at hand. "So, anyway, boys, I called you both in here because I have a job for you. There is going to be a Nazi meeting in Madison Square Garden next week." Then Laevsky called out loud enough for Lenny who was sitting in the front of the restaurant to hear him, "Lenny, bring me another bottle of whiskey and two more glasses."

"Yes, boss," Lenny answered.

"Anyway. I'm gonna get right to the point. Yesterday, I was having lunch at Fine and Shapiro's, best pastrami in the city. In walks this fella who I recognize from my old neighborhood. His name is Izadore Greenbaum. I used to go out with his older sister. Nice kid, but she wasn't for me. This fella's quite a few years younger than me. So he comes over and asks if he can sit down with me. I say, sure, why not. I ask him about his sister. He tells me she's fine, married, with three kids, all grown." Laevsky smiles. "But then he starts talking all about this Nazi meeting that is going to be held in Madison Square Garden. He's all hot under the collar about this crazy meeting. Finally, I said, 'Listen, I don't think you oughta go.' Then he tells me that he's going no matter what anyone says. He says he knows that they'll be spreading all kinds of hate about the Jews.

"I said, 'You can't save the world, Greenbaum.' But he's not listening. Anyway, I don't like the sound of all this, so I try again to stop him from going. I am afraid if he goes, he's gonna get hurt. But he won't listen to me. He's not a part of the Mafia. In fact, he wouldn't even know how to use a gun. So I figure that since I can't stop him from going to fight the whole damn American Nazi Party unarmed, I'll send you boys to that meeting, so you can keep a watch on him. If things get ugly, pull out your guns, and take care of it. You understand me?"

Sam and Yankel both nodded.

"Besides, I think it would be good for us to know what the Nazis are up to. It's not a bad idea for us to keep a watch on them."

Then Laevsky pulled out some pictures of himself as a young man with a pretty girl standing beside him and a young child sitting on the ground. "The handsome one is me," Laevsky said. "The girl is Judith, Greenbaum's sister. The kid is Greenbaum." I know this picture is old, but I think he looks pretty much the same, so you should be able to recognize him."

Sam and Yankel exchanged a glance between them. "I hope we can recognize him from this picture. I mean it's an old photograph, and he's just a kid in it," Sam said.

"You'll be able to recognize him," Laevsky said, and his tone of voice told Sam not to question him anymore. Then Laevsky continued, "I'll get you all the details on the meeting, the date and time, and then I'll have one of my boys buy you both tickets. Both of you boys, just go into the auditorium and keep your mouths shut. Act like you're goys. But keep an eagle eye out for Greenbaum. Once you find him, stay where you can see him. Then don't do anything. You don't need to stick your neck out unless there's trouble. And unless something happens, I would prefer that you don't even let Greenbaum know who you are and why you're there. Understand me?"

"Yes, boss," Sam and Yankel both said.

"Now," Laevsky said, lighting a cigar, "if I were to make a bet, I would put money on the fact that there will only be a handful of people at this meeting. New Yorkers don't like Nazis congregating in their city, if you know what I mean. Greenbaum even said as much, that the folks in New York City tried to stop the meeting from taking place. But they couldn't stop it. So I figure Madison Square Garden shouldn't be too crowded. That should make it easy for you to find Greenbaum."

"A Nazi meeting, huh?" Yankel asked.

"Yeah, I heard something about this thing with the Nazis. They call themselves the German—American Bund," Sam said.

"Idiots," Laevsky said. "They hate Jews. And ya see, I can still remember Greenbaum getting into fights about being a Jew. He used to pal around with his cousin who was the same way. Some dumb shegetz would make a remark, and the two of them had their dukes up. His cousin ended up in the hospital twice. And I heard that Greenbaum got the shit knocked out of him plenty. But you gotta give these fellas credit. Nobody could call them yellow."

"Don't you worry about a thing, boss. We'll take care of it. Won't we, Shatzy?" Yankel said.

"Sure thing." Sam nodded, trying to sound confident and convincing. But inside he was worried.

CHAPTER SEVENTY

Izzy made sure he maintained a friendship with Yankel so that he was always aware of Sam's activities. Izzy wasn't certain, but he felt that Laevsky was suspicious of him, and he was certain that Laevsky was searching for evidence to back up his theory that Izzy was responsible for the robbery all those years ago. But even though he knew it was beyond foolish, he still could not help but wait and hope for another opportunity to rid himself of Sam. When Lenny told him in passing that Yankel and Sam had been called in for a meeting with Laevsky, he immediately made it his business to have a drink with Yankel to find out what was going on. Izzy didn't have to wait long. Two nights later he saw Yankel sitting at the bar alone and went over to sit with him.

"Nu? So how are things with you?" Izzy asked.

"Can't complain," Yankel said.

"I heard you had a meeting with the boss the other day."

"Yeah. He wants Sam and me to go to some Nazi meeting so we can watch over his friend."

"A Nazi meeting? Really?"

"Yeah, it's some kind of big rally at Madison Square Garden on Monday night. I can't tell you how excited I am to spend an evening with all of those Jew-hating sons of bitches," Yankel said, sarcasm dripping from his tongue.

Izzy had all the information he needed. But he couldn't get up and leave. It would be too suspicious. So he bought Yankel another drink, and they talked about Yankel's younger sister. She was a homely girl that Yankel had been trying to talk Izzy into dating. He had no intentions of it. But he let Yankel think he might consider the possibility. Finally, after an hour, Izzy said he had to get home. "I have to feed my dog."

"You have a dog?"

"Yeah. His name is Lancelot."

"Damn!" Yankel said, smiling.

CHAPTER SEVENTY-ONE

Monday, February 20, 1939

Sam picked Yankel up at his apartment at 7:30 p.m. the night of the rally. Then they drove together to Madison Square Garden.

"You got the tickets?" Sam asked.

"Yeah, I picked 'em up yesterday from Laevsky's office."

"Good."

"You know, this thing gives me the creeps. I read some shit about Nazis, and I'm not looking forward to meeting a whole room full of 'em," Yankel said. He was toying with the mezuzah that he wore around his neck.

Sam noticed him. "Is that a mezuzah?" he asked.

"Yeah, I always wear it. Why do you ask?"

"Take it off, you idiot. We're going to pretend like we're Nazis."

"Yeah, you're right. I forgot. Guess I am a little nervous," Yankel said.

"It's all right. Just take it off, and leave it in the car so you don't lose it."

"What do you know about Nazis?" Yankel asked as he slipped the necklace off.

"I think they are a lot like the KKK."

"I haven't ever met anyone who was in the KKK."

"I did," Sam said. "I had a run-in with those bastards when I was living in Medina before I moved to the city."

"They're mean, I hear."

"Yeah, that's for sure," Sam said.

They pulled into a parking space a block away from the stadium.

Yankel turned to Sam and said, "Well, we got a job to do. So are you ready?"

"As ready as I'll ever be," Sam said.

When Yankel and Sam were given this job they both agreed that it would be in their best interest not to wear flashy suits that made them stand out. Sam didn't own anything that was not custom made anymore. He scanned his closet searching for something that made him look like a working man, but he found nothing. As he looked through his clothes, his thoughts went to Irving, who had been buried in the only suit he owned. It was an ill-fitting garment, which Irving had worn when he married Goldie. Thinking about it made Sam want to cry. He wished his father were still here beside him so that he could buy him a custom-made suit. Chana had found him thumbing through his closet with tears rolling down his face. "What is it?" she said, concerned.

"I have to wear a cheap-looking suit for a job I am doing for Laevsky."

"And you're crying about that?"

"No, I was thinking about my dad. I feel like an idiot for crying. But I can't help wishing that he'd had a better life. You know what I mean?"

"I know, honey. I know." She put her arms around him.

"He worked hard and never had anything to show for it."

"He had you. You loved him."

"Alma did too," Sam said.

"He knew that."

Sam managed to smile. "Yeah, you're right." He put his arms around her. "Have I ever told you how much I love you?" he said.

"You tell me every day, and I never get tired of hearing it." She kissed him, then she said, "What is this about you needing a cheap-looking suit?"

"I need a suit that looks like a hand-me-down. Something that doesn't fit right. Lousy fabric."

"I'll make it for you," she said. Then she giggled and added. "But you have to promise not to tell anyone that I was your seamstress."

It took Chana less than a week to create a suit that was too small. The pants were too short, and the jacket sleeves revealed Sam's wrists. When he saw it he let out a loud guffaw. "You did a hell of a good job," he said. "I hope you won't mind that as soon as I finish this job, I am going to throw it out."

She smiled. "I expected as much."

Now Sam sat beside Yankel in the car. He was wearing the suit Chana had made. Yankel was wearing a jacket that he'd purchased at a secondhand store. When they both climbed out of the car, Yankel looked at Sam and shook his head. "You look like shit, Shatzy," Yankel said jokingly as they walked toward the door.

Sam just nodded. He was on edge. He was remembering the beating he'd suffered at the hands of the KKK. And he felt like every step he took toward the rally was a step closer to danger. Yankel was rambling on about something. But Sam wasn't listening. He was remembering what those sick KKK boys had done to his sister. They were a heartless group. And from what he'd heard about the Nazis, he was fairly certain they were not much different. Sam felt as if every nerve in his body were on fire. He could sense the danger all around him.

Attending a rally with these men and praying his real identity was not discovered was more terrifying than running illegal whiskey. That was because he knew that men like these would get great pleasure out of killing a Jew. Especially when the Jew was outnumbered. And although Laevsky had assured them there shouldn't be too many people attending this meeting, Sam realized that even if there were only a few, he and Yankel were still outnumbered. Sam felt for the gun in his pocket. The cold steel gave him a sense of security. But even so, as he and Yankel entered the auditorium, his heart was thumping wildly, and his palms began to sweat.

The room was overflowing with men dressed in brown shirts and black pants, the uniform of the Bund. They had swastika arm bands. Nazi flags hung over the podium surrounding a picture of George Washington which was next to a poster of Adolf Hitler. A small musical band, dressed in traditional German garb, played German folk songs. Yankel elbowed Sam. "How many people you think are here?" he asked nervously.

Sam shook his head. He didn't answer. He had to stay alert. He dared not allow Yankel to distract him. Sam was watching every move of everyone around him, and at the same time he was searching for Greenbaum. *Laevsky was wrong: there are thousands of people at this rally.*

At eight o'clock on the dot a woman walked up to the podium. The room grew quiet. She began singing the "Star-Spangled Banner." The crowd began to cheer. Sam and Yankel cheered too. Sam felt the back of his neck tingling as he waited for the song to end. When it did, everyone sat down. Then a man took the stage and introduced himself. "Let's have a big hand for Margarete Rittershaush for her wonderful rendition of our country's theme song. Everyone clapped. The man raised his hands in the air to quiet the crowd. Once the applause stopped, he introduced himself. "For those of you who don't know me, my name is James Wheeler-Hill . . ." He was still speaking, but Sam couldn't hear him; the audience began clapping again. Wheeler-Hill raised his hands in the air, and after a few minutes the crowd grew quiet.

"If George Washington were alive today, he would be friends with Adolf Hitler. It is our responsibility to return America to the true white Americans. We must act now to take our country back from the kikes and the colored who've stolen it from us. They have ruined our land. We, the Bund, must save our country. We must band together, you and I. Only in numbers will we have the power to restore America to the true Americans," Wheeler-Hill said. And then he continued to make a longer speech. Sam wasn't listening; he was searching the crowd for Greenbaum. *Damn Laevsky. He gives us a picture of a kid and expects us to find the man he grew up to be. How can he think we could recognize this fella from the picture he gave us?*

Wheeler finished his speech, and another man stepped up on the stage. The crowd cheered and raised their hands, pointing them straight at the man. He returned the gesture. Sam recognized this as the Nazi salute he'd seen in magazines.

The speaker introduced himself as George Froboese, and when he began to speak, Sam felt a bubbling up inside of him. Froboese's hatred for Jews was the essence of his speech. "The Jew is cunning. Make no mistake, his aim is world dominance. He wants to rule the world, to steal everything of value from the rightful owners." Froboese went on for almost a half hour spewing anger and hatred. When he finished, the crowd roared with applause and raised their hand in the Nazi salute.

Sam wished it would end, but another speaker took the stage. This one warned that the Jews controlled the newspapers and Hollywood. *If I weren't outnumbered, I would take my gun and break the guy's jaw*, Sam thought. But he was outnumbered, by thousands. So he controlled his temper and searched the crowd for Greenbaum.

"Let's move around here, and see if we can find Greenbaum," Sam whispered to Yankel, who nodded.

"You think you'll recognize him from that picture Laevsky gave us?"

"No, do you?"

"I don't see how it's possible. But I know we gotta give it a try. I am hoping that nothing happens, and Greenbaum doesn't need us. That way the boss can't be mad at us for not finding his friend."

They began to move through the crowds when Sam looked to the left and saw a familiar face. He recognized the man immediately. He was a little older and had gained a little weight, but Sam had no doubt that it was John Anderson, Betty's old boyfriend from the KKK. The man who had beaten Sam up and broken his ribs. Sam knew better than to approach John with this crowd of Nazis around him. So he moved far enough away so John would not see him, but kept his eyes on John.

"You see Greenbaum anywhere?" Yankel asked.

"No, but I need to take care of something."

"What? What could you possibly have to do here at this crazy rally?" Yankel asked.

"None of your business. Keep looking for Greenbaum. I'll meet you at the car when this over. Wait there for me."

"Sam?" Yankel said.

"I've got something I have to do," Sam said, and he walked away.

Sam was consumed with the desire for revenge, so consumed that he couldn't think about anything else. He knew Laevsky would be mad if he didn't assure Greenbaum's safety. But he also knew that Laevsky would believe him if he said he couldn't find Greenbaum using the picture he was given. So Sam stood in the darkest corner of the room watching John, and waiting. Yankel found Sam and grabbed the sleeve of Sam's coat. "The boss won't be happy if we don't find Greenbaum."

"Leave me alone," Sam said, shaking him off.

"Are you nuts?" Yankel said. "You want Laevsky mad at you?"

"I said, get outta here. I'll see you later."

Yankel left Sam, who was still hiding in the corner. *If I stay here until this is over, the crowd rushing the door to get out will be too big for me to get close enough to follow John. If I wait outside, I can watch as he comes out. The crowds will be dispersing, and I should be able to follow him.* Sam slipped out the door and then found a hiding place on the side of the building. He shivered from the cold in the coat that Chana made for him.

Izzy had driven to Madison Square Garden before the rally began. He parked on a side street where he could not be seen, but he had a clear view of the door of the building. He'd watched as people lined up to enter the auditorium. It took over a half hour for him to spot Sam. He'd almost thought the job had been canceled. But as he watched Sam and Yankel get in line, he was surprised to see them both dressed so strangely. Izzy had waited for over two hours until he saw Sam come walking out of the building. He knew the rally hadn't ended because no one else was outside. He watched Sam with curiosity as Sam sneaked into an alleyway and lit a cigarette.

At least ten minutes passed. Sam almost considered going back inside when, from where he stood, he could hear a large roar of applause. Groups of men came rushing out the door. Sam knew the meeting was over. His eyes scanned the crowds frantically for John. But there were too many people blocking his vision. He'd almost given up when he saw John and four other men walk outside. They stood on the sidewalk talking, shivering, laughing, and smoking.

Sam felt a rush of hatred fill him. He no longer felt the cold as he hid behind a group of people and watched as John said goodbye to his buddies, who all went in different directions.

John started walking. Still hiding in the shadows, Sam tailed him. He waited until John was far away from the crowds. Just one man alone in the dark casting a shadow on the ground from the streetlight. Sam looked around him. No one was there. John stopped to light a cigarette. The flame of the match was a tiny orange spark in the darkness.

Izzy ran back to his car and got in. He followed Sam, staying far enough back so Sam would not see him or hear his footsteps. He watched as Sam walked over to a man who was smoking a cigarette. He couldn't hear the words that were exchanged between the two of them.

"Got a light?" Sam walked over to John.

"Yeah, sure," John said, handing Sam the matches. "Were you at the meeting?"

"Yeah, I was," Sam said, every nerve ending in his body tingling. Sam looked directly into John's eyes. But he saw no recognition. Then he said, "Do you remember me?"

"I don't think so. Did we meet before?" John said.

"You beat the living shit out of me, and you raped my sister. I'm Sam Schatzman, remember? I'm the Jew that Betty was dating."

John grew pale as he remembered. "All right. Yeah, I remember. So what?" he said, trying to sound brave. But John was only brave when he was with a crowd.

Sam pulled the gun out of his pocket and aimed at it at John.

"Take it easy," John whimpered. "That stuff happened a long time ago."

"And you're still the same Jew-hating son of a bitch that you were then," Sam said, firing the gun into John's face. The angular features became nothing but a blur as blood flew in every direction. Some of it came flying back at Sam. *I killed a man*, Sam thought. *I broke God's Commandment.* The anger that had consumed him only moments ago was gone. His face was spotted with blood. His soul felt dark and deeply sickened. He turned away and vomited. Then he ran back to his car where Yankel was waiting, and climbed in.

Izzy stayed hidden. He had not heard what was said, so he had no idea why Sam had killed this man. But he had witnessed the entire crime in all of its brutality. Now all he had to do was pay someone to turn Sam in for the murder. And then Sam would be arrested, tried, and executed. But most of all he would be out of Izzy's way for good.

"What the hell happened to you? You've got blood all over you," Yankel asked.

"I don't want to talk about it," Sam said.

"I found Greenbaum," Yankel said. "Do you remember that guy that ran onto the stage when that Jew hater, Kuhn, was speaking?"

"I guess. I'm sorry I wasn't paying attention at the time," Sam said. He was suddenly worried about facing Laevsky. His anger had blinded him to the job he had set out to do. Sam had finally gotten his revenge on John. But it turned out not to be as satisfying as he had thought it would be. He was thankful that no one had seen him.

"That fella was Greenbaum. The Nazis knocked him around a little, and then I saw the cops take him away."

"Oh shit," Sam said. He was worried because he knew he'd failed Laevsky. And Laevsky didn't appreciate it when someone didn't carry out his orders.

CHAPTER SEVENTY-TWO

Chana was awake sitting in the kitchen when Sam got home.
"Sam." She looked up, and her eyes flew open wide. "What the hell happened to you?"

"Oh, you mean the blood?"

"Yeah, the blood."

He sank down onto the sofa and looked into her eyes. "I messed up," he said. Then he told her everything. But he added, "I didn't kill John because of Betty. I want you to know that I don't have any feelings about Betty anymore. I killed him because of what he did to Alma."

Chana nodded. "And Greenbaum is at the police station?"

"Yeah. Laevsky is going to be furious," he said. "Chana, I killed a man tonight, and I disobeyed the crime boss. I think I am in serious trouble."

"You said nobody saw you shoot the guy."

"Nobody saw."

"Are you sure?"

"Yeah, I'm sure."

"Well, that's good, at least. And you said the picture he showed you of Greenbaum was like twenty years old?"

"Right," Sam said.

Chana sighed. Ida was asleep in her room. She was glad her daughter hadn't seen Sam covered in blood. She got up and went to Ida's room and closed the door. Then she returned to the living room and sat beside Sam. "I'll go and talk to Laevsky tomorrow. I'll make him understand," she said.

"I love you, Chana."

She touched his cheek. "Go wash off all this blood."

He nodded and went into the bathroom. When he returned, he laid his head in her lap, and she smoothed his hair. "I love you too, Sam," she said.

CHAPTER SEVENTY-THREE

When Yankel told Laevsky that he and Sam were not able to find Greenbaum before Greenbaum got into trouble, Laevsky was angry. But when he saw the papers that said that there were twenty thousand people at the rally, he understood that it was almost impossible to find one man in such a large crowd So when Chana arrived at Laevsky's office with a box of his favorite salt bagels and a kiss on the cheek, she was able to convince Laevsky to forgive Sam again. She told Laevsky that Sam had done his best to carry out Laevsky's orders. And since Greenbaum wasn't badly hurt, Laevsky decided that Sam and Yankel had not really defied him. Greenbaum was sentenced to ten days in jail and fined twenty-five dollars, which Laevsky paid anonymously.

John's murder was in the paper, but it never made the front page.

CHAPTER SEVENTY-FOUR

In his everyday life, Izzy had run into plenty of men who would do anything to make a buck. They were drunkards who spent their days in the bars. Izzy would see them sitting on the barstools, when he went to collect his payment for the liquor that the local bars had been forced to purchase from Laevsky. Sometimes he would see the drunks and feel sorry for them. So he would buy them a drink. They all liked him.

He considered all of the possible barflies he'd met, until he decided which one would be able to do the job for him. Once he made his decision, Izzy drove to the local bar where he knew he would find Mickey Dinkelman. He walked in, and there was Dinkelman sitting at the bar.

"I can't wait for baseball season to start. Love them Yankees. Love the Babe," Dinkelman said to another drunk who was sitting on his other side.

"You been to a game lately?" the other drunk asked Mickey.

"Nahh, but I am gonna go this year. Yes, I am. I am gonna take my kid to a Yankees game. I sure am."

"How you doin', Mickey?" Izzy interrupted. Then he turned to the bartender. "Give him a drink," Izzy said as he threw a bill on the counter. The bartender poured Mickey a drink.

"Can I get you anything?" he asked Izzy.

"No, thanks," Izzy said.

Mickey turned around and looked at Izzy. Then he downed the shot of whiskey Izzy had just bought him and said, "Nu? How should I be doing? I can't find a job. The wife is always hounding me for drinking too much. She hides her money from me because she's afraid I'll drink it all up. But she oughta understand, she's working, I'm not—"

Izzy cut him off in midsentence, "Listen. I need to talk to you . . . alone."

"Yeah, sure. What do you need, Izzy? By the way, thanks for the shot."

"Let's go outside," Izzy said.

They walked outside. "What do you want to talk about? It's fucking raining out here," Mickey said.

"Yeah, so a little water won't hurt you," Izzy said. "I have a job for you. How would you like to make a hundred dollars?"

"Wow! A hundred bucks? Are you serious? That's like a fortune."

"Yep."

"What do I gotta do?" Mickey said, suddenly skeptical. "I don't gotta kill nobody, do I?"

"Nope. All you gotta do is go to the police station and tell them that you know who murdered that Nazi. The one that was killed after the rally at Madison Square Garden on Monday. You gotta tell the coppers that they can't connect you to the investigation because the guy who did the killing is in the mob. You tell them that you saw the whole thing."

"That's it? That's all I gotta do?"

"Almost. But here is the most important part. If you want to live to drink another bottle of your favorite whiskey, you better make sure that no one ever finds out that I gave you the information or that I paid you to turn this guy in. Make sure that my name is never mentioned, or you can be sure I'll find you and make you sorry. You got it?"

"Yeah, sure," Mickey said.

"Here's your money," Izzy said, counting out a hundred dollars.

"But don't get smart and think you can take my money and run away without doing the job. I know where you live. And even if you don't ever go back home, I know where to find you. So if you don't do this thing the way I want it done, I'll be back."

CHAPTER SEVENTY-FIVE

Eight-year-old Ida and her father were busy doing Ida's homework. They were working with the new set of World Books that Sam had just purchased for his daughter. Ida was the first girl in her class to own her own set of World Books and she adored them. "They smell so new and the pages are so clean and pretty," Ida said.

Many times since Sam bought the encyclopedias, they would start doing Ida's homework but then become distracted by something in one of the books and find that they'd spent hours reading all sorts of fascinating material. Sam was glad to see that his daughter was studious. In that way she reminded him of his sister, Alma, and that made him proud. Her grades reflected her love of school. And whenever there were conferences with the teachers, they raved about how much they enjoyed having her in their classes.

Sam wished Chana would come and look through the World Books with him and Ida. He thought it was important for a little girl to feel that her mother took an interest in her schoolwork. But Chana did not have the time. Her business had grown so much that she had started to take work home with her in the evening in order to keep up with her deadlines. She was cutting fabric for a dress that she was in the process of custom making for a client, when there was a knock at the door.

Laying the fabric down carefully so as not to lose her place, Chana got up and went to see who was there. Before she could open the door there was another, louder, stronger knock. She decided to look through the peephole before she let this person inside. Two uniformed New York City police officers stood at the door. They knocked again. Chana took a deep breath, and then she calmed herself and opened the door.

"Good evening, Officers. What brings you here tonight?" she said. "Are you collecting for the police association?" She walked over to grab her handbag. "Here," she said, taking out a few bills. The officer ignored her.

"Is this the home of Samuel Schatzman?"

"Yes," Chana said, smiling. She put the purse and the money back down on the table. Then she smiled and added, "How can I help you?"

"We need to speak with Samuel."

"Of course. Won't you gentlemen please sit down? I'll call my husband. He's in the bedroom doing homework with our daughter." Then Chana called out. "Sam, can you come in here, please. There are some gentlemen here to see you."

"I'll be right there," he said, sounding casual. But Chana knew him well, and she could hear in his voice that he was worried.

"Can I offer the two of you officers some coffee or tea, perhaps?" Chana said.

"No. Thank you. We have work to do."

"Of course. But I have some lovely cookies that I bought at Fannie's this afternoon. I'm sure you know Fannie's bakery. She is the best in town. Don't you think? So I know you'll enjoy them." She winked.

The policemen eyed each other. "Well, if you insist," one of the officers said.

"Of course I do. Would you prefer coffee or tea?"

"Coffee."

"Make yourself at home. I'll be right back," Chana said.

Chana put on a pot of water. Then she put the cookies on a plate and pulled the bodice of her dress down to reveal her ample cleavage. She removed the tortoiseshell combs from her long, red hair and let the hair fall across her breasts. Once the water was boiling, she quickly made the coffee and brought out a tray with the refreshments.

CHAPTER 75 | 249

Sam had come out of the bedroom and was already sitting on the sofa. He looked stunned, like a deer caught in the headlights. The police were questioning him when Chana walked in.

"Where were you on Monday night?" one of the policeman asked.

"I don't remember," Sam said.

"Do you remember a Nazi rally?"

"No? I don't know what you're talking about." Sam sounded nervous.

Ida was standing in the corner watching. She was twisting her hair the way she did when she was uneasy. Her mother gave her a smile of confidence and a quick wink that told Ida "Don't worry, I have everything under control."

"So have you heard anything about a fella being killed after that rally?" the officer said, eyeing Sam.

But before Sam could answer. "Gentleman," Chana interrupted, "try these cookies," she said, bending over so they could get a good glimpse of her breasts. She passed the plate to each of the officers. Just like she'd hoped, they stared at her bosom. "So," she said in a breathy voice, crossing her legs suggestively, "what is this all about?"

"Where was your husband last Monday evening?"

"Here . . . at home with me." She winked and smiled. "Now, come on, fellas, if you had a wife like me, where would you be when the sun went down?" She slid on the sofa so her movement forced her skirt to rise a little higher, revealing her shapely thigh.

One of the officers smiled, but the other one asked, "With all due respect, you say your husband was at home with you?"

"Yes, Officer," she said innocently.

"He was accused of being at a Nazi rally, where he is accused of murdering another man."

She laughed, and her laughter sounded like the tinkling of tiny bells. Then she said, "Forgive me, please, Officer, but we are Jewish. The last place either of us would ever go would be to a Nazi rally. Nazis hate Jewish people. We would have no place there. Besides, we would be afraid with so many gathered together. If my husband were foolish enough to go to something like that, he would have been severely outnumbered."

"She has a point there," the officer said to his coworker. "Well, thank you for your time and for the cookies."

"Wait, let me wrap the rest of these cookies for you, so you can take them with you."

"Are you sure, ma'am?"

"Positive." Chana smiled. "Enjoy them." She handed the cookies, wrapped in a cloth napkin, to the officer.

When she closed the door, she thought, *Thank God for Fannie.*

CHAPTER SEVENTY-SIX

After the police officers got back into their vehicle, they talked about the meeting with Sam and Chana.

"I believe her," one of the cops said as he took another cookie.

"Yeah, I do too. She doesn't look like a liar. Besides, that idiot who came in and told us that he witnessed the murder is a known drunk. His name is Mickey Dinkelman, and I've arrested him plenty of times. I'd say he probably made the whole thing up to see if he could get a reward."

"Or maybe he did it. Maybe he was the one who killed the guy. I mean he is a drunk. He always needs money. He probably robbed him."

"Now, that sounds more like it."

And so Mickey Dinkelman was arrested for the murder of John Anderson. Dinkelman's wife told the police that he had not come home on Monday night.

"He's a heavy drinker. He spends all his time in taverns. He's gotten into plenty of trouble," Lillian Dinkelman said. She had weathered skin resembling a sheet of paper that had been balled up, then opened to reveal a map of wrinkles. Deep lines hung over her angry brow. She may have been pretty at one time, but her pretty years had been thwarted by the hard life she'd lived.

Then Mrs. Dinkelman added in a gritty voice, from too many years of heavy smoking, "I don't know if this means anything, but I did see Mickey burning some clothes outside on Tuesday morning. I happened to look out my bedroom window, and there he was standing right at the back of the building throwing a shirt and some pants onto a fire he made in a metal garbage can. Then, again, I don't know if this means anything, but I did see some blood in the bathroom sink down the hall that morning. But I didn't think anything of it. I figured someone might have cut themselves shaving. But who knows, it coulda been blood that Mickey was washing off his hands." She shook her head as she uttered the words that signed her husband's death sentence. *I'll be rid of him at last*, she thought as the police officers left.

Mickey could not afford a decent lawyer. The public defender who was appointed by the court to take the case had recently graduated law school. He was overwhelmed with cases of indigents. And since Mrs. Dinkelman had given such strong testimony and all the evidence pointed to Mickey's guilt, Mickey was easily convicted. He screamed as he was taken from the courtroom. "I need an appeal. I need help. I didn't do this. I didn't kill anybody." But he was dragged away. And he never revealed Izzy's name because he knew that if he did, he was as good as dead.

Mickey Dinkelman was executed for the murder of John Anderson.

Sam watched the case unfold in the papers. He wondered who this Mickey Dinkelman was and how he'd ended up taking the rap for John's murder. But Sam never tried to find out. He was glad to be exonerated of the crime. So he put away the execution of an innocent man in the back recesses of his mind and went on with his life.

Izzy, too, watched the case unfold. At first he was angry that his plan had gone sour. He was furious that Sam had somehow gotten away with murder. But then as the trial wore on, he began to worry that Dinkelman would draw him into it, and if he did, Laevsky would find out everything. He'd find out Izzy had been responsible for Dinkelman turning Sam in. And Laevsky would be livid that Izzy had turned another member of their gang in to the police. That would destroy any drop of trust Laevsky still had for Izzy. And Izzy would be as good as dead. When the papers announced Dinkelman was dead, that he had been executed by electrocution, Izzy breathed a sigh of relief. His secret was safe now; it would be buried along with Mickey Dinkelman.

CHAPTER SEVENTY-SEVEN

Europe, 1939

Several months later, Germany rained a flood of bombs on Poland, crippling the country. Then on the first of September 1939, German troops marched into Poland and conquered the land as well as the people. What followed was a plunge into hell for the people of Poland. Their culture would be destroyed. Their religion would be controlled by the Nazis. Their blonde children would be stolen from their rightful parents and sent to homes for the Lebensborn, where their names would be changed. They would be conditioned to reject anything Polish and taught how to become good Aryan Germans. Once the Nazis were satisfied that the children had relinquished any memory of their families, they would be adopted and raised by the SS officers and their wives. After the war ended, many of them ended up in mental institutions, and very few of them would ever find their families again. Oh yes, Poland would suffer. But no one in that country would suffer as greatly as the Polish Jews.

CHAPTER SEVENTY-EIGHT

New York City, July 1941

It was a bright, hot Sunday morning. Chana was in the kitchen making pancakes. She'd promised Ida blueberry pancakes, and she never made a promise to her child that she didn't keep. Sam came up behind her quietly startling her. Then he leaned down and kissed her neck.

"It's a gorgeous day. Why don't you cancel your appointments and come to Coney Island with Ida and me?"

"I would love to, Sam. But I can't," she said as she checked the batter for bubbles. "Why don't you two go, and then when you get back, we can all go out for a nice dinner?"

"The beach isn't the same without you. I want all the fellas to envy me when they see my gorgeous wife in her bathing suit."

"Sam, I really wish I could go. But I have a full day of appointments. Maybe next time?"

He nodded, disappointed but resigned. He still didn't like it, but he'd become accustomed to her putting her work before her family.

Ida came into the kitchen.

"I'm making you the blueberry pancakes I promised you," Chana said.

"Oh good, Mom!" Ida said. "Did Dad ask you to come with us to Coney Island today?"

"He did. But I can't. I have a full day. Fittings from the time I get in to the time I leave."

"Oh, Mom," Ida said. "One day you have to take off from work, and go on some kind of an outing with Dad and me."

"She's right," Sam said. "It's Sunday today. Who else but you works on a Sunday?"

"Sam, I can't help it. I don't want to lose the customers, and there just aren't enough hours in the week for me to handle all these appointments."

"So all you do is work. It seems to me that you are busy working seven days a week every week, and we never see you," Sam huffed.

"Yes, Mom, it's true. We hardly ever see you," Ida said.

"Please, don't start this again," Chana said. Then she smiled and took down three plates. "Pancakes are ready."

"This is Ida's first time at the beach. You don't want to miss this," Sam said.

"Come on, Mom," Ida crooned.

"I really wish I could."

Sam looked away as she put the plate in front of him. They ate in silence, and then Chana washed the dishes and went to take a shower. She was in a hurry to get ready for work.

"Put on your bathing suit with a pair of shorts. Pack your towel, and let's get going," Sam said to Ida, trying to sound enthusiastic.

"Should we bring anything for lunch?" Ida asked.

"Nope. They have the best darn food you ever ate right on the boardwalk. But . . . I am bringing a pail and a shovel," Sam said, forcing a smile.

Ida giggled with excitement. "What for?"

"You'll see," Sam said, winking at her.

When they arrived at the entrance to the boardwalk, Ida saw a sign that pointed to the left and read "This Way to the Sideshow." There were pictures of a bearded lady, a man who was unusually tall, and a pair of women who were conjoined twins. "Look at that, Dad," Ida said. "Is that stuff real?"

"Yeah, most of it is."

"Can we go? I want to see it."

"I'd rather not. I hate to gawk at those unfortunate creatures."

"Creatures? Are they even human?"

"That's the point. They are human, honey. They feel pain and love and all the things that we do. But people don't see them as human and that's awful sad. At least I think so," Sam said. Then he added, "I shouldn't have called them creatures. That was wrong of me," Sam said, then he knelt down so that he was at eye level with Ida. "When I was a boy, a traveling show came through the small town where I grew up. All the kids were so excited. I was too, and I wanted to go. My father didn't like the idea. He said the kind of people who ran those shows exploited the less fortunate. I didn't know what that meant at the time. All I knew was that I wanted to do what all the other kids were doing. So my friends and I sneaked out when our folks thought we were in bed. We met at the park and then walked half of a mile to an open field where the show was set up. I'll have to admit, some of it was the bee's knees."

"Bee's knees." Ida giggled "How do you know those words?" she asked.

"Your dad knows lots of things." Sam smiled. "Well, anyway, like I said, some of it was fun. There was a dancing bear and a group of gypsy musicians. But there was also something called a freak show or a show of oddities. It was just like this sideshow. The pictures on the caravan were frightening and fascinating at the same time. So my buddies and I bought tickets. We went in. I was expecting to be scared but I wasn't, Ida. I was sad. These were deformed human beings. One man in particular stands out in my memory. His body was twisted like a pretzel. I felt like throwing up as I looked at him and wondered what kind of a life he might have. That night when I got home, I thought about that fella, and I suddenly understood why my father didn't want me to go."

"I think it's sad too, Dad. I am glad you told me that story. I don't know what kind of life those people will have. But I hope they will be all right," Ida said.

"Me too," Sam said, squeezing her shoulder.

Then Ida spotted the Ferris wheel. "Look, Dad! Can we go on that?" she asked.

"Absolutely. Come on," Sam said, then he took her hand, and they ran all the way to the Ferris wheel.

A barker stood at the entrance to the ride, calling out, "Step right up, folks. Try the wonder wheel, the biggest, the most sensational Ferris wheel in the world. Only five cents a ride." Sam bought tickets and they got on.

When the ride began to move, Ida screamed with delight, but as the cabin rose high in the air, she buried her face in Sam's chest. Round and round they went. And each time they hit the top Ida screamed, but after the ride was over she wanted to ride again.

"I promise. We will ride again, right after lunch," Sam said.

"Can we eat by the water?" Ida asked.

"Sure, let's go down to the beach and get set up. It's awful crowded, so we want to get a spot as soon as possible. Right?"

"Yep."

"All right. And once we have our place on the beach, I'll go and get us some food."

"Hot dogs!"

"Yes, ma'am."

Sam set up the towels and the blanket. Then he turned to Ida. "Now listen, sweetheart. I am going to go and get us some hot dogs. Don't you like yours plain?"

"Yep. Nothing on it," she said.

"Now, Ida, you stay right here and don't move. You promise?"

"Yes, Dad. Can I just put my feet in the sand?"

"You can. But that's all. Don't leave this blanket. And if anyone comes up to you and asks you to go with them, don't. You stay here and wait for me. Am I making myself clear?"

"Yes, Dad, Mom already told me about how I am not supposed to go with strangers," Ida said as she slipped her sandals off. She sank her toes in the sand and giggled.

Sam ran up to the boardwalk and got in the line in front of Nathan's Hot Dogs. He ordered two hot dogs with french fries and two orange sodas. The girl who took his money at the hot dog booth gave Sam a flirtatious look. But he didn't respond. He just waited until his hot dogs were bagged up. Then he thanked her, paid, and left.

Ida had removed her shorts and was sitting on the blanket in her pink-and-white bathing suit. Her red hair shined in the sun. Sam's heart swelled with pride. *She is so pretty; she looks just like her mother*, he thought.

"Are you having fun?" Sam asked.

Ida nodded.

When they finished eating, Sam took Ida down to the water. He carried the pail. They got their feet wet and filled the pail with water. Then Sam carried it back to their blanket. "Watch this," he said as he poured the water on the sand. Then he filled the bucket with the wet sand and made a poor attempt at building a sandcastle.

Ida laughed as the castle folded.

"I tried," Sam said.

"You did a very good job, Dad."

They walked back to the blanket together. Once they were seated, Sam turned to Ida and said, "How about some frozen custard?"

"Yes, please!" Ida said.

"I'll be right back," Sam said.

Ida smiled and waved at him.

Sam climbed the stairs up to the boardwalk. He found the sign that said, "Borden's Frozen Custard, 5 Cents." He walked over to the stand. The line at Borden's was long. It was no surprise on such a hot day that frozen custard was the most popular item on the boardwalk. While Sam waited, he noticed that a woman was glancing at him. She was a tall, slender blonde with a scarf in her hair, and she wore a skimpy bathing suit. Her lips were covered in blood-red lipstick. And she wore black sunglasses like a movie star. Sam tried not to look, but he couldn't help but notice her large breasts and the way the suit rode up her thighs. *Damn, would you just look at that*, he thought, but Sam forced himself to look away. When he turned his face away from her, she walked over to him. "Hey, handsome," she said. "Mind if I cut in line?

This line is so long that it could take at least an hour to get a cone here."

He was at a loss for words. "The line is moving pretty quickly," he said, but then he added, "All right. Sure. Get in line in front of me."

Someone in the back of the line called out, "Hey, who do you think you are, lady? Why don't you get to the back of the line like everyone else?"

The blonde ignored that comment. Instead, she turned to Sam. "So do you live around here?" she asked, cocking her head.

"Not far. I'm from New York. Manhattan. I live in the city," he said.

"I'm here visiting my cousin. I'm from Virginia."

He nodded.

"You ever been there?"

"Where?"

"Virginia. Aren't you paying attention to me?" she asked.

"Yeah, sure. Sure I am. But no. I've never been to Virginia."

Then she pushed her breasts out, and Sam couldn't help but notice.

"It's pretty in Virginia. You know why they call it Virginia?"

"No, why don't you tell me?"

"Because all the girls are virgins."

He smiled. "So that makes you a virgin?" *She's one hot tomato*, he thought.

"Why don't you try me and find out?" she said coyly. Then she added, "I wouldn't mind spending an evening with a handsome fella like you."

Sam knew a lot of men who cheated on their wives. In fact, most of the married fellas in the mob had girls they kept on the side. But even though this woman was very attractive, and she was throwing herself at him, and he couldn't help but wonder what she would be like in bed, he knew he would never act on it. He loved Chana. And he wasn't willing to do anything to put his marriage in jeopardy. "Sorry. I'm married," he said.

"What a shame all the good ones are taken," she scoffed.

"What can I get for you?" the man behind the counter asked the blonde.

"A vanilla cone, please."

CHAPTER 78

Out of nowhere a rush of people were running toward the beach. More followed. It looked like a film clip Sam had once seen of the running with the bulls in Spain. Sam grabbed a teenage boy's arm as he tried to run past. The boy stopped and looked at Sam. "What's going on?" Sam asked.

"I'm not sure," the boy said, "I heard that some kid drowned."

Sam let go of the boy, and he started running with the rest of the crowd toward the beach.

Sam felt his heart sink. A chill shot through him. He left the line and ran as fast as he could toward the beach with bile rising in his throat. He had to get back as fast as he could. He couldn't stop running until he was able to see that pink-and-white bathing suit in front of him. But when he got close enough to see the blanket where he'd left Ida, he saw that she was not there. *No, dear God, please, noooo. I beg you . . . don't let Ida be the kid that drowned.*

He pushed through the crowd and ran down to shore where he saw all the lifeguards gathered in a circle. And before he even got close, he could see a tiny figure on the ground wearing a wet pink-and-white bathing suit. Tangled red hair fanned out across the sand. It was wet with drops of water that sparkled like tiny crystals in the sunshine. Sam gagged as he pushed the crowds out of his way.

"Is she all right?" Sam asked the lifeguard as he bent down to take his daughter in his arms. Her body was lifeless, and he knew even before they told him that she was dead.

"Who are you?" the lifeguard asked.

"I'm her father."

"She's not breathing." The lifeguard was trembling. He was a young man. "I tried everything I could do to revive her. But she was already gone. I'm so sorry."

The hot sun felt like a weight on Sam's shoulders. The taste of salt from the ocean on his lips made him want to vomit. He heard the blaring horns as an ambulance arrived. Leaving his car at the shore, Sam rode to the hospital with Ida.

She was pronounced dead on arrival.

CHAPTER SEVENTY-NINE

Izzy walked into the shop. He had come to visit Chana. He still came to see her all the time. But Chana believed that he had finally accepted that they were just old friends and would never be anything more. He told her that he had dated several women, but he still had not married. And she wondered if he would ever settle down. Chana never told Sam that Izzy came to the shop. That was because she knew Sam, and she knew he would be afraid that something more might develop between herself and Izzy. Chana knew for certain that it wouldn't.

"Where's Lance?" she asked.

"I left him at home. It's so darn hot outside. I didn't want to take him out in this. I figured at home he could sleep and have water whenever he wanted it. He's getting old, so I try to make life as easy as I can for him."

"Yeah, he's is such a good dog," Chana said.

"He sure is, isn't he?" Izzy smiled.

"I've been thinking about getting a dog for Ida. I think it would be good for her."

"I couldn't agree more. I didn't have one when I was a child, and

I'll tell you what, if I had a kid of my own, I'd make sure they had a puppy to grow up with."

The phone rang interrupting the conversation. Jake, Chana's father, answered it.

"Chana," he said, "it's Sam."

Chana walked over to the black telephone that was sitting on the front counter and took the receiver from her father.

"Hello, Sam. Are you and Ida home already?"

"No. I am at the hospital in Coney Island. You have to get here as soon as you can." His voice was shaking.

"What is it, Sam?"

"Ida. It's Ida."

"What happened? Did she get hurt at the beach?"

"She's dead, Chana. Our Ida is dead."

Chana turned white. She put her hand to her forehead. Then she dropped the phone and passed out. When she regained consciousness, Izzy and her father were standing over her. "Izzy," she said in a weak voice, "is it possible that you can drive me to the hospital in Coney Island? I can't drive myself."

"Sure. Of course, I'll drive you. What happened, Chana?"

"Ida is dead."

CHAPTER EIGHTY

When Chana and Izzy arrived, Sam was so distraught that he didn't even pay attention to the fact that Izzy had driven Chana. He was sweating and biting his nails, walking the floor, talking to himself... blaming himself.

"Where is she?" Chana screamed. Her eyes were wide with terror.

"In there," Sam answered, pointing to a door.

Chana walked to the door that Sam had indicated. Sam didn't follow her. He sat down on the chair in the waiting room and began to weep. Izzy ran over to Chana. "Don't go in there alone. Let me go with you," he said.

"No. You don't have to," she said, but she stumbled. Izzy took her arm and gripped her tightly.

"Come on. I'll help you. I'll go in with you," Izzy repeated.

Chana nodded. "All right."

Izzy held her up. Her knees were buckling, and she felt that without his strength she would fall to the ground. Chana had always been strong. But not today. Today she needed someone stronger than herself to lean on.

When Chana saw her daughter looking so small and helpless, still wearing that pink-and-white bathing suit that she'd wanted so badly,

Chana almost fainted again. She fell into Izzy's arms. He held her up. "What am I going to do? How am I ever going to go on living? I wish I could die instead of her. God, take me instead," her voice cracked, and she broke down like a wounded animal, tearing at her hair. She was weeping so hard that Izzy could hardly understand the words she was saying.

Izzy didn't speak. He just held her and smoothed her hair.

CHAPTER EIGHTY-ONE

Chana and Sam were both in a state of shock. They were incapable of taking care of anything practical. So Izzy made all of the funeral arrangements. Chana's parents went to her apartment during the funeral. They prepared and laid out the food for shiva. They covered the mirrors and set up boxes for Sam and Chana to sit on. Then Mrs. Rubinstein put a pitcher with water and a towel outside the main door of the apartment building so anyone who had been at the cemetery could symbolically wash the grief from their hands before entering the house.

Fannie had attended the burial at the cemetery, but there was a large crowd, so she did not have a chance to speak with Chana. However, she was one of the first people to arrive at the shiva house, bringing with her boxes and boxes of cookies and cakes.

"I am so sorry, honey," Fannie said, laying all of the boxes on the table and taking Chana in her arms.

Laevsky paid his respects, and so did Lenny and Yankel. Screwy came too.

Chana sat silently in her stocking feet with the collar of her dress ripped by the rabbi to indicate she was in mourning. She stared blankly at the wall. Sam sat beside her weeping. The lapel of his black suit had also been torn.

The Shiva lasted for seven days. Each night during that period of time, ten men, including Sam, made a minyan. They said kaddish for the little girl. Friends, neighbors, and family were coming and going all day. And by the time everyone had left for the night, Chana and Sam were too exhausted to think.

However, on the night after the shiva had ended, Chana was thrown back into the reality of her loss. Depression and pain descended upon her like a cloud of black dust.

Sam lay in his bed curled up on his side and staring at the wall. Since the day she and Sam first met, Chana had always been Sam's savior, his comforter. But she couldn't find it in her heart to comfort him now. She realized she was angry at him. She blamed him. And once she made this realization, she couldn't bear to lay in bed beside him.

"I'm going to sleep in Ida's room," she said, not looking at Sam.

"No. Please Chana. Stay with me. I need you now. We need each other," Sam said.

She shook her head. "I can't, Sam."

He looked at her in disbelief. He couldn't understand what had happened. "Chana?"

"Leave me alone."

He got up and followed her. His face was tear stained. She turned around to look at him, and for the first time since she'd met him, she found him repulsive. "How could you let this happen? Weren't you watching her?"

"I told her not to leave the blanket. She didn't listen." Sam threw his hands up in the air.

"You left her on a blanket, Sam? Where were you going that you left her alone at the beach sitting on a blanket. Are you a fool? Anything could have happened. Anything . . . and it did." She was screaming hysterically.

"I went to get her ice cream. She promised me she wouldn't move. I'm sorry, Chana. I am so sorry." He was pleading with her for forgiveness.

"You idiot," Chana said. "This is all your fault."

She had never talked to him that way. Sam's face turned red with anger. He clenched and unclenched his fists. "My fault? Is it all my fault, Chana? Maybe if you would have been more of a mother instead of going to work all the time, you would have been there with us at the beach, and you could have prevented this. But I'll bet you were with Izzy. I'll bet you weren't working. In fact, I think you have been with Izzy a lot. Maybe all the time that you told me that you were working, you were really with Izzy."

"Damn you, Sam. Don't you dare try to make this my fault. You were there with her. You should have been watching her. This was all your fault."

"And you, Chana? You were not there because you were too busy cheating, weren't you? But what else should I have expected from a whore, a curva? You were a whore when I met you. A whore could never be satisfied with only one man."

"You bastard," she said and walked into Ida's bedroom slamming the door behind her.

That night Chana slept in Ida's bedroom.

That night when Sam was alone, he went through an box of all of the things he'd kept as memories. In that box he found ticket stubs from films he'd seen with Ida. He found an old photograph that had been taken one day when he and Ida went to the theater. And then he saw the picture that Ida had drawn for him on her first day at school. In his mind's eye, he remembered how she ran to him and jumped into his arms. "Daddy, I made this for you," she said. Sam fell onto his knees and wept.

The next morning, Chana heard Sam moving around in their bedroom. When he came out, he carried a suitcase. "I'm leaving," he said. "I'm moving out. You can spend all your time with Izzy now. Maybe you should have married him in the first place."

Chana was overcome with anger. The anger turned to sadness which engulfed her. She longed to stop him. But she didn't. She wanted to scream. But she didn't do that either. She just watched as he walked out the door. Then she ran to the window and looked outside.

Sam threw his suitcase into the back of his car. Then he got in and drove away.

Chana lay down on her bed and cried. She had been strong for Sam for so long that now she felt as if she were cracking like an eggshell into tiny pieces. Her head hurt, and her heart ached with regret. *Maybe Sam was right. He wanted me to sell the store, to be a full-time mother. Maybe I should have sold the store. Or given it to my papa. I had a husband who loved me and a beautiful child. So many women would have given anything to have what I had. We had plenty of money. And Ida was such a precious gift from God. If only I had spent more time with her when I had the chance. It wasn't that I didn't love her. I did. I loved her more than life itself. But I was afraid to lose everything and be poor again. So she was with Sam all the time. The two of them were so close and me? I was so busy trying to grow that business. Why? Because I grew up poor? Because I had been forced into prostitution when I was just a teen? I was so afraid of falling back into that life that I never realized what I had. And now . . . it's gone.*

CHAPTER EIGHTY-TWO

When Sam left the apartment, he drove around for an hour. Then he stopped at a liquor store and bought a bottle of whiskey. He checked into a cheap hotel and threw his suitcase in the closet without unpacking. For the three days he lay in bed drinking without taking a shower, brushing his teeth, or changing his clothes. Sam didn't eat, and even though he was exhausted, he could not sleep. The alcohol dulled his pain, but it could not erase his desire to see Chana again. Only she could understand the grief he was feeling.

They had both loved Ida, and he knew she was suffering the loss too. When he closed his eyes, he saw his beloved Chana come running into the hospital with Izzy at her side. He had been so paralyzed by his grief that he could not speak at the time. But why had Chana come with Izzy? What was he doing at the shop? The thoughts whirled in his drunken mind. Finally, he fell asleep. His dream was so vivid he wasn't sure if he was asleep or awake. Ida came to him. She was dressed in that little bathing suit. Her hair was in a ponytail the way it had been when they left the house on that fateful day. She smiled, and he smiled back reaching out for her. "Daddy, I am all right here. It's a nice place. There are other children to play with. I'm sorry for going down to the water. I know you told me not to, but there was another girl my age who asked me to come and play with her at the shore. I thought it would be all right for just a few minutes. But then she dared me to come into the water. I went. I wasn't going to go in that deep, but something swept me away. It was like a wave. At first, I was afraid, but then . . . it was so beautiful. There was a white light, a very bright white light. But it didn't hurt my eyes. It felt good. Inside the light was Grandpa Irving. I knew it was him from the pictures on our wall. He said, 'Come with me, mine kind. I'll watch over you.' I took his hand, and then I looked back, and I saw you on your knees by my body. You were crying. I wanted to go to you, but Grandpa said you would be all right. So I came as soon as you fell asleep. I wanted you to know that I love you, and you didn't do anything wrong."

"I did, Ida," he said. "I should have watched you better. I should have . . ."

"It's all right, Daddy. You did the best you could. I love you and I always will. Whenever you miss me and you feel sad, just look at that picture that I drew for you on the first day I went to school. It will make you feel better."

"Ida . . ." He put his arms around her. "Ida . . ."

"Take care of Mommy. You have to make up with her. She loves you, and I know you love her."

"Ida . . ." he said, but she had begun to turn to light.

"No. No, please don't leave me . . . come back."

Sam woke up, wet with sweat, and the sheets were twisted around him. His face was covered with tears.

Several days later Sam returned to pick up the rest of his things. Before he left, he washed his face and combed his hair, but he still had not changed his clothes. He could have gone to the apartment early in the day when he thought Chana would be at work, but he didn't. He went at night when he knew she would be at home. She was sitting on the sofa with a book beside her when he walked in.

"Sam," she said, startled to see him.

"I came for my things."

Sam looked at Chana. In all the time he'd known her, he'd never seen her look disheveled until now. Chana had always been meticulous about her appearance. Her nails had always been manicured; her hair had always been perfectly curled. But tonight, her nail polish was chipped, and her hair was uncombed. She wore an old robe that Sam had never seen before. There were so many things he longed to say. But he couldn't bring himself to say them. His heart ached to take her into his arms and hold her. Instead, he went into the bedroom and began packing another suitcase. He hoped that she would follow him, but she didn't.

After Sam finished packing, he went into Ida's room. He looked around. His eyes fell upon the desk and the encyclopedias. Memories of helping Ida do her homework came to him. Then he glanced at her dresser and saw her box of hair ribbons. He took a white ribbon out of the box and held it to his chest. The emptiness inside of him was unbearable. He lay down on her bed and buried his head in her pillow. The sweet smell of her shampoo still lingered. "Ida," he whispered, "you left us much too soon." He lay there for a long time, until he saw the lights go out in the living room and the door close to the bedroom. *Chana's gone to bed. I should leave.*

Sam picked up his suitcase and walked out the door, locking it quietly.

CHAPTER EIGHTY-THREE

Chana lay in bed wishing Sam would come into their bedroom. All the anger she'd felt the other night had dissipated like water that had been boiled into steam. It had been replaced by grief, which felt like a black hole in the pit of her stomach. And now she wished more than anything that Sam would come and hold her. That they could bear this terrible loss together. She heard him moving around in the other room, and she considered calling his name. But she couldn't bring herself to do so. After all, how could she call to him and beg him to forgive her after the horrible things she said the other night. He had said horrible things too. Perhaps there was no going back for them. But if they were ever going to find a way to work this out, Chana felt that he would have to come to her.

As she lay there in the darkness shivering in spite of the July heat, Chana heard the door close and the key turn in the lock. She knew Sam had gone. Tears burned her eyes. *How can something like this happen? How, in an instant, can my life have changed so drastically? When I left for work that morning all was well. My greatest worry was being late for my fitting. And now? Now it feels like my life is over. Ida, my poor precious baby, is gone forever. And I have had no idea if, or when, I will ever see Sam again.* She did not sleep at all that night.

At first Chana tried to throw herself into her work. But she couldn't concentrate. Her designs were no longer the stylish innovative creations that the clients had come to expect from her. And her fittings were not as perfect as they had been in the past. The clients began to complain that they found her dresses to be unflattering. She kept trying to please them, but she couldn't. And then they stopped coming. She worked fixing shoes with her father for a while, but there wasn't enough work on that end of the business to sustain them both. Finally, she gave up and offered to give the business to her father. He had benefited so much by working with her. Before she'd hired him, he'd been an alcoholic with no ambition. The job had given him purpose. But when she offered him the store, he refused because he told her that it wouldn't be the same without her. "I've earned enough money working with you to take care of your mother and me." He said, "I'm old. I guess it's time to retire."

For a moment, Chana felt that she should keep the store open for her father's sake. He needed it. But she was drained. She had lost all of her ambition. Chana called a real estate agent and put the store up for sale. It sold quickly for a nice sum of money. And between what Chana had saved over the years and the money from the sale of the store, she had enough. She knew if she ever needed money Sam would send it to her. But if she was careful, she could live the rest of her life comfortably without ever having to ask him for anything.

CHAPTER EIGHTY-FOUR

Sonnenstein Institute, Late summer 1941

The transfer to Sonnenstein was a blur for Goldie Birnbaum. She vaguely remembered riding a bus filled with other patients, some of them ranting noisily, others whimpering softly. Due to her medication she drifted in and out of sleep during the ride. But she did remember opening her eyes and seeing what looked like an old castle looming in the distance. She couldn't be sure if the castle was real or if she was still asleep and dreaming.

The next memory she had was of waking up in a brightly lit room filled with nurses and doctors in white uniforms, all of them smiling at her. There was a receptionist at the desk, a young pretty girl who told her the doctor would be there to assess her within a few minutes. Goldie tried to smile. There was a window in the room. She gazed outside enjoying the change of scenery. She was glad about the move. It was like being on a new adventure. Goldie had endured enough of the same boring routine at the other hospital. Every day, for what seemed like a lifetime, she saw the same people, and was given the same medications. Then she slept until she was awakened and forced to eat. She hated food. It always seemed to have a metallic taste that made her gag. But she was grateful for the drugs that kept all the painful memories of her life at bay.

Once in a while the nurses would be late with her pills, and her mind would drift back to her home in Medina, or to her children, or even to poor Irving and what she'd done to him. Sometimes she would be plagued by visions of Leni laying on the floor covered in blood in that makeshift art studio. When this happened, she could smell the filth and mold in that rotten hotel. Goldie would cry out until one of the nurses came and grabbed her arm, stabbing her with a hypodermic needle. Then she would feel the heat of the drug as it entered her veins, warming her body as the blessed relief of sleep overcame her. And so she was able to get through another day.

Goldie was in a waiting room again. She wasn't sure how she'd gotten there or why she was there. *I'm still groggy, but I can feel that the medications are beginning to wear off.* "Nurse" she cried out. "Nurse. I need a nurse." The room was full of other patients, and everyone who was in a white uniform was rushing around. They didn't seem to hear her. Goldie wondered if she was invisible. One man was laying on the floor kicking his feet and crying. Another man who was sitting on a chair in front of her had urinated, leaving a pool of urine on the floor. A woman was holding a baby doll and cooing. "Nurse!" Goldie yelled out even louder this time. "Nurse."

A young nurse with curly red hair and a frown on her pretty face walked over to Goldie. "What is the problem?" she said, her voice filled with disdain.

"I need my medications. I can feel that they are starting to wear off," Goldie said, her heart racing and skipping. Sweat covered her brow as it often did when she had to face reality. "I can't be without my medication," Goldie demanded. But then she added, "Please. Please . . ."

The nurse stood up and took Goldie's arm. "Come on, I am going to get you right in to see the doctor."

Goldie lay on a table as the young doctor examined her, squeezing her breasts, and putting his fingers inside her. Goldie winced and looked away from him. Once he'd finished, he said, "So what is this that you are demanding medications? The nurses know what you need. You don't tell them you want medications. They tell you what you are expected to take. They know their jobs."

Goldie began to cry. The doctor was the same age as Sam. He brought back unwanted memories of her son. "Please," she begged. "I've ruined my life. I need the medication. I can't be without it. It's the only thing that keeps me from going out of my mind." Tears filled her face, and snot ran out of her nose. She wiped it with the back of her hand. The doctor gave her a look of disgust.

"I've read your records from the previous institution where you were kept like a useless animal in a cage. You really are nothing but a filthy, disgusting pig. You do know that, don't you? Just look at yourself. You have track marks all over your arms. And would you just look at the bruises and sores on your face. I look at you, and I want to vomit. You should be ashamed of yourself," the doctor said.

Goldie looked at him, shocked. She'd never heard a doctor speak that way before.

He smiled as if he felt clever, then shook his head. "And . . . by the way, I believe you are a Jew."

"I don't know. I don't remember. Please, help me," Goldie said, not knowing what to say or do around this very strange and frightening man. "All I know is I am begging you to have mercy on me and give me my medications."

"Of course, Miss Birnbaum. We will do whatever you ask. Everyone always has catered to you, isn't that right?" the doctor said, smiling wickedly. He glanced over at the nurse, who stood in the corner and winked. "And by the way . . . Goldie Birnbaum, in case you forgot, I didn't. You are a Jew. I know who you are. You're a rich Jew. The daughter and heir to the Birnbaum fortune." He laughed. "But even if I didn't know that, I can tell you are Jewish. You know how I can tell?"

"Please . . ."

"I can tell because you make demands as if you are in charge, when in fact you are a nobody here. You know why? Because you are nothing but a useless eater. You are Jewish swine. And you are certainly not in charge. But I am," the doctor said. Then he called out to the nurse. "Nurse, take her to building two, C sixteen. Give her a sedative once you check her in." He winked, and the nurse nodded.

The nurse helped Goldie into a wheelchair. Then Goldie was taken to building two. Once inside, the nurse helped her out of her chair and sent her into a large room. "You be a good girl, and stand right here and wait for me. I will be back shortly with a needle to sedate you," the nurse promised.

The room was filled with other patients. Goldie stood in the corner trembling. It looked like a shower room with showerheads along the top of the wall and drains on the floor. *If they want me to shower before I can get my medications, then why are there men and women in here together? Are we all going to take a shower together?*

Just then someone called her name: "Goldie Birnbaum."

Goldie's head whipped around to see an old familiar face. It was Luisa Eisenreich. She wore a white nurse's uniform and cap. There was a wicked half smile on her face. "I am sure you must remember me, don't you?"

Goldie nodded, wishing the other nurse with the red hair would return. "Go away. I want the other nurse to treat me," Goldie said.

"Still thinking you have the power to make demands, you rich Jew," Luisa said. "Well, you can make all the demands that you like. But no one is going to listen to you anymore. You want to know why? Because I have some inside information. Can you guess what is about to happen to you? Can you guess?" Luisa taunted her.

Goldie had enough of talking to Luisa. She called out, "Nurse, nurse..."

"I told you, no one is coming. You see those showerheads above you, Goldie Birnbaum? Look up. Go on. Look up."

Goldie had seen the showerheads already, but she looked up anyway.

Then Luisa let out a laugh. "I'll tell you what is about to happen. The beautiful, rich Goldie Birnbaum is about to be gassed to death. The gas that will steal your breath is about to come right out of those showerheads. And there is nothing you can do to stop it. You will never have another chance to wear your fur coat or your pretty dresses. This is the end of the line for you: you'll never leave here alive."

Goldie was shaking. She said, "Please, I'll do anything. I just want to go home. I need my mother. Please, Luisa, take pity on me."

Luisa laughed, and then she turned to leave. But before she walked out of the room she turned back and looked at Goldie. Then she smiled and took Goldie's arm. "You're coming with me," she said.

"Thank you, Luisa. I always knew you were a good person at heart," Goldie said.

"Did you?" Luisa laughed. Then she took Goldie into a small private room with a cot and a chair. She quietly closed the door behind her. Then she looked at Goldie and said, "Now the time has come for you to pay back an old debt. Goldie Birnbaum, a quick death is too good for you."

CHAPTER EIGHTY-FIVE

December 7, 1941

Japan sprang a surprise attack on America on December 7, 1941. They bombed Pearl Harbor. The Japanese were part of the Axis which consisted of Germany, Italy, and Japan. America was stunned and horrified. Until now, the United States had managed to stay out of the war. But now she was all in. There was fighting on two fronts, in the Pacific and in Europe. Almost every able-bodied man in America enlisted. The attack had only served to strengthen the United States. And her citizens were ready to fight for their country.

CHAPTER EIGHTY-SIX

February 1942

Sam had not worked for months. He never told anyone, but he had a secret fear that God had taken Ida as punishment for his killing John. Many times he thought about the night he'd murdered John, and he wished he could go back and change his actions. If it would bring Ida back, he would do anything. Once, in a drunken stupor, he'd begged God to exchange his life for his daughter's. He'd waited for God to answer him. But no one answered. Instead, he woke up the following morning on the floor in a pool of his own vomit.

Most of his days were spent staring out the window of the cheap hotel he'd come to call home. Once in a while Lenny or Yankel would stop by to visit him. Every so often he would take a drive over to the restaurant to see Laevsky. Four times a week he went out to pick up food from a nearby restaurant, which he hardly ate. Food containers, still mostly full, lay scattered around the room, their contents moldy and rotting. His unwashed clothes were strewn across the chairs. Towels lay balled up in the corners. He refused to allow the maid to come into his room until the smell got so bad that the other hotel guests complained. Finally, the management knocked on the door to his room and demanded that he allow the maid to come in and clean up his mess.

The first time he'd gone to see Laevsky after he'd quit working, was two weeks after Ida's death. He hadn't wanted to go. But Laevsky had always been kind to him; he felt obligated to make the trip. Sam forced himself to get out of bed and take a shower. Then he'd headed to the restaurant that had once been the speakeasy. After not driving for two weeks, the wheel felt unsteady in his hands. And twice he almost turned back. It was so much easier not to face people. He wanted to hide in the darkness of the small, dirty hotel room.

Lenny was the first person to greet him when he walked inside. "Shatzy. Good to see you," Lenny said. Sam could see the sympathy in Lenny's eyes. "How have you been, my friend?" Lenny patted Sam's back.

"I'm getting by. But it's good to see you too," Sam had answered, trying to smile.

"I went by your apartment the other day. Chana said you moved out. Where are you staying?"

"A small hotel off of Delancey."

"Which one?"

"Gittleman's Hotel."

"Why there, Shatz? That place is a dump."

"I don't care. It's what I deserve."

Lenny looked at him. "Come on, Shatzy. Don't say that. You can come and stay with me for a while if you want. Or I can give you some money if you need it."

"That's real nice of you. I appreciate your kind offers. But I can't come and stay with you. And I have plenty of money," Sam said. Then he went on. "Listen, I can't stick around here for too long. So I'm going back to the office. Is the boss here?"

"Yeah, he's back there."

"Thanks again for the offer," Sam managed to say as he walked toward Laevsky's office. Laevsky was sitting behind his desk. He smiled warmly when he saw Sam. "Shatzy, I'm glad you came. How are you doing?"

"I've been better, boss."

"Yeah, I can imagine, kid. You've been through hell. I understand."

Sam sat down. "I came because I have to talk to you," he said.

"You want a drink?"

"Yeah. Sure."

"Whiskey?"

"Sure."

Laevsky poured two glasses of whiskey and pushed one across the desk to Sam. Sam drank the shot in one gulp. Then he took a deep breath.

"I don't know how to tell you this. You've been a great boss to me. And not only a boss but a friend."

"So what is it, Shatzy? Tell me what you came to tell me."

"I can't work anymore. I don't trust myself to be cautious and careful enough to do these jobs. My hands shake. I don't get enough sleep, so I'm always tired. I guess what I am saying is I have to quit."

"You can take some time off if you'd rather do that," Laevsky said as he eyed Sam's deeply wrinkled brow.

"I can't promise I'll ever come back. But I sure appreciate everything you did for me. I hope you're not angry."

"Angry? Nahh. I'm feeling many things but not anger. I don't mind if you want to quit. That's your choice. But you gotta pull yourself together, Shatz."

"I'll try, boss."

"Listen, how about you don't quit outright. You just take an indefinite leave of absence. I'll keep your job open for you. When you're ready, you'll come back."

"I can't say how long that will be. Right now, I can't do anything."

"Yeah, you're grieving. It's to be expected," Laevsky said. "I know grief very well."

"Thanks for understanding."

"Listen. If you want, you can just come and work the bar at the restaurant. It would get you out. What do you say?"

Sam shook his head. "I can't. I'm sorry, boss. I'm just not ready to be around people right now."

For a moment Laevsky was quiet. He tapped his pen on the desk. Then he looked up at Sam and nodded his head. "I understand. You take as much time as you need to pull yourself together," Laevsky said. Then he added, "How's your wife doing in all of this?"

"We split," Sam said.

"Oh shit. I sure am sorry to hear that," Laevsky said, shaking his head. "You broke up over losing your little girl?"

"Yeah. It pulled us apart."

"I know how the death of a child can kill a marriage. Believe me, I know. I never told you or any of the boys about this, but I lost my only son to polio. It destroyed me and my wife. Things were never right with us afterward. We're still together, but things were just never the same between us."

Sam nodded. "Yeah, it's like you almost don't know each other anymore. And yet there is so much history between you . . . and so many unspoken words."

"You still love her."

"Yeah, I sure do," Sam said.

"You know, Sam. I've always favored you. I put up with a lot more from you than I ever have from any of the other fellas. And up until now, I never told you why. But in view of all that's happened, I think I should tell you now. It's because you remind me of my son. I believe he would have grown up to look like you. He had your same coloring. He was tall and had a smile just like yours. A smile that could melt you. Damn, Shatzy, he was a handsome kid. Just like you are. I sometimes tried to substitute you for him. I gave you the fatherly love I couldn't give him. I still can't believe he's gone."

"I'm sorry, boss. I had no idea."

"Yeah, I was never the type of fella to wear my heart on my sleeve," Laevsky said. Then he added, "If you want my opinion, you ought to try to talk things over with your wife. You should at least make some effort."

"I don't know how to talk to her. Chana blames me for what happened to Ida. And she's right. It was my fault. I took our daughter to the beach, and I should have been doing a better job of watching her."

"Things happen," Laevsky said, shaking his head. "The two of you love each other. You'll work it out. You'll find a way."

"I wish I could believe that. You see, I was a real jerk. She hurt me and I lost my mind. I said some terrible things to her. Things I should never have said. I don't know if she'll ever forgive me. I'm afraid that there is no going back to what we were before all of this. But what I do know is that she was the best thing that ever happened to me."

"I'll tell you what I know. I know that Chana loves you. You'll work it out, Shatzy. I have faith in you."

That conversation had taken place last summer, but it seemed like a lifetime ago. He'd gone to see Laevsky several times since, but they had never discussed Chana or his working for Laevsky again. Now it was mid-February; icicles had formed on the window. The hotel where Sam was staying didn't have a good heating system. It reminded him of the first apartment that his family had lived in when they moved from Medina to Manhattan. *That was a lifetime ago,* he thought. *My parents were alive. I didn't even know Chana yet. And Ida? I never knew I would have a child who I would love more than my own life.*

The phone rang. It was rare for Sam to receive calls. For a moment his heart fluttered. *What if it's Chana. What if she talked to Lenny or Laevsky, and they told her where I am and how to get in contact with me,* he thought and ran to pick up the receiver.

"Shatzy." It was Lenny. His voice sounded solemn. "I thought I should let you know that the boss died a few hours ago. He had a heart attack."

"What happened?" Sam felt another dark cloud descending upon him as he threw the clothes off of a chair and then sank into it. He had seen Laevsky a month ago. He'd gone early in the afternoon and brought Laevsky his favorite salt bagels. They talked for a couple of hours. Laevsky told him the gossip from the neighborhood, and for a short while he'd forgotten his troubles. Sam had never suspected that visit would be the last time he would see Laevsky alive.

"The boss was in a foul mood all day today. He had me call Izzy and tell him to come in. I did. Izzy came to the club and went into the office. I could hear things getting heated. I couldn't make out everything they said, but I heard Laevsky mention the ambush and say something about the Italians. Then, bam, just like that Izzy came out of the office and yelled for me to call an ambulance. But the boss was already dead when they got there."

Sam was silent for a few moments. Then in a soft voice he asked, "When is the funeral?"

"The funeral is Wednesday morning at Weinstein's. There's gonna be a shiva at his house right after the burial."

"Thanks for calling and letting me know," Sam said.

"Shatzy, I can pick you up and take you to the funeral if you want me to," Lenny offered.

"No, but thanks," Sam said. He felt as if all the people who he'd cared for were leaving his world one at a time. Sam felt so empty and alone. He wished he could call Chana. If only he could call Chana. He felt hot tears run down his cheeks. Squeezing his eyes shut, in his mind, he saw his father, then Ida, then Laevsky. Each of them were smiling, alive, happy. And then as he watched, one by one they were erased from the imaginary picture.

"Are you gonna come to the funeral?" Lenny asked.

"I don't know. I suppose I should."

"I talked to Chana. I called and told her about Laevsky. She said she would be there," Lenny said.

Chana. Thank God that at least she was alive. But he was miserable when he thought that she was no longer a part of his life. He'd lost her, and without her he felt he couldn't go on. "You said you called her?" he asked. Just hearing her name made his heart skip a beat.

"Yes, I called her."

"How did she sound?"

"All right. We didn't really talk too long. I just told her about Laevsky and asked her if she was going to come to the funeral. She said yes. That's all."

"Did either of you mention me?"

"No. Like I told you, that was all we said. She was pretty stunned by the news about Laevsky."

"So she was upset?"

"Yeah, of course she was. You know Laevsky always had a soft spot for Chana."

"He sure did," Sam said. "He was a hell of a guy. He was as smart as a fox. He knew every one of his men. He knew our strengths and our weaknesses. And he always knew what to say. I sure am gonna miss him. Anyway, I'll be at the funeral. So I'll see you then." Sam hung up the phone. He lit a cigarette. *Damn it*. Sam poured himself a shot of whiskey. Laevsky was gone. Sam downed the whiskey. He felt like he'd lost his father all over again.

CHAPTER EIGHTY-SEVEN

On Wednesday morning Sam forced himself to get out of bed and take a shower. He washed his hair with a bar of soap because he'd run out of shampoo a month ago and had never bothered to replace it. He towel dried his hair as best he could because it was wickedly cold outside. Then he dressed in a black suit, a black shirt, and a dark gray tie. Since he knew Chana was going to be at the funeral, he even put on some cologne. Sam hadn't worn cologne since he'd left home. When he was completely dressed, he looked in the dirty, cracked mirror that hung on the door. The handsome man he'd once been had been replaced by a stranger who stared back from the mirror. This was a man he didn't recognize.

Sam was painfully thin. His hair, that had been lustrous and as raven black as a pair of newly shined shoes, was now dull and sprinkled with gray. There were fine lines around his eyes and deeper ones between his brows. His dark eyes had lost their sparkle. *I look so old*, he thought. Then he sighed and put on his dark wool coat and scarf. He hadn't been paying attention to how much weight he was losing. But now he could see that all of his clothes were hanging off of him. If he'd had more time, he would have had a new suit made, one that fit. But this was the best he could do right now. He took his hat off the coatrack and put it on his head. Then he walked outside.

The bitter, cold wind that came down from the north greeted him. He shivered. Then he walked to his car and got behind the wheel. Sam turned the key in the ignition, but the car wouldn't start. He'd hired a woman to go to the store for him when the weather got cold. So the last time he'd driven the car was three weeks ago when he'd gone to see Laevsky. His breath was white in the frigid air as he put his foot on the gas pedal and pumped the gas several times. The engine only sputtered. He tried again. Still nothing more than a few grunts from the engine. *Slow down,* he told himself, *or you'll flood it.* Sam waited a few minutes, then he tried to start the car again. This time the engine roared to life. He gave thanks and then maneuvered the car out of the parking space and headed to town.

It was a Jewish tradition that one must bring something sweet to a house of mourning. So he stopped at Fannie's bakery. Sam had been in such a hurry that he hadn't considered how painful it would be to stand in line at the counter where his late father had worked before he died. *I shouldn't have come here. I should have stopped for a box of candy instead,* he thought as a man he didn't recognize behind the counter asked, "How can I help you, sir?"

"What's good today?" Sam managed to say.

"Everything. This is Fannie's bakery. Everything is always good here."

"Do you have a strudel?"

"I have apple and cherry."

"Give me a cherry strudel," Sam said. He waited while the man put the strudel into a box and tied it. Then he paid the bill and was just about to leave when Fannie came out from the back.

"Why, if it isn't Sam Schatzman. I thought I heard your voice," Fannie said. "How are you?"

"I've been better," Sam answered.

She nodded. Fannie was best friends with Chana. She already knew that the two of them were separated. "Listen, come on back to my office; let's have a cup of hot coffee and a nice piece of fresh babka. I just took the chocolate babkas out of the oven, and they are heavenly this morning. What do you say?"

"I don't know. I have to get going. I'm on my way to a funeral."

"Laevsky, right?"

"Right."

"I was sorry to hear about it. He was a nice fella, always nice to me. Respectful. You know he came in here at least twice a week. Always soft spoken. Who would have ever thought he was the powerful man he was. He never threw his weight around. You know?" she said, sighing. "Anyway, I can't make the funeral. I just hired a new baker, and I can't leave him alone. But I'm going to the shiva later tonight. I'm going early to help set things up. However, if I recall correctly the funeral doesn't start until eleven this morning. It's only nine thirty. You have plenty of time. Come on back to my office. I need to talk to you."

Sam considered it. She was right. He did have time. He had left the house early because he wasn't sure how slippery the roads might be. Once he started driving, he discovered the roads were pretty clear. So he wasn't in any hurry, and he did have the time to have a talk. And besides that, he hadn't eaten, so the idea of some hot coffee and a piece of cake appealed to him. "All right. You convinced me," he said, smiling.

They went back to Fannie's office where she already had a pot of coffee brewing and an open babka on a shelf behind her desk. She cut him a slice and poured him a cup of steaming coffee. Then she poured herself a cup as well. Sam took a sip of coffee. "Damn, this is good coffee."

"Only the best. I get it on the black market. It's expensive. But worth it." She smiled. Then she added, "So, you handsome devil, tell me, how have you been?"

"Eh, not so good," he said.

"I can imagine. I know you've had your share of troubles losing your dad and then Ida."

"Yep," he said, "I sure have. And now, Laevsky. Sometimes I think I'm cursed." She was so easy to talk to, he found himself telling her things that were very private and close to his heart. "The hardest thing for me to bear is the breakup of my marriage."

"Cursed, nahh. You've just run into a patch of bad luck," she said, then she added, "Chana and I have always been the best of friends. And, well, I know that she still loves you."

"Did she tell you that?"

"Not in so many words. But I know her, and I know that she misses you terribly. She gave up the store. You know that, don't you?"

"Yeah, Lenny told me."

"She couldn't work like that anymore. Losing the child and losing you broke her. She needs you, Sam. And . . . I don't know if you want to hear this or not, but I've never been one to keep silent . . ."

"What is it?"

"You need her too."

Sam looked at Fannie. She was a strong woman, but her heart was pure gold. "I don't know what to do, Fannie. How can we get back together after the terrible things I said to her. She'll never forgive me."

"You gotta try, Sam. You said things to her that were hurtful. She said things to you. But the fact is, you were both grieving the loss of a child. A terrible loss. You were angry with each other. But that doesn't mean that you don't need each other."

"What should I do?"

"When you see her at the funeral today, talk to her. Just talk. Don't dive into the past. Don't bring up anything that could make her uncomfortable. Apologies will come later. Right now, just keep the conversation light. Then after you talk for a while ask her to go out for coffee or lunch sometime. You two need to rebuild what you had, but you need to do it slowly."

He looked into her eyes. "Anybody ever tell you that you're brilliant."

She let out a loud laugh. "Brilliant. Nope."

"Thanks, Fannie," he said.

"Anytime, Sam."

CHAPTER EIGHTY-EIGHT

Sam left Fannie's and drove to the funeral home. He left the strudel he'd bought in the car. He would take it into the shiva house after the burial.

The Laevsky funeral was taking place in the largest room in the funeral home, and it was overcrowded. People were congregating in the lobby as well as in the room. Laevsky had a lot of friends and business associates. By the time Sam arrived, there were no chairs available. He had to stand in the back of the room. Quietly, he took his place in the corner and looked around. Chana wasn't there. His heart sank. He'd hoped that he would have a chance to speak to her. When Lenny and Screwy saw him they both nodded. Sam nodded back. Then the rabbi began to speak. Sam could hear Laevsky's widow weeping. He felt dizzy. The air was hot and stuffy. It smelled of a mixture of many different men's colognes and women's perfumes. Sam wished he could go outside and get some air, but it was rude to leave while the rabbi was speaking.

When the rabbi finished, he called Laevsky's brother up to the podium to speak. Until today, Sam hadn't even known that Laevsky had a brother. Glancing across the room, Sam saw Yankel and his wife sitting quietly holding hands. And then the door creaked open. Sam glanced over and saw Chana with a lace covering on her head. She was so beautiful that he ached to hold her in his arms. But then he saw that Izzy was with her. Izzy took her arm and led her to the other side of the room. They stood there, close together. The room was hotter than before. Sam's head was spinning. Vomit rose in his throat. He swallowed hard. Sam left the room quickly, afraid that if he stayed, he might throw up. He ran outside and took deep gulps of air. Then he got into his car and left.

CHAPTER EIGHTY-NINE

Sam trembled as he drove to Laevksy's home where the shiva was being held. *Chana was with Izzy. They are together. Just the way Izzy always wanted it*, he thought as he parked the car. Then he went to the door and poured the water over his hands and went inside.

Fannie was in the kitchen setting things up. She'd brought several cakes and cookies with her. When she saw Sam, she ran over to him and hugged him. "Samelah, how are you?"

"Not good."

"It's never good to go to a funeral. Nu?"

"No, it's not. And I sure am gonna miss that fella. He was a good friend to me."

"He was tough, but he was also fair, and he could be kind too."

"Yeah, that's so true," Sam said. Then he hesitated for a moment.

"What's the matter, Sam? You look terrible all of a sudden. Do you feel all right?"

"Fannie . . . Chana was at the funeral with Izzy. I saw them together, and it broke my heart. When I saw her sitting beside him, I knew it was over for her and I. It's killing me."

"Listen, you need to eat something. You don't look right. Let me get you some food," Fannie said

"But the mourners are supposed to eat first," Sam said.

"We'll make an exception today, huh?" Then she smiled. "Here, sit down. I'll be right back."

He nodded. She walked into the kitchen. Sam slumped onto the sofa. Fannie was right; he did feel sick to his stomach. He leaned on his elbows and put his head in his hands. Closing his eyes for a moment, he felt like he was drowning in pain and loss. When he heard Fannie's heels on the wood floor, he opened his eyes. There was newspaper in front of him on the coffee table. The article read: "Men across America are enlisting in the army every day. We must defend our country. Uncle Sam wants you!"

Sam read the lines twice. "Uncle Sam wants you!" He read it softly aloud to himself.

"Here you go. Eat this. You'll feel better."

Sam took a bite of the roast beef sandwich she'd brought him. Then he said, "I've gotta go."

"Where are you going? You didn't touch your food."

"I can't eat. I'm going to the recruiting office. I'm going to sign up."

Fannie looked at him distressed, but before she could speak he was out the door.

CHAPTER NINETY

The people who had been at the cemetery began to trickle into the shiva house. Among them were Izzy and Chana. When Fannie saw Chana come in, she ran over to her. "Izzy," she said, "I need your help putting these knishes out on the table. Can you do that for me, please?"

He shrugged. "Sure."

As Izzy began laying the knishes onto a serving platter, Fannie grabbed Chana's hand and pulled her out of the room and into the bathroom. "I have to talk to you," Fannie said. "Sam was here. He wanted to make things right with you, but then he saw you with Izzy at the funeral. He's distraught."

"I only went with Izzy because he was so upset. He was with Laevsky when he died."

"Chana," Fannie said, "listen to me. You might only have a few minutes left to change everything. Sam left here. He said he was going to the recruiting office to join. If you still love him, you'd better get there in a hurry."

Chana was still holding the box of cookies that she'd brought to the shiva house. She looked at Fannie. The cookies fell from her hands. And she ran out of the house.

As she dashed down the street, her high heels were slipping on the ice. But she dared not stop, not for a second. Her heart was racing. *Sam, please, Sam, I'm coming. Don't do this. I love you . . .*

CHAPTER NINETY-ONE

Sam sat across from the army recruiter, who looked him straight in the eye. "How old are you, son?"

"Thirty-two. I don't know if it matters, but I speak fluent German."

"Sure does. Do you have an accent?"

"When I was in Germany I was told I sounded like a native," Sam said.

"Good. Very good," the recruiter said. Then he laid the paper and a pen in front of Sam. "Once you sign this paper, you're in for good. Are you ready to fight for your country? Are you willing to die for America?"

Sam picked up the pen. It felt cold in his hand. Then he thought, *I have nothing left to live for* . . .

AUTHORS NOTE

I always enjoy hearing from my readers, and your thoughts about my work are very important to me. If you enjoyed my novel, please consider telling your friends and posting a short review on Amazon. Word of mouth is an author's best friend.

Please Click Here to Leave a Review

Also, it would be my honor to have you join my mailing list. As my gift to you for joining, you will receive 3 **free** short stories and my USA Today award-winning novella complimentary in your email! To sign up, just go to my website at www.RobertaKagan.com

I send blessings to each and every one of you,

Roberta

Email: roberta@robertakagan.com

Please turn the page to read the prologue of the next book in this series, *The Syndrome That Saved Us…*

THEY SYNDROME THAT SAVED US EXCERPT

Rome, Italy, April 1938

The room smelled of sweat and fear as Lory and Alma Bellinelli stood side by side in the long line to register at Rome's main synagogue. Lory cast a worried glance at Alma. But she returned his glance with a reassuring smile. *My sweet wife. She is always trying to make the best of everything.* Lory forced himself to return her smile, but his eyes were still narrowed with worry. And the wrinkle between his brows had deepened. As they stood waiting, they could hear the soft pitter-patter of rain on the roof outside.

"We should have worn our raincoats," Lory said, acknowledging the sound.

"Yes, we should have. But we didn't. Oh well, so we'll get wet," Alma whispered to him as she gently squeezed his arm. "Nothing like walking in the rain in the springtime."

"You're right. Even if it is still cold outside."

"We'll put our arms around each other, and that will keep us warm," she said.

"I can't help it, I still get a bad feeling about what is going on here,

Alma." Lory was suddenly serious again. "Why would it be that all of a sudden, out of nowhere, Jews are forced to register and report everything they own?"

"I don't know. But look around you. Everyone else who lives in the Jewish Quarter is here with us. And we are at the Jewish synagogue. No one else seems concerned they are all reporting their assets. If all of the others think it is all right, then it must be."

"Ehhh, I just don't know," Lory said, shaking his head.

"We don't have that much, really, to worry about. Heaven knows we aren't rich. If the Nazis are looking to take valuable things from people, they will find that all we have is a small flat filled with secondhand furniture. It they want it that badly, they can have it," she said.

From across the room, a deep baritone voice called out, "Bellinelli, is that you?"

Lory let out a belly laugh when he saw the familiar face of his old friend. "Sacerdoti, I haven't seen you in years. How are you?" Lory walked across the room and put his arms around his old friend, taking him into a bear hug.

"I'm all right," Sacerdoti said, "but you sure look good."

"You look good too. What have you been doing with yourself these days?"

"I was working at the Civil Hospital Umberto 1 of Ancona, but they let me go because I am Jewish. Then my uncle introduced me to Dr. Borromeo, who offered me a job at the Roman Catholic hospital, Fatebenefratelli. It's on Tiber Island. Are you familiar with it?"

"Yes, of course," Lory said.

"Dr. Borromeo is a wonderful man. I wish you could meet him. You two would get along well. I know it. Anyway, I have been so busy that I hardly ever get out and see the light of day. And what are you doing these days?" Sacerdoti asked.

"I'm working at the Israelite Hospital. And . . . I got married. Come, follow me, I want you to meet my Alma."

The two men walked back to Alma, who was still in line.

"This beautiful woman is my wife, Alma. She works as a nurse at the Israelite Hospital, and we are also doing some private medical work in the ghetto. So many people need help, and they are unable to get to a hospital," Lory said, then he put his arm around Alma proudly.

"I'm Vittorio Sacerdoti. My friends call me Vito. It's a pleasure to meet you. Your husband and I have been friends for a long time. In fact, he kept my spirits up all through the time we spent at the University of Bologna together," Dr. Sacerdoti said, smiling, then he embraced Alma and kissed her on either cheek.

"It's nice to meet you too," Alma said.

Then Vito looked at Lory with a puzzled expression on his face and asked, "I don't mean to pry, but I never knew you were Jewish."

"I'm not Jewish; I'm Roman Catholic, but my Alma is Jewish, so we have come to register."

"Ahhh, all right. That makes sense. I think you knew that I am Jewish, so that's why I am here."

"I didn't remember, quite frankly. But it's so good to see you."

"When I first got out of school and came back to Rome, I thought about getting a job at the Jewish hospital. But then I got such a wonderful offer from the Roman Catholic hospital that I couldn't refuse it. They are a wonderful bunch of monks who run the place. And that's what I have always loved about Italy. Here we can all live together in peace. Not like in Germany where they are treating Jews worse than dogs. I think it is disgraceful."

Lory nodded, but then he added, "My wife's mother and her grandparents are from Berlin. They are still living in Germany."

"Oh, I am sorry. I hope I didn't offend you. I certainly didn't mean to," Vito said. Then not wanting to upset Alma, he changed the subject. "You and I have lost touch for far too long, Lorenzo, my friend. We must arrange to have dinner together soon. And, of course, you must bring your lovely wife," Vito said as Lory and Alma came up to the front of the line.

Lory took out a small book of paper and a pencil from the breast pocket of his shirt. He scribbled down his address, then he handed it to Vito. "Here is my address. Please come by. Alma and I would love to have you over for dinner. Our apartment is nothing fancy. But you are always welcome in our home."

"As you would be in mine. However, right now I don't have a place of my own to invite you to. What does a single man need with an apartment? So I am living in a room at the hospital."

"Well, not to worry. You'll come to our place," Lory said. Then he added, "I can still remember that year that I went home from school for Christmas with you. Do you remember?"

"Of course I do. How could I ever forget? We went to my friend Marco's house next door where we had the Feast of the Seven Fishes. We ate so much that we both got sick."

"I remember, my friend," Lory said. "We were rolling on the bed holding our swollen bellies." He laughed.

"And then you accompanied me and Marco to his church for midnight Mass even though you're Jewish," Lory said.

"That is because I loved you both, and I would never let religion get in the way of that love. I may not be a Catholic, but the service was quite beautiful."

"Midnight Mass is always very special." Lory smiled, then he continued. "Even though I would never want to change a single thing about my Alma, I love her just as she is: I would really like for her to see a midnight Mass one Christmas Eve."

"Let's keep the line moving," a man, who was standing behind Lory and Alma, said in a frustrated tone.

"So come by our house and see us soon. Don't be a stranger. My Alma is a good cook."

Alma smiled. "I try anyway," she said.

"Next . . ." the clerk at the desk said. He was tapping his pencil impatiently.

Lory shrugged. "I suppose it's our turn now," he said, and then he and Alma walked up to the desk to fill out and sign the registration papers.

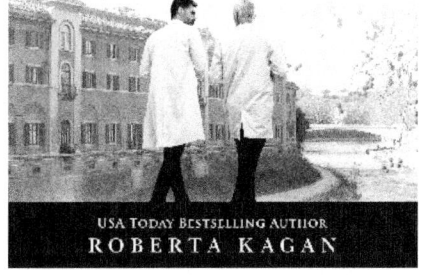

Click Here To Purchase The Syndrome That Saved Us By Roberta Kagan

ACKNOWLEDGMENTS

I would also like to thank my editor, proofreader, and developmental editor for all their help with this project. I couldn't have done it without them.
   Paula Grundy of Paula Proofreader
   Terrance Grundy of Editerry
   Carli Kagan, Developmental Editor

ALSO BY ROBERTA KAGAN

Available on Amazon

A Jewish Family Saga

Not In America

They Never Saw It Coming

When The Dust Settled

The Syndrome That Saved Us

A Holocaust Story Series

The Smallest Crack

The Darkest Canyon

Millions Of Pebbles

Sarah and Solomon

All My Love, Detrick Series

All My Love, Detrick

You Are My Sunshine

The Promised Land

Michal's Destiny Series

Michal's Destiny

A Family Shattered

Watch Over My Child

Another Breath, Another Sunrise

Eidel's Story Series

Who Is The Real Mother?

Secrets Revealed

New Life, New Land

Another Generation

The Wrath of Eden Series

The Wrath Of Eden

The Angels Song

Stand Alone Novels

One Last Hope

A Flicker Of Light

The Heart Of A Gypsy

Copyright © 2020 by Roberta Kagan

All rights reserved. No part of this publication may be reproduced, distributed, or transmitted in any form or by any means, including photocopying, recording, or other electronic or mechanical methods, without the prior written permission of the publisher, except in the case of brief quotations embodied in critical reviews and certain other noncommercial uses permitted by copyright law.

DISCLAIMER

This is a work of fiction. Names, characters, businesses, places, events, and incidents are either the products of the author's imagination or used in a fictitious manner. Any resemblance to actual persons, living or dead, or actual events is purely coincidental.

Printed in Great Britain
by Amazon